MW01462275

City
of
End

The Tree of Life Series Vol. 1

Gwen,

My Hawaiian beauty! Your smile and personality is totally infectious. I have so enjoyed getting to know you over these years. I hope you are blessed by this book. Thank you for your friendship and support!

KATELYN E MCCALLUM

iUniverse®

CITY OF END
THE TREE OF LIFE SERIES VOL. 1

Copyright © 2018 Katelyn E McCallum.

All rights reserved. No part of this book may be used or reproduced by any means, graphic, electronic, or mechanical, including photocopying, recording, taping or by any information storage retrieval system without the written permission of the author except in the case of brief quotations embodied in critical articles and reviews.

This is a work of fiction. All of the characters, names, incidents, organizations, and dialogue in this novel are either the products of the author's imagination or are used fictitiously.

iUniverse books may be ordered through booksellers or by contacting:

iUniverse
1663 Liberty Drive
Bloomington, IN 47403
www.iuniverse.com
1-800-Authors (1-800-288-4677)

Because of the dynamic nature of the Internet, any web addresses or links contained in this book may have changed since publication and may no longer be valid. The views expressed in this work are solely those of the author and do not necessarily reflect the views of the publisher, and the publisher hereby disclaims any responsibility for them.

Any people depicted in stock imagery provided by Getty Images are models, and such images are being used for illustrative purposes only.
Certain stock imagery © Getty Images.

ISBN: 978-1-5320-5874-5 (sc)
ISBN: 978-1-5320-5876-9 (hc)
ISBN: 978-1-5320-5875-2 (e)

Library of Congress Control Number: 2018912275

Print information available on the last page.

iUniverse rev. date: 10/17/2018

This book is dedicated to the woman who brought me into this life, and first stoked the fiery love of reading and writing within me. To my mother, my guardian angel who departed too soon from this world, you instilled a deep love of the written word in me from my earliest beginnings. I love you now and forever.

Chapter One

Thunder rumbled in the distance.

Aoire lay in the warm sun, the tall grass soft under her body. Not a cloud was in the blue sky above her, and a gentle breeze ruffled the red and gold leaves in the tree she lay under. She chewed lazily on the end of a stalk of sweet onion grass, with her eyes closed and her arms crossed behind her head. The clean smell of earth filled her nose as she breathed steadily, drinking in the peace and tranquility of the hill she was lying on.

Thunder rumbled again in the distance. This time a stronger wind ruffled her shirt.

Wake up, my child.

Aoire's brows knit together as Father's voice filled her head.

Wake? Why? She thought, blinking in the bright sunlight and then closing her eyes lazily. The soft grass bent and folded under her arms as she swept her hands in lazy circles at her sides. She could hear the sounds of crickets and the movement of the trees in the distance, as a cool breeze swept through them. The air was clean and crisp and every time it brushed against her skin, she could feel Father's gentle presence. *Why would I wake from this?*

Thunder rumbled a third time, but this time closer.

Wake up, my child.

Aoire felt confused by hearing the same command. *But this is our spot. This is where I come to be with you. Why send me away?*

As if to reply, thunder clapped directly over her, darkness rolling in and blotting out the warm sun. The grass under her body began to harden, growing cold and sharp. All sounds stopped and the air grew thick. Aoire's eyes snapped open as a foreboding presence that she couldn't quite place filled the pit of her stomach. Above her towered a mountain of a man, the grass around his boots turning black. His lips curled into a sickly grin as he looked down at her. He began to reach toward her and her body froze.

Wake up! NOW!

Father's voice filled her mind at the exact same time that cold fire radiated up her arm from where his fingers wrapped around her slender wrist. Pain exploded behind her eyes, another voice pushing Father's out of the way and filling her mind.

I AM COMING FOR YOU AOIRE. I HAVE FOUND YOU AND I AM COMING FOR YOU.

With barely any effort, he pulled her up violently from where she lay until they were eye level, her hand limp in his grip as her arm began to go numb. Her toes dangled a few feet from the ground. She squirmed in his grasp, trying to claw his fingers off from around her wrist as his smile widened. His jaw came unhinged as if to devour her whole.

I AM COMING FOR YOU.

His voice echoed in her head as he pulled her closer to him. As the darkness closed in, she could hear millions of screaming voices coming together to form one dark laugh.

WAKE UP!

Aoire jolted upright in her bed with a gasp as Father's voice shattered the nightmarish dream. The harsh smells of the world came crashing down around her, helping to push away the lingering cobwebs of the dream. The sharp smell of earth and the sounds of the city outside were all around her as she sat in her bed. In the dim light, Aoire traced her fingers lightly over where he had grabbed her by her left wrist. Her skin was burning, ice cold to the touch and felt cracked. She could feel blood seeping through the cracks in her skin.

I am coming for you.

His dark voice echoed in her head, sending chills down her back. Aoire ran her hands through her long auburn hair as a thin layer of sweat began to collect on her brow. He was familiar to her, but any thought of him vanished the moment she grasped onto it.

Who is he, Papa?

A single thought entered her mind:

All will be made known in time.

Sighing, Aoire forced all thought of the nameless man out of her head. It was infuriating to her that she didn't know him – Father had never kept things from her before, so why would he keep this man secret?

He must have his reasons. Aoire told herself.

Swinging her feet to the floor, Aoire strode to the trunk at the foot of her bed and quickly dressed. The packed earth was cool under her feet, and the pale green algae from the lanterns on her walls gave off just enough bluish-white light that Aoire could see around her room. The sounds of the city outside drifted through her glassless window, more muted at this time of day than others.

Between the light of the lanterns and the sounds from outside, Aoire knew it wasn't much past sunrise – or what sunrise was for them. This day was the most important day in the city she lived in, one that only came around once a year. To the rest of the city, it was business as usual. For her, it held much more significance. She knew the timing of the dream was no coincidence.

Moving to her window, Aoire gazed at the city spread out before her. They called it City of End - or End City - and not many alive knew why except Aoire. It was a bustling metropolis of earthen houses with flat roofs, set into four distinct sectors. Endians moved about the city at all times, their paths lit by the algae that grew on the walls of the cavern or lanterns that hung all around End. The intensity of light that was emitted changed depending on the time of day.

The ever-present power - *opari* as she called it - that flowed through Aoire's veins allowed her to simultaneously see the city in its present, and past states. Pale white trails ran in every direction throughout the city, marking the paths that the early inhabitants had walked. Everything swirled before her eyes in layers of color, shape, and sound. She saw what End had once been, what it was currently, and what it could become.

Most of the colors in End were muted - houses of brown, grey, and red - but every now and again a burst of color would intersect with another path. She could see a bright orange-yellow leaf floating on the wind in the fall, or a streak of green as a child long dead and forgotten ran through a meadow that no one alive knew had existed.

From her small room, Aoire heard the sharp ring of the blacksmiths hard at work and could see the glow of their forges that never died out. The fires had been a gift from the Red Sihir, and it was only this fire that could purify the rocks from the lake. It was these rocks in their purified and melted state that created the ionaithe metal that ran throughout all of End. They had even found a way to mold the algae into delicate bulbs that were attached to ionaithe lanterns around the city, allowing each building to have light.

Aoire preferred to stay in this part of the city because she could easily hide. The constant bustle of the blacksmiths' quadrant allowed her to slip in and out unseen. Aoire had managed to be a specter in End her whole life, but it hadn't been easy. Now that this day had arrived, she was taking extra precaution.

Staying invisible in a city like End was nearly impossible, especially for a young woman, but it had its merits. Aoire had come to know the Endians in a special way, and she had never been completely alone. Her adoptive mother was overjoyed every time she came to visit, especially since her husband had died, but even she had to be careful. Neither of Aoire's adoptive parents had been unable to conceive – "Unborns" as they were called – so if anyone knew Aoire existed, it could raise questions that would be impossible to answer. End was a complicated city, full of a multitude of rules, so at times it could also be very dangerous.

This was one of those times.

Looking out upon her beloved city, Aoire's thoughts drifted to the past. To the people of End, it was the start of their seventy-seventh year, even though it was actually the year 4085.

End City had been built as one of five refuge cities, during a time when the human race knew nothing more than what the most powerful company in the entire world – LiquiTech – wanted them to know. LiquiTech was a humanitarian organization that had risen from obscurity. They gained in power until all government officials across the globe were appointed by them, all media outlets were owned by them, all medicine was produced by them, all business had been bought out by them, and all information given to the people was filtered by LiquiTech. They controlled what people wore, what they were taught, and what art was acceptable to look at, even how many children they could have and when. The people lived as slaves, but they were unaware of that fact.

By the year 2590, just as word was spreading about LiquiTech and it's secretive - but powerful - founder, Bitcoin grew to heights no one could have expected. The value of the dollar zeroed out and shortly after Bit Coin collapsed, causing a worldwide market crash far worse than the one that preceded the Great Depression in the Americas in 1929.

Around the same time, a solar flare of epic proportions melted the polar ice caps, flooding thirty percent of the world almost overnight. Another solar flare followed about fifty years after, this one evaporating the earth's oceans and lakes. In reply, LiquiTech's scientists mass-produced water synthesizers that eventually were in every home across the world. Mr. Saoirse, the leader of LiquiTech, refused payment, stating that, "when people are in need, they shouldn't be denied help due to an inability to pay." Overnight, LiquiTech became a household name.

Near the end of 2795, a strange disease appeared, ravaging only the animal kingdom. It wiped out every species on land, in the sea, and in the air. No one knew if it was a new form of chemical warfare, because the disease could not be traced to any particular lab or scientist. It held no markers of any kind when examined, or any clues as to where it had come from. It seemed to spread through bodily contact or through excretions of the flesh, but it had no effect on humans. Within months the world's animal population vanished. LiquiTech began producing a new form of protein to replace what was lost, rationing it out to every family in the world.

With no currency or ample food supply, along with population increase, worldwide panic set in. LiquiTech built glass factories at the edge of every dry lakebed across the globe to create a new form of currency. The factories lifted the air pollution to record levels, forcing humans to stay indoors as much as possible. The times they did have to leave home, they had to use breathing masks even to travel a short distance.

Every home now came equipped with a LiquiTech breathing mask for each person and an air purifier as the climate outside grew more hostile. LiquiTech provided every comfort that each family may need, and because they controlled all information, it was impossible for an uninformed and misguided people to refute them. Even still, rumors and fear have a way of spreading even among the blind. Chatter about growing nuclear arsenals and World War III began to spread.

By the year 3080, the human race had grown to nearly 15 billion people. The President of the World, appointed by LiquiTech, instigated a worldwide population control of two parents and one child. No one left their homes unless they were going to work in the factories. Unable to quell the rumors of a nuclear attack, LiquiTech equipped each home with airtight metal doors and windows that would lock down. They then began running propaganda to calm the masses.

For a time it seemed to work. Humanity knew that the homes they now lived in were crafted to withstand any attack, nuclear or otherwise, but above that they knew that LiquiTech would always find a way to save them. Security and peace settled in and the rumors began to vanish, ushering in a golden era of sorts. But all golden eras have come to an end at some point.

No one was prepared.

No one knew where the first attack had come from, but it was powerful enough to eradicate all of the Middle East and half of Africa. After, it was sheer chaos. Every nuclear arsenal across the globe was set off and LiquiTech went dark. Mr. Saoirse was nowhere to be found and the news coming from LiquiTech stopped. The ones lucky enough to be in their homes were safe when they locked down, but the warning system that LiquiTech had created didn't have enough time to alert others to find shelter.

Overnight the population of the world dropped to a few hundred thousand. Those in their homes had no contact with the outside world. Even without any way to find out what had happened, the weight of that many souls killed overnight could be felt by all. No doors or windows would open until the radiation levels dropped enough, so for two years the people of the earth were confined to their homes, waiting, with nothing but food and no news of the outside world. As the years dragged on, some want mad and others took their lives. Those who survived did so with no information coming from LiquiTech. It was more than anyone could bear.

One day, a single image simultaneously appeared on every television across the globe. It was a silhouette of a mountain with a white lake under its base, and a grey city rising behind the lake. A crisp, clear voice accompanied the broadcast, slicing through the heavy silence. The voice sounded similar to Mr. Saoirse, the long-vanished owner of LiquiTech, but it had changed. The message was simple and repeated on the hour every day.

A HIDDEN SANCTUARY HAS BEEN FOUND. FREEDOM HAS BEEN DISCOVERED. IF YOU ARE LISTENING TO THIS, TUNE TO CHANNEL ONE TO FIND YOUR FREEDOM. WE ARE WAITING FOR YOU. THE END TO YOUR SUFFERING IS WAITING FOR YOU.

End City: the city whose purpose was to end to all suffering and bring salvation.

The message had promised freedom and an end to suffering, but the road had been a harsh one, filled with hardship after hardship. The surface of the earth had changed, barren and cold with sharp winds and sudden lightning storms. Yellow mushroom clouds obscured the sun from view during the day and the stars at night. Rainstorms appeared on a moments notice, dumping acid rain upon the earth with no regard for it, or the people trying to find salvation.

Wrapping her arms around her chest as she gazed upon End, Aoire's thoughts returned to the first settlers of End. She could see their transparent forms entering the city, moving slowly down the long slope that led from the earth's surface and into the cavernous city. Some had collapsed along the way, exhaustion killing them before they could set foot in their new home. Many carried their children, wounded, and their nearly dead, on their backs. Others mustered what energy they had left and raced with complete abandon into their new home. Above, death had been everywhere, but soon after leaving their homes they discovered an even deeper evil that plagued them.

Bashers. The darkest of humans at the time of the attack, the radiation had done something to them, twisting them into the sub-human creatures they were now. There were seven groups of Bashers, and it seemed like their soul purpose was to hunt down all humans and eradicate them.

Aoire shuddered. She had always known evil. Father and Brother had fought against evil their whole existence and Brother even died fighting it. But evil kept coming back and she had a feeling that the nameless man from her dream had some kind of connection to the Bashers. Even with her vast knowledge of the past, present, and future, he was a shadow on top of a lake to her.

Gazing at End, her eyes focused on a section of the wall where the Protectors were training while other Endians worked on the repairs. Years ago Khalefo had attacked, destroying much of the wall and taking many lives. These Bashers were the embodiment of wrath, their attacks always swift and brutal. Aoire admired the resolve of End to continue pushing forward, no matter what happened, but their wasn't a family in End that hadn't been affected by the Bashers.

Aoire put all thought of Bashers out of her mind. Take

every thought captive - that was one of the things Father had taught her. She absently fingered her left wrist, the skin still on fire. She could feel some strength returning to her hand, but the numbness had nearly spread to her elbow.

Hearing her foster mother downstairs, Aoire pulled her hood up. She knew where she needed to go to find help, but she couldn't risk saying anything. Her foster mother wouldn't let her go there, not on this day.

Glancing at her door to make sure it was still shut, Aoire crouched in her window. The street lay far below her, a violent drop if she slipped. Grabbing hold of the bottom of the roof, she hoisted herself onto it.

Moving swiftly and silently, Aoire moved from rooftop to rooftop towards the Birthing House that rose like a sentry at the apex of End City. The rest of the city expanded out like a half wheel from its base. Even from here she could see the blue glow of the lake behind the Birthing House, a lake so large that not even the enormity of the Birthing House could obscure all of it. Unlike the rest of End, the walls of the Birthing House had been whitewashed to resemble the flat stones at the bottom of the lake. Its roofs were the same flat style as the rest of End, bright blue in color to match the lake. Some algae grew on the walls of the Birthing House, making it glow like the starlight of legends told to the children of End.

Finding her way to the east end of the city, Aoire dropped quietly down from the roof into a narrow alley between a home and the wall. Not many came here, unless you were marked an Unborn or had become an Undesirable, and so this part of the city was quieter.

Hearing a sound from within the house to her right, Aoire stopped. Two large eyes peered at Aoire from a low window of the house. Smiling gently, Aoire reached out a hand and pressed two fingers against the child's forehead.

A thin trail of *opari* flowed from Aoire's fingers into the girl's body. Her eyes unfocused, blinking, as Aoire made her forget. Aoire quickly darted down the alleyway before the girl saw her again.

Pulling her hood a little further down around her face, Aoire glanced over her shoulder. Protectors were on top of the wall every minute of every day. Even the Guardians that watched over the Birthing House had eyes on the wall and everything around it. It was easy to make one young child forget she had seen Aoire, but adults or multiple people presented more of a challenge. This was not the time that she could chance being seen or followed. Not yet.

Kneeling before a crack that ran up the wall, Aoire strained as she rolled aside a large rock to expose a hole and the Dhunni forest behind. Glancing back over her shoulder once more, Aoire slipped through. Just as she straightened up on the other side, the main bell at the Birthing House began to chime.

Feeling eyes on her, Aoire wrapped her cloak around herself before entering the forest. She counted the bells as she moved away from the city.

Four.

It's starting, Father. It's time.

Aoire could still feel eyes on her back, but didn't dare to look behind her.

The forest whispered as it closed behind her and blotted End City from her view. The bells still rang loud and clear, cutting through the air sharply.

Nine.

Even in the thick cover of the forest, she could feel the eyes following her movements.

It's almost time. Father's voice whispered through the trees.

Fifteen.

She could begin to see the bright blue glow of the lake through the branches. Behind her she could hear the trees whispering more urgently.

Eighteen.

The last of the forest opened up, and Aoire walked out of it to see the lake spread in front of her. From here she could see the rear of the Birthing House rising up towards the roof of the cavern like a bright white sentinel, the forest pressed tightly against the wall that encased all of End. The bells still rang clearly, but in this place, things were more serene.

Twenty-one.

Aoire knelt next to the lake and dipped her raw and blackened wrist into the water as the last bell rang clear and crisp. Black ooze began to seep slowly from her wrist. Hearing boots shift in the soft sand behind her, she pulled her wrist from the water before it was fully healed. Wrapping a thick strip of cloth around her wound, Father's voice filled her head.

It's time.

Aoire turned to look at who had followed her through the forest.

Chapter Two

Retter Twinblade gazed out over the people gathered below in the courtyard of the Birthing House. His stormy deep-grey eyes were masked, appearing unfeeling as he watched the young women below saying goodbye to their families. The bells had not yet begun to toll, so they still had time. Every year, and with every group, Retter could see the hope in their eyes that they would see their families again. They never did.

He shifted his weight slightly as Eimhir came to stand next to him on the balcony, her blonde hair a stark contrast to his dark. She pressed her fingers together in front of herself, her bright grey eyes scanning over the crowd below. She was a beautiful woman, young and full of life, with intelligent grey eyes. A simple black glass bead hung from a delicate silver strand around her neck.

"These are the hopefuls?"

Her voice was calm, but Retter could hear the edge of authority in it. She was much younger than her post as Amesi, head Mother over all of the Birthing House, the Birthers, and Seeders within would suggest, but she was a powerful figure to the people in End. No Amesi had ever been as young as Eimhir was, something she carried with pride. More pride than Retter thought she deserved.

Retter nodded curtly, his arms crossed across his large chest. He stood at least a head taller than her, but she had a way of making him feel like he was two inches tall. Eimhir turned towards Retter and he could feel her eyes boring into him. They traced over every inch of his body, finally settling on the beads in his braid that marked his rank within the Guardians. He didn't have to look at her to feel her disdain.

"They look promising," Eimhir stated, turning her gaze back to the women below.

Behind them the Birthing House rose to towering heights, a wide building with a spiral tower in the middle. At each of the corners tall turrets stopped when they reached half the height of the main spiral. Walkways connected the turrets to the house, and balconies like the one that Retter and Eimhir were standing on jutted out at different intervals. It had the effect of mushrooms growing up the side of a large tree in a spiral.

Retter's muscular arms tensed. "They look promising every year, Eimhir."

Retter could feel her hot stare on his face, as if trying to will him to show her an ounce of respect. He set his jaw and kept his eyes on the women below.

"Do your duty and make sure they get settled in properly," Eimhir said as Retter's silence grew, turning on her heel. The golden hem of her white dress swirled around her ankles as she vanished into the House.

Retter let out a deep breath and griped the ledge in front of him. Eimhir hadn't always made him uncomfortable, they had even grown up together. She had been a merchant's daughter and he a blacksmith's son. He had been five when he left home to train with the Guardians, and would not see her again for sixteen years. When she came to the Birthing House to train, Retter saw ambition within her eyes instead of hope.

That ambition paid off well for her. Eimhir became the youngest ever Amesi, and from that moment forward her pride grew stronger year after year, but so did her hold on End. She even tried to extend her grip as far as the Guardians, but it stopped with Retter. Eimhir maintained the highest rank within the Birthing House and the city, but Retter maintained the highest rank within the Guardians. He knew that it infuriated her that he did not show her the respect she demanded, but that did not stop him. He would not show respect to someone who ruled through fear.

Today was Collection Day – Retter's least favorite day of the year. It marked the beginning of a new year in End, and Retter had seen many Collection Days since becoming a Guardian. On this day, the women who have turned twenty-one are called to the Birthing House for a year of training. During that year they have no contact with anyone outside of the walls of the Birthing House.

Then, on their twenty-second birthdays and the next Collection Day, the Amesi decides who will be branded as Birthers and who will be named Unborns. After the ceremony, the Unborns are cast out into the streets to make a life for themselves. Some are given the children of Birthers and Seeders to care for, but many end up living close to the wall, forgotten and unwanted.

Once the Birthers are named, they are moved to their new quarters in the Birthing Wing. Cast into a life of bearing children year after year until they cannot, they have been taught from birth that this is their duty. No one tell them that they are then cast into the streets to live as paupers once used up for the glory of End. Many ex-Birthers find themselves living destitute by the wall, forgotten and unwanted. No record is kept of the women who are forced to serve their city in this way, or the children they bear. Only the names of the Amesi are recorded.

It turned his stomach. This was no life for any young woman to live, but Retter had been trained since the age of five to protect the walls of the Birthing House, not to question Ends entire way of life. He had heard the Collection bells ring every year for the past twenty-eight years, reminding him of his place in this world.

Muttering under his breath, Retter turned his back to the courtyard as the first of the bells rang out, but movement on the east side of the wall caught his eye. Retter's brows furrowed as his sharp gaze caught sight of a hooded figure in a long brown cloak slipping through the wall. Memories of seeing that cloak before in various places around the city sprung up, but it was as if the memories had been changed – like they had been fragmented.

"Watch the women. Make sure they get processed," Retter said to a Guardian standing beside him on the balcony. Without waiting for a salute, he entered the Birthing House.

Inside, it was a hive of activity. Current Birthers, their midsections now swelled with life, watched the new prospects enter through the main doors. They stood on various balconies that connected to the spiral staircase rising from the floor of the Grand Hall. The staircase connected everything within the Birthing House together.

The Birthers closest to Retter grew quiet as he drew near, their conversations starting up again once he had passed by.

Even though Retter's steps were heavy, his boots made no noise on the thick black and white carpet that covered the staircase. It matched the carpet running down each hallway that branched out like limbs from staircase. Guardians saluted him as he moved past, but he was so focused on the hooded figure that he did not notice. Large lanterns with delicate ionaithe bases anchoring them to the walls were set at regular intervals along the long hallways, casting everything in a bright, bluish hue.

Retter paused a moment at the main door and looked over his shoulder. Behind him he could see Eimhir standing on the second-floor balcony that stretched across the whole of the grand hall, overseeing everything. He felt her eyes lock onto him, boring into his back as he left the Birthing House.

It didn't take long for Retter to cross the empty courtyard, and find the hole in the wall that he had seen the figure slip through. Stooping down to slide through the hole, Retter looked at the forest in front of him. Each ring of the bells of End pierced through his heart. With each toll, he was reminded of the unwanted sacrifice the young women joining the Birthing ranks were being forced to make. Stepping towards the forest, Retter hesitated a moment as the trees moved to make a path for him. Hearing the bells behind him, he plunged into the forest. Retter wanted to be anywhere but in End this day.

* * * * *

Aoire looked across the lake back towards her beloved End City. By now, her foster mother would have found her room empty, and Aoire knew the panic she would be feeling to find Aoire missing on Collection Day.

This was the day that all mothers feared, but to Aoire this day was much more important. Father had been talking to her about this day her whole life, preparing her for what had to happen. This day was the day that everything would begin to shift, and his plans would fall into motion. The man from her dream had a part to play in all this, that much Aoire knew about him.

The last of the bells faded away and by the light of the algae growing on the cavern walls, Aoire could see that the day was nearly half over. The newest prospects would all be inside the Birthing House by now, waiting to be processed and placed in their new home. Tomorrow they would start a year of training in childbearing. When that year was over, Eimhir would decide their fate. Most believed that being branded a Birther was one of the highest titles you could earn in all of End, but Aoire knew it was just another form of slavery.

After the nuclear attack had subsided and they were safe in End, the original settlers took a census. It was another dark day, revealing that only ten thousand souls had made it to End. Shortly after, another devastating blow was discovered - over half the population was unable to bear children.

The original settlers of End knew that the human race would not survive long if Bashers found them, or if they had no children, so they created a new system of government. They appointed the wisest of their female elders to be the first Amesi, a woman with an affinity for prophetic wisdom. She was named Unua and it was she that chose the first

Birthers and the first Seeders, young women fertile enough to bear children and young men who carried the life spark.

With this new program and way of life, the first generation of Endians began work on the Birthing House. The first of the Protectors and Guardians were named, each one given their different domains. Protectors were created to protect the wall being built around end and the Guardians were entrusted with the protection of the Birthing House. They had originally intended for the Amesi, Protectors, and Guardians to all work together to police End and secure their way of life. They were a tri-form of government, meant to protect End and allow it to thrive.

The Protectors were a rag-tag group of soldiers, consisting of both male and female, learning to fight with whatever they had. They lived in the city and worked on top of the wall, their job as Protector marked by a golden earring through their left ear. Anyone could join the ranks of Protectors and the earring granted them access to anyplace in the city that they wished – except the Birthing House. They were stationed all throughout End, carrying out the daily tasks of protecting its people.

While Protectors acted as a police force for End, Guardians were tasked with protecting Ends' most important asset – life itself. They came to train, live, and protect the Birthing House from the age of five. Only the most elite male children were chosen to be Guardians. Like Birthers, Guardians left behind any family they may have had, living out their lives in service to their duty. They have no wives or families of their own - unlike Protectors - because they know that their calling is what is most important. If Bashers ever got through the Protectors, it was the Guardians they would be met with next, and no Bashers had ever gotten past the courtyard wall to the Birthing House. With these two protective forces, the Amesi was allowed to care for her charges in the way that she saw fit.

With the three entities working together, things improved for a time. Eventually Bashers found them, but they were unprepared for the wall or the resistance that met them. It stalled their attacks for a bit, but only that. Sometimes their attacks would come in waves, and other times they waited months or years before attacking again. It was as if the Bashers were testing Ends defenses to learn more about them.

Many souls were lost over the years, but this only steeled the resolve of the Endians. They became even more resilient, and more set on the idea of Birthers as their numbers dropped. The last Basher attack had been one of the worst. Among many others, Aoire's foster father had been killed doing his duty as Protector. Not a single person in End had been spared the heartache of losing a loved this time.

A sharp stab of pain brought Aoire out of the past. She cringed as she pulled the hem of her sleeve up to expose her left wrist. In the light, she could see the shape of a hand wrapping around her wrist, the skin blackened and blistered. Underneath her charred flesh, she could see the bright red of exposed flesh.

Kneeling down, Aoire plunged her wrist into the lake with a deep breath. The water was warm and thick, wrapping around her arm. Aoire whimpered softly, biting her bottom lip and blinking away tears as the water washed her burns. Aoire felt a tug within her wound, blinking as black ooze began to seep from her wrist. The ooze twisted and turned in the water as it was pulled out, like it had a life of its own.

Barely able to withstand the pain any longer, Aoire pulled her wrist from the lake as she heard boots on the sand behind her. No water ran down her arm or clothing. The burn had begun to heal, the blackened skin now replaced with a sickly pale scar. It was still in the shape of a hand.

Gritting her teeth, she attempted to make a fist. Her fingers curled weakly, but she was happy to feel she had more of her strength and control back. Unclenching her fist, Aoire felt her stomach churn for a moment from a wave of pain, but she recovered quickly.

Wrapping a thick strip of cloth around her wrist, Aoire turned around to face the man behind her. He stood at the edge of the forest, his black leather outfit signifying his rank as Guardian. Four beads, not the usual three, were woven into the braid that hung down from behind his left ear. The rest of his hair was cropped short in the normal Guardian style, intense eyes gazing at her from underneath dark eyebrows. Their eyes locked as the last bell faded away.

It's time. Father's voice echoed in her head.

Chapter Three

Retter wasn't quite sure what happened once he entered the forest. It was as if all thought left his mind except one – *find her.* He wasn't sure who 'she' was, but it seemed as if his feet knew the way. The forest was thick around him, but the trees moved out of the way to reveal a path. Hardly any light from the algae was able to penetrate the thick forest, but Retter saw that the trees gave off a glow of their own. At the end of the path, he could see the blue of the lake clearly.

Looing around, Retter realized he had never looked at a Dhunni tree up close before, even though he saw these trees every day in the courtyard of the Birthing House. They were beautiful, both in a stately and wild way. Each tree was exactly like the other even down to the shape of their roots.

Running a hand across the smooth grey trunks, Retter could see a small amount of light glowing within each white leaf on the branches. The branches all started at the same point on each tree, the groups of leaves clustered to resemble glowing orbs. Retter had seen some of the young Guardian recruits cut into the trees in the courtyard to eat the sap for food and a healer at the Healing House boil the leaves into a medicinal tea for infections. Pulling his hand away, Retter pushed on towards the lake.

Stepping out of the forest, Retter paused. He had only ever seen the lake from the Birthing House, and the size of it had never struck him before now. Now that it spread out in front of him, he could see its size dwarfed End City. The water was crystal blue, and didn't look very deep. He could see directly down to the bottom of the lake, large flat white stones covering the lakebed. Nearly no noise from End could be heard here - here it was quieter and more serene.

As his boots fell on soft sand, his gaze was drawn to the small figure standing at the lake edge with their back to him. Immediately Retter knew this was the person he was supposed to find. Their hood was still up, a long cloak made of various shades of brown leather patched together hanging around them. Even from behind, Retter knew it was female.

The figure straightened up and turned around slowly. Retter couldn't see the face under the hood, but he felt their gaze. Pale, slender hands reached up and pulled the hood back.

Retter was not prepared for the face that greeted him as the hood fell away. Bright auburn hair spilled out, waves of curls, cascading around her shoulders. Her features were a perfect mixture - soft, powerful, feminine, fierce, youthful, and wise. Bright, light grey, eyes fixed him with an unwavering gaze that seemed to take all of him in, but look right through him at the same time. Unlike Eimhir, her gaze put him at ease. It was as if she knew everything about him and still wanted to know more.

She stood at the water's edge, her back straight with the

lake framing her. The blue glow from the lake illuminated her hair like fire. She was the most regal creature that he had ever seen in his life, and Retter felt completely disarmed by her. Her eyes were what drew him in the most, eyes much older or wiser than her features would suggest, but gentle and kind as well.

"I see you found the way here safely, Retter," she said, breaking the silence.

Retter looked behind him, seeing that the path he had traveled was gone. At a loss for words, he turned back to her.

Clasping her hands in front of her, she fixed him with a steady gaze. "I know why you have come."

Retter cleared his throat. "What? How?"

The girl shrugged nonchalantly. "It's Collection Day. Do you see any other young women around here? It's no accident that you are here, Retter."

"How do you know my name?" Retter asked.

"Being a ghost in a city this size has its perks. I have known you for a long time."

Retter crossed his arms over his chest, suddenly feeling exposed. "How long have you been a ghost here?"

The girl looked at him, her head to the side with a slight smile on her lips. "It bothers you that you don't know me, doesn't it?"

"It bothers me that I don't know your name," Retter replied, his voice lowering.

The girl continued to smile. "In time."

"What are you doing down here on Collection Day?" Retter asked, deciding to change the subject. "Didn't you hear the bells? All women of age are supposed to gather at the Birthing House. If you really grew up here in End than you would know that."

The girl absently tugged at a leaf on a nearby tree. "Your laws do not pertain to me. They never have."

Retter blinked at the subtle bluntness of her remark. Anyone else would have been arrested for such a statement, but she held a gentle authority to her voice that made her statement believable.

"If our laws do not pertain to you, whose laws do you follow?"

"Father's."

Retter's mind raced. He knew all the men in End who could possibly have had a daughter with hair like hers. No one had hair like hers.

"Your father," Retter repeated slowly. "Who is he?"

She spread her hands out around her. "Many call him Creator, but only I call him Father. He watches over everyone and everything, and I do nothing without his permission or instruction. He is all things to one person, but then nothing to another."

Retter watched her face change as she spoke about her father. He had heard others in End speak of their gods as she did – End was a polytheistic city – but he had never heard anyone speak with such conviction. Something inside his heart stirred. Immediately he knew that he could never leave her side.

"Will I get to meet this mysterious father of yours?" Retter asked.

She stroked the trunk of the tree and for a moment the glow in the leaves brightened.

"One day," she replied, walking towards Retter.

Passing by him, the forest opened up as she neared its edge to reveal a path back towards End. She paused, looking back at Retter expectantly. "We should get going. It's time."

Retter fell in step next to her and they walked in silence back towards End. She was a tiny thing, her head barely coming up to his chest, but it was Retter who felt smaller. Looking back over his shoulder, Retter watched the trees fill in behind them, obscuring the way they had just come.

"What happened to your wrist?" Retter finally asked, pointing to her left wrist. He could see the edge of the burn peeking out over the top of the thick cloth that bound her wrist.

"I had a run-in with an old foe last night," Aoire replied.

"Last night?" Retter asked. "Shouldn't you go to a Healing House?"

Aoire waved his question away. "It'll be fine. It's already starting to heal."

Retter put a hand on her shoulder, stopping her. "I can tell that this is a burn and a bad one at that. There is no way that it should be this healed already. Is this another thing that your father is able to do for you?"

She absently fiddled with the ends of the cloth around her wrist. "No. Not overtly at least. The lake was able to heal most of it."

Retter's eyebrows arched, but the rest of his face was blank as normal. "That lake?"

She smiled up at him. "That lake is not just pretty to look at, nor is it only for providing water for the Bath Houses. It has other attributes as well, powerful healing attributes."

"I never knew that," Retter grunted.

The girl ducked under the hole in the wall, waiting for Retter to join her on the End side. "Not many do. It's unfortunate that the proper use of the lake has not been utilized."

"It doesn't surprise me. Information is power here, and the ones who wish to be the most powerful work to keep things like that hidden. It's a way for them to control others. The same people might take offense when they learn about you."

She and Retter began moving through the alleyway back towards the Birthing House.

"I revealed myself to you first for a reason, Retter. I hope bringing me to the Birthing House will not cause problems for you."

"No more than I am already in. There is a growing darkness here in End, and has been for a while now. It is especially bad within the Birthing House. Many secrets are being kept, not only from Guardians, but also from the rest of End. Your unknown presence in the city, and your appearance here today, will no doubt cause ripples throughout End. Eimhir especially will not like this."

"The Amesi," she said, her eyes darting to the Birthing House that loomed over them.

Retter nodded. "She prides herself on knowing *everything* that goes on in End, especially when it comes to the young woman who may become Birthers."

The girl stiffened at the word Birther, pulling her hood tighter around her face. The tip of her nose vanished. She readjusted the thin strips that hung down in front of her body to wrap around her slender neck. Seven colored beads hanging at the end of them were the only splash of color to her ensemble.

"It's time," she said, taking a deep breath as they crossed

the main courtyard and came before the main doors to the Birthing House.

Retter did not strain as he pulled on the heavy doors. They opened without a sound, allowing the bustle from inside to spill out. No one seemed to notice them yet. Eimhir was still overseeing the prospects from her place on the second-floor balcony, two tall Guardians behind her. A small murmur spread throughout the hall as they caught sight of Retter and Aoire. Quickly all eyes turned towards them.

From under her hood, Aoire kept her gaze straightforward and steady as they moved further into the Grand Hall, trying to keep her heart from beating out of her chest. A dull ache in her wrist began, intensifying the closer to Eimhir she drew. Drawing closer to Eimhir, Aoire heard Father's voice in her mind.

Tread lightly Daughter, and be aware. He is always watching and searching for you, and his spies are everywhere.

Stopping in the middle of the hall, Aoire could feel all eyes on them both. Not a single sound could be heard. Aoire's eyes took in the tapestry that hung under the balcony Eimhir was on, a picture of a black mountain with a white lake under its base and a grey city behind the lake. Aoire's eyes shifted up to Eimhir. The effect of her standing above the image that had driven so many from their homes, and down to the City of End, was not lost on Aoire.

Aoire closed her eyes, quickly finding her *opari* deep within her. The ever-present swirling mass of power was soft and warm behind her navel. In her mind's eye, she could see the opalescent ball of fire lazily spin and twist within the tree roots that encircled it. Each of the eight roots had vines wrapping around them, a different color for each root. Focusing on the root that had blue vines, it pulsated and the ball of flame turned blue. Her senses immediately sharpened.

"And what have you brought us today, Commander?" Eimhir asked, her voice slicing through the silence.

Retter opened his mouth to reply, but Aoire lifted her hand slightly, silencing him. Without a word, Aoire gracefully took down her hood. A murmur rapidly spread through the crowd as her red curls spilled out around her shoulders. Aoire lifted her chin to stare directly at Eimhir, her round eyes unblinking. Questions echoed through the hall.

"Who is she?"

"Is she a Prospect?"

"Have you ever seen hair like that?"

"Where did the Commander find her?"

"Where did she come from?"

Aoire kept her hands clasped loosely in front of her, keeping her eyes on Eimhir. Eimhir raised her hands to try and gain control over the room. It grew quieter, but Aoire could still hear hushed whispers float around.

"What is your name?" Eimhir asked.

Her voice rang out clearly in the hall, but Aoire could detect a slight waver to it. Glancing at Retter, she knew he heard it too.

"Aoire Ah'Rhyss," Aoire replied. Her voice was softer than Eimhir's, but it filled every inch of the hall and commanded immediate silence.

Aoire saw Eimhir's eyes flick around, her jaw flexing as she saw the effect Aoire's voice had on the crowd. One hand absently began twirling the bead around her neck.

Aoire breathed in sharply, quickly grabbing her wrist.

Red-hot pain flashed up her left arm from her wrist. She could feel the man from her dream on the edge of her mind, trying to force his way into her thoughts. Aoire heard his dark laugh again, all the hair standing up on the back of her neck.

I CAN SEE YOU. I KNOW WHERE YOU ARE AND I AM COMING FOR YOU.

"Dleihs," Aoire whispered softly.

Her eyes flashed bright blue and then turned back to grey as she spoke the spell. The air around Aoire thickened, shielding her. Immediately his dark presence left, but Aoire still reached out with her mind to make sure he was truly gone. She searched for his voice, or his presence, and felt nothing. Realizing that she was holding her wrist too tightly, Aoire loosened her grip. The pain had ebbed as well.

"It is nice to finally meet you, Aoire Ah'Rhyss," Eimhir said a little too politely. "Who are your parents?"

Aoire looked up at her. "My parents are not important to you. They serve you no purpose. Father is the one who sent me."

"Your father? Who is he? A Seeder?"

Aoire paused a moment before answering. "None of my parents are."

A sharp murmur went through the crowd as Aoire's words hung in the air.

Eimhir's eyes flashed, angry at losing control over the room again. "Silence!" Immediately the room quieted.

Eimhir turned her cold gaze back to Aoire. "In a way, you are right. Your parents are not my concern, but you are. You are obviously past or near the age of processing," her gaze shifted to Retter, "and thankfully my Commander finally remembered his sacred duty and brought you here.

How he ever could have overlooked someone with hair like yours for so long is beyond me. But now that he has done his duty, he is no longer needed today."

"Excuse me?" Retter asked, uncurling his crossed arms. "What gives you the right to order me around Eimhir?"

Eimhir's cold gaze lingered on Retter before she turned her emotionless eyes back to Aoire. "Now that he has brought you here, here is where you will stay. We will figure out your lineage later, but for now you will be trained as a Birther. My Commander will go back to his duties, because that is where he belongs. Seeing as his duties are numerous, I doubt the two of you will see each other again for a while, if ever. Guardian Caz will show you to your quarters, Aoire, and *Commander...*you and I will speak at a later time."

Retter moved instinctively closer to Aoire. "I would like to escort her to her quarters. After all I found her, and it is my right as Commander."

Eimhir's top lip curled back as she looked down at them both. "I think you lost that right when you abandoned your post. Perhaps we can find a way to remind you of the duty you swore your life to. There are consequences to your actions, Commander, and your choice today could prove costly."

Without waiting for a reply, Eimhir snapped her fingers. "Caz!"

One of the Guardians on the balcony stepped forward. Caz was dressed in the same black leathers as every other Guardian, but they were worn slightly looser. Dark chestnut hair was cut in the traditional Guardian style, intelligent dark eyes darting around the room constantly. Aoire tilted her head to the side as she took in all of Caz. There was something different about this Guardian.

"Amesi?" Caz asked.

"Please escort Aoire to her room," Eimhir said.

Nodding, Caz moved to leave the balcony, but Eimhir placed out a hand. Speaking softly so that only Caz could hear her, Eimhir looked at Aoire with disdain. "Put her in one of the original cells. Twenty-one should be adequate."

"Amesi?" Caz asked again, confused. No one used those cells, ever.

Eimhir's gaze never left Aoire. "I believe our guest deserves a special place to lay her head."

Caz hesitated, but finally nodded in obedience. Aoire watched as Eimhir motioned for the other Guardian – one with a crooked nose, and bright blonde hair – to come to her as Caz descended from the balcony.

Stopping in front of them, Caz motioned for Aoire. Aoire could see the protective way Caz stood, putting as much distance between them as possible. Stepping forward, Aoire stopped when Retter put a hand on her wrist.

With his other hand, Retter took Caz by the elbow. "Don't do this, Caz. Let me take her."

Caz was almost tall enough to look Retter in the eye. "I'm sorry, Commander. Not all of us have the luxury of being able to disregard Amesi's orders like you do."

Caz's gaze deepened, eyes intent. "Be careful, Commander. There are things going on here that even you don't know about. I would suggest that you tread lightly."

Retter opened his mouth to reply, but was stopped as the blonde Guardian appeared in front of him. Taking Aoire tightly by the arm, Caz led her away from Retter. Aoire went with Caz quietly, leaving everything behind them. She could feel Emihir's hot gaze lingering on her back until they vanished from sight.

Chapter Four

Caz walked silently down the long corridor with Aoire by her side. They had not said a word after Eimhir had ordered Aoire into Caz's custody, but Aoire had gone with Caz willingly. She studied Caz the entire way, and what made Caz different from all the other Guardians finally sunk in.

Caz was not a young man, but a young woman. Even though she dressed like a Guardian, cut her hair like a Guardian, and carried herself like a Guardian, there were feminine aspects about her that were impossible to stay hidden now that Aoire figured it out.

Aoire knew that Guardians were never female. It was unheard of, and yet here she was. Aoire wondered how Caz had managed to stay hidden in plain sight for this long. Caz's true name flashed through Aoire's mind, and for a moment, memories that were not Aoire's replaced her thoughts.

The thick carpet ended as Aoire and Caz descended steep stairs. Continuing down a long hallway, the smooth walls changed to rough stone. The sound of Caz's leather echoed dully through the hallway, coupled with the sound of their footfalls. There were fewer lanterns on the walls here, spaced further apart, and they were barely emitting any light.

Aoire and Caz's forms cast long shadows down the hall as they walked. The hallway grew darker, old wooden doors appearing on both sides. Crude numbers were scratched into them and dark brown stains had spread up the walls between the doors. The air thickened, becoming stale and oppressive. From behind one of the doors, Aoire thought she could hear a woman scream but Caz made no motion that she had heard it as well. Shivering, Aoire pulled her cloak tightly around herself.

Finally, they stopped in front of a door with a twenty-one scratched crudely into it. There was no door handle, only a rusty ionaithe lock bolting the door to the wall.

"Eimhir's bright idea to put me in here?" Aoire asked, her fingers tracing the number. She could feel an angry presence behind the door, pushing against her hand. Caz did not reply.

"Do they know about you, Ahearn?" Aoire asked, turning around. She fixed Caz with a gentle gaze.

Caz stiffened. It had been nearly twelve years since she had heard anyone speak that name. "I don't know what you are talking about. My name is Caz."

Aoire smiled gently. "You and I have both been in hiding for far too long. Be careful, Ahearn. Your true identity will always find its way to the surface."

"I don't know what you are talking about," Caz repeated more firmly. She reached around Aoire and unlocked the door. The bolt rang out sharply in the empty hall as she pulled it free from the wall, the rusty hinges creaking as the door swung open.

What little light was in the hallway fell upon a bare room

just large enough for a single bed, with a hole in the floor underneath a glassless window. The window was barely large enough for Aoire to see outside. Rusted lanterns lay where they had fallen from the walls, blanketed with years of dust. Aoire could feel the presence in the room grow stronger. Caz did not look at Aoire, but silently held the door open.

Taking a deep breath, Aoire stepped into the cell. She turned around to face Caz. "Please be careful, Ahearn. You are very important and if Eimhir was to find out your secret, everything would change. This place may not be safe anymore, even now."

Caz raised her eyes to meet Aoire's, her jaw set. "I don't know what you are talking about."

Without another word the heavy door swung shut, and Aoire was plunged into complete darkness. From within her cell, Aoire could hear the bolt scrap against stone as it slid into place. The sound of Caz's heavy boots faded away, the silence in Aoire's cell resonating off the walls like the breath of a living creature. Aoire shivered, pulling her cloak even more tightly around herself.

Sitting on the hard bed, Aoire's eyes slowly adjusted to the darkness. Pulling her knees to her chest, Aoire did everything she could to ignore the old, faded stench of human that still lingered in the room and the growing feeling of anger and panic that she felt all around her.

Something tragic had happened in this room. What had been left behind was just as angry.

Opening her mind, Aoire's surroundings melted away like smoke, and she now saw the room in its original state. It was a simply furnished and beautiful room. The two lanterns were now on either side of the window, burning brightly. Lush pillows and blankets lay on the bed with a small carpet in the middle of the room. A wispy form of a young woman stood with her back to Aoire, staring out the window. Waves of despair, anger, and pain washed over Aoire.

The woman turned around to face her. Wild hair framed a plump face that had become emaciated from starvation. Equally wild eyes looked at her, her stomach round with child. Dark scratches ran from her eyes to her chin. Her clothing, which had once been made of beautiful finery, was now tattered and stained. The woman tore at her face, screaming soundlessly, and hurled herself at Aoire.

A rush of wind hit Aoire as the woman passed through her, pushing her back against the wall of the cell. All the air was driven from her lungs, pulling her from the vision. Aoire felt hot tears begin to fall down her cheeks as her heart broke for the woman who had suffered long ago, alone and with child, locked in the tiny cell. Shivering uncontrollably, she wrapped her cloak tighter around herself and collapsed onto the bed.

* * * * *

Memories flooded Caz's mind as she walked away from the old cells - memories that she had forced away long ago. The face of Commander Bearn, her foster father, flashed before her eyes. Caz swallowed back the hard lump that formed in her throat. She could still hear his voice, hear the lessons he had taught her that had stayed with her all these years later.

Strong family ties are the key to survival.

Knowing who you are is more important than what others think of you.

I push you harder than any other recruit not because you are my daughter, but because I know the greatness that you hold within.

Push yourself past your boundaries. You will always be your greatest enemy.

Learn every way you can to protect and defend yourself. One day you will be called to a greater purpose than being a Guardian. One day your future will come for you, and even if you do not feel ready, you must be.

Never turn your back to your enemy! Learn your surroundings! Learn the weaknesses of your enemies so you can use those to your advantage.

Be strong my daughter, not just in body, but also in mind.

Protect yourself, Caz. This is your name now. No one can know who you really are, or everything will be chosen for you. This is where you belong, but you have to protect yourself.

"Guardian Caz?"

Caz blinked, turning around. She was so consumed with her thoughts that she didn't realize she was nearly to her room. Guardian Cayden, who had been next to her in the Grand Hall, stood behind her. His crooked nose hung over his top lip slightly, and a shock of white-blonde hair made his pale grey eyes look even paler. The edges of his mouth mimicked the downward turn of his nose.

A white bead was woven below the other two in his braid, signifying his standing as a Major within the Guardians. Caz wore a similar bead with a silver stripe through the middle, signifying her rank as First Lieutenant. She nodded her head in salute.

"Did you do it?" Cayden asked.

Caz blinked. "Do what?"

"Put that girl, Aoire, in an abandoned cell instead of a Prospect's chamber?"

"How did you know that?" Caz asked.

Cayden put his hand on the pommel of the sword at his hip and looked sharply at her. Caz carried no weapons except for a knife she kept hidden up her sleeve. She was in the hand-to-hand combat camp of the Guardians, whereas Cayden was a master swordsman like Retter.

"It should not matter to you, First Lieutenant, how I come to know this. Answer the question. Did you do it?"

Caz's jaw clenched but she nodded curtly. "Of course I did, Major Cayden. Amesi commanded it and I obeyed."

Cayden leaned forward. "Our orders are to obey the Commander, not her. I find it worrisome that I need to remind you of that fact. I hope Amesi's special interest in you hasn't made you think you are better than you are."

Caz felt anger rise up within her. "You forget who *you* speak to, Major Cayden. Of all the Guardians and the people in End, I am the last to want special treatment. I simply made the decision that I thought was best. After witnessing the Commander blatantly disregard Amesi's orders, I wasn't about to challenge her."

"Guardians don't have that luxury, Caz. We follow only the Commanders orders. Do I really need to remind you of that as well? Amesi may oversee the Birthing House, and everything that goes on within, but we are the ones who protect this house. There is a hierarchy to our family, and we are separate of her command."

Caz didn't reply so Cayden stepped forward, looking her up and down. "You have always shown a rare amount of initiative, but since Amesi has taken an interest in you, your growing disregard for the rules is what will ultimately keep you from the rank that others believe you deserve. You might even make a good Commander one day...if you would simply learn your place."

Caz nodded. "Yes sir. Noted sir."

Looking Caz up and down once more, Cayden walked off.

Breathing a sigh of relief as he left, Caz all but ran the rest of the way down the hall to her room. Shutting herself in her small room, Caz collapsed onto her bed. Overwhelmed by the memories and emotions that were resurfacing, Caz ripped at the tiny buttons on the side of her jacket. It opened, and for a moment Caz felt like she could breathe.

Caz traced the thick web-like scar that splashed across her left shoulder and up her neck. It partly vanished beneath the black bands around her torso that gave her a more masculine figure. The scar ran the entire length of her left side.

In her mind she could hear a woman screaming. Fire flashed before her eyes. Caz had been seven when Bashers had set fire to the section of the city she lived in with her parents. The fire had spread quickly, jumping from home to home like a living creature. She still had no idea how she had been pulled from her home before the fire completely consumed it. All she remembered after passing out from the smoke was waking up to Bearn's face, full of concern, as he tended to her burns. It was Bearn that had nursed her back to health and given her a new family.

A knock at the door pulled Caz from her thoughts. Buttoning up her jacket quickly, Caz opened her door. "Amesi! What brings you here?"

Eimhir stood framed in her doorway, her face devoid of emotion. Without a word, she pushed past Caz and entered her small room.

Stopping in the middle of the room, Eimhir turned slowly around before shifting her cold gaze back to Caz, her nose wrinkled slightly. Not sure what to do, Caz stood by her open door.

"You may close the door," Eimhir said.

"What brings you here Amesi?" Caz asked.

"Do you know that I have never actually been in a Guardian's chambers before? You do live simply, don't you?" Eimhir asked, her voice snide.

Caz glanced around her small room, brightly lit by two lamps that stood on either side of the round glassless window opposite the door. From here, she could see the training courtyard below and look out across the rooftops of End - a view Caz had always loved. A bare chest made of Dhunni wood sat at the end of her bed, and a small washbasin sat to the right of the window. It was a sparsely furnished room, but Caz had never felt shame in that.

Caz shrugged. "Our duty is not to a life of fanciful items, but one of servitude. This room serves me so I can better perform my duty."

Eimhir clasped her hands in front of her, and tilted her head slightly. "And what duty is that, Caz?"

"May I first ask you a question, Amesi?"

Eimhir nodded.

"What will happen to Aoire?"

Eimhir's eyes hardened. "That girl-child is none of your concern, Guardian. She will be dealt with as needed, as will Retter."

"The Commander? Why?"

"It appears as if Retter has forgotten his duty. He constantly undermines me at every turn. I have no way of knowing if his insubordination has spread, and he has forced my hand. If there is a disease within the Guardians, I will need to cut away any infection I find."

Caz could sense a trap. "Is that why you came here, Amesi? To see if I know anything?"

Eimhir smiled reassuringly, but her smile did not reach her eyes. "I came here to get an answer to my original question, dear Caz. What is your duty?"

Caz chose her answer carefully. "To protect the Birthing House and put Ends needs above my own."

"Would you do anything for that duty?"

"As long as I wear the black leathers of the Guardians, I will."

Eimhir studied Caz for a moment before her smile widened. "That's exactly what I needed to hear."

Caz could feel the hair on the back of her neck stand up. The room suddenly felt very cold. "Was there anything else that you needed, Amesi?"

Eimhir didn't reply, but moved towards the door. Opening it for her, Caz stopped closing it when Eimhir turned back around in the hallway.

"There was one more thing, dear Caz. Stick to your duty as Guardian. I have taken a special interest in you for a reason, and if you continue to do as well as you have in the past, there could be a promotion in your future. But if you disappoint me, you will not like the alternative. I too, know many of the secrets around this place," her eyes darted to Caz's chest and then back to her face.

Caz swallowed, trying not to let her fear appear on her face. "Yes, Amesi."

With one final long look at her, Eimhir strode away. Caz closed her door, leaning her forehead against it. She took a few deep breaths to try and calm her racing heart. Caz wasn't sure if Eimhir actually did know her secret, but her threat wasn't very veiled.

The benefit to having such a large secret to hide was that Caz had long since perfected the art of anonymity. She had learned how to make herself so unassuming that others did not often realize she was in the room with them. Knowledge was power, and while Caz was not looking to rise to power, she did find a sense of security in knowing valuable information.

She had long since heard whispers that Eimhir was changing, becoming more strict and harsh in her role as Amesi. Eimhir had been a very beloved Birther, sharp in wit and gentle in spirit, and she originally brought that to her role as Amesi. Over time though, Eimhir had begun to change.

The change could be felt like ripples running through the Birthing House, and even the Guardians had been more on edge - Retter especially. She had heard him speak often of Eimhir's threats, but Caz had never been on the receiving end of one until tonight.

Making sure her jacket was fastened securely, Caz began to make her way to the Guardian Tower. Training always seemed to clear her head.

Called that for as long as anyone could remember, the Guardian Tower didn't resemble a tower at all. Instead, it was a one-story, stone building built along the entire west side of the Birthing House. The inside was broken up into three large training rooms, one for each of the Guardian houses of swordsmanship, hand-to-hand combat, and archery. Once a Guardian had proven which house they most excelled at, they only reported to that room. No Guardian was named into their house until they turned eleven years of age, allowing for six years of training. Once named, their first beads were braided into their hair - one for their age bracket and a second one to signify which house they belonged to.

Caz had come to live at the Birthing House at the age of seven, only allowing for four years of training, far less than any other Guardian. Her natural talent allowed her to excel within each of the houses and she rose quickly through the ranks, but her upward momentum stalled when her body began to change. Caz didn't care that her secret held her back. A higher rank meant more scrutiny, less privacy, and she couldn't risk being found out. No woman had ever been named Guardian. If they found out what Bearn had done...

Caz shuddered to think what could happen to her.

Exiting the hallway, Caz quickly descended the narrow staircase. It led her out of the Birthing House next to the training courtyard of the Guardian Tower. The familiar ring of training met her ears and immediately she felt her whole body relax.

Weaving her way through the courtyard, Caz slipped through the arched opening to the hand-to-hand combat room. A simple brown tile had been placed in the wall above the opening, colored glass beads for each of the Guardian ranks set around the tile. A matching light blue tile was above the entrance to the archery room, and a grey tile with three gold stripes was set above the swordsmanship room.

Entering the training chamber, Caz took it all in quickly. A few Guardians were in the room, but these Caz ignored. Instead she zeroed in on the two Guardians in the back. The light from the lanterns played off the golden beads in their braids, signifying their rankings as Major Generals.

Moving quietly, Caz positioned herself as close to the two of them as she could get. She knew they were always aware of their surroundings, as all Guardians were, but Caz also knew she could get as close to them as she wanted to. Not even Retter knew every time she was near him.

"...and she is still detaining him?" Major General Mannix asked.

He was a short, burly man, with a flattened nose from a training incident when he was younger. It had never healed properly, causing the rest of his face to look flat as well. He had dark grey, almost black, eyes that were perpetually stormy. Mannix had the ability to get any recruit, or Guardian, in line with just a look.

"Yes. No word has been given as to when he will be allowed to return," Major General Tol replied, his clear grey eyes also stormy under his thick eyebrows.

Tol was a stark contrast to Mannix in every way. Half of his blonde beard had turned grey over the years, adding to his stately features. Tall and lean, he stood a whole head taller than Mannix, his blonde hair streaked with grey at each temple. He was a handsome man, far more compassionate than his counterpart, however both had earned the respect of more than just the men they commanded.

"Gods. She is getting out of control," Mannix swore. His eyes darted to Caz, and she immediately straightened her back.

"Is there something you need, First Lieutenant?" Mannix barked.

"I simply wanted to see if the Commander was around. I need to speak to him," Caz replied, her eyes straight ahead.

"If there is something that you need to ask, it can wait.

Anything you need to know, you will be informed of," Mannix said, turning back to continue his conversation with Tol.

Caz lifted her chin defiantly. "I don't need to ask anything, sit. The Commander wanted to be the one to take Aoire to her chambers, and I thought he should know where she ended up."

"Why?" Tol asked, turning to look at her.

Caz's eyes darted between them for a moment and then back to the wall behind them. "Because Eimhir ordered me to take Aoire to the first Birthers' cells."

Mannix opened his mouth to speak, but Tol lifted a hand. His studious eyes fixed on Caz. "Eimhir told you not to take her to a Prospects chamber?"

Caz nodded her head. "Yes, Major General. I thought it odd that she wanted the girl housed there, but after what happened in the Grand Hall, I thought it pertinent to obey Amesi. I didn't want to make things worse for the Commander, however it may not have made much of a difference in the end."

"What do you mean, Caz?" Tol asked.

"Amesi came to see me tonight. She told me that the Commander was going to be dealt with, and she did not answer me when I asked where he was. She also would not answer why she wanted Aoire in those rooms instead of with the other Prospects," Caz replied.

Tol rubbed his mustache with two fingers for a moment, thinking deeply. "It was odd for Eimhir to command you to escort Aoire away instead of allowing the Commander to do it, especially in front of everyone. It seems even stranger that she wanted the girl in those cells. They have not been used since before any of us were born."

"Is the Commander around? He has known Amesi the longest, perhaps he can say why she would do such a thing," Caz asked.

Tol shook his head. "Shortly after you left, she ordered that the Commander be taken to her chambers, but did not say for how long."

"Who took him?" Caz asked.

Mannix's reply took Caz by surprise. "Guardian Major Cayden."

Caz blinked, trying not to let the surprise show on her face, but she could tell by Tol's studious gaze that he had seen her shock. Caz thought rapidly, looking for a way to pull herself out from under his gaze.

"Why are those cells empty? Why not use them for something else?"

Tol hid a smile behind his hand. *You are quick on your feet, aren't you child? Bearn chose well when he brought you here to be his prodigy.*

He still doesn't miss a thing. Caz thought, studying Tol in turn.

Caz had known Tol as long as she had been at the Birthing House. He and Bearn had been the closest of friends. Tol had even helped to raise her at times. Sometimes she wondered if he knew her secret, but he had never alluded to if he did or didn't.

"Those cells were used for Birthers who had broken under the stress of their duty. There was a time when Birthers suffered great mental distress from seeing their children snatched away, days after giving birth, and they had to be hidden away for their own safety and the safety of all the people of End," Mannix said.

Caz felt her stomach turn. "They went insane?"

Told nodded, his voice quiet. "Sadly, yes. This was when their role was still being mapped out. Unfortunately, the first Birthers could not mentally process what was expected of them, or what was being done to them. The madness was transferred from generation to generation and it grew, especially among their fertile female offspring. Every option to help them eventually was exhausted. The cells were the last resort."

"So we locked them away?" Caz asked.

Even Mannix's voice was gentler. "It was the only option there was at the time. They were a danger to themselves, and to countless others. The cells were meant to be a saving grace, a place where we could bring in reinforcements to help heal their minds."

"Sihirs." Caz supplied. There was only one group of women that had the power to heal not just wounds, but also minds. They did not show up often, and only when the need was great, appearing mysteriously and vanishing just as quickly.

Caz had seen the Sihir Sisters - women who had powerful magic – only once before, on the day that Bearn had died. A group of red and orange robed Sihirs, called Reds and Oranges, had come to help End when Bashers attacked. They had somehow known End would need them. Caz often wondered if it had been a Sihir that had pulled her from her families burning home.

Tol nodded. "Yes. A group of Yellow Sihir came, but the generational damage to the Birthers' minds was too great. We lost them to their madness, however, the Yellows were able to treat the children of the afflicted and stop the affects. We have not needed those cells for the last twenty generations."

"What happened to the Birthers who first stayed in them?"

Tol and Mannix exchanged a look, before Mannix spoke. "They all died."

Caz swallowed back the lump that rose in her throat. "How?"

Mannix's voice seemed to cut right through Caz. "The damage was too great, and the Birthers shut down after the Yellows came. Some took their lives before the Sisters could reach them. Those they were able to reach were taken back to their Temple, but we got word later that the Birthers did not live much longer."

"And Eimhir ordered me to place Aoire in that hell hole!" Caz spat.

Tol looked sharply at her – in all his years, he had never heard Caz call Eimhir anything other than Amesi.

Finally he spoke. "It seems like she wants to make a point about Aoire, but what? None of us has ever seen Aoire before, and Eimhir seems threated by her somehow."

"It's not just Aoire that she may feel threatened by," Caz said.

Mannix frowned. "What do you mean?"

Caz spread her hands. "Amesi believes that all of this, the Birthing House and the way End is run, is somehow her doing. If she really believes that, then a young woman like Aoire would pose a threat. On top of that Retter seemed to defer to Aoire and not to Amesi."

A small smile played at the edge of Mannix's lips. "Well observed, First Lieutenant. You may make a good General, or Commander, yet."

Caz's expression soured as Eimhir's words from earlier rang in her ears. "Thank you, sir."

"For now though, you should get back to your duties," Mannix added. "We have a group of new recruits that could use some training."

Caz started to nod in salute but Tol shook his head. "I have a better idea of how we can use young Caz."

He fixed her with a deep, knowing gaze. "You have always had a penchant for the covert, haven't you Caz?"

"Yes sir," Caz replied hesitantly. Her ability hadn't missed the attention of the higher-ups - or Eimhir apparently. Caz wondered what Tol was thinking as he looked at her.

"I think we could use that ability. It would be beneficial if you can figure out anything about where the Commander is, and why Eimhir has him detained. You will only report back to us. If anyone asks you what you are doing, you are not to expose yourself. Especially not to Eimhir."

"Yes, sir." Turning on her heel, Caz slipped out of the training chambers as quietly as she had come in.

"Think he can pull it off?" Mannix asked.

Tol watched Caz as she left the training chambers. "Caz carries more secrets within himself than either of us are capable of understanding. He is the right man for the job, and furthermore, he is a man of duty and principle. He will always do what he believes is right. If any Guardian can do this, it's him."

Chapter Five

Slipping back into the Great Hall, Caz's mind was focused on where she needed to go, ignoring all else. A few of the prospects were still getting processed, but most had been shown to their chambers. Her eyes fell on a seasoned Birther who was rubbing her swollen belly in expectation. Before this day was done, she and all the other Birthers would meet their children and share just a few short days together before they would be snatched from their mother's arms.

Some of their offspring were give to Unborns to raise, until the girls were called back to the Birthing House. Caz would see the children in the streets, living with no idea of their true lineage. She could also see the longing for their children in the eyes of the ex-Birthers who had been thrown out, aching to be reunited with the ones they had never gotten the chance to know. Every year that Caz stayed in the Birthing House she grew more fearful her secret would be exposed, but she had no other place to go.

Scanning the hall, her eyes fell on a long tapestry that hung across the hall. It was the image of the first Amesi, Unua, bringing forth the first of the Birther children. She was sitting on a plush bed with multiple faces looking up at her, bright light rays radiating out from her head like a crown. Unua's face was serene, not twisted with the painful screams of childbirth that had already begun in the north wing. Caz hated those screams and she hated this tapestry. It was meant to be an inspiration to all who looked at it, but it was just another shackle on the wrists of all fertile young women in End.

Slipping her hand behind the tapestry, Caz felt around. Feeling a small, rough stone underneath her fingers, Caz pressed it firmly. She heard a tiny click and a rush of air ruffled the tapestry slightly. Slipping behind it, Caz stepped into the hidden corridor before anyone noticed she had even been in the hall. Small holes were drilled into the walls, allowing light, sound, and fresh air in.

"Thank the gods it is still here," Caz muttered, half to herself and half to Bearn. It had been years since she had last been in any of the corridors in the Birthing House, but she remembered immediately where to go.

As a small child, she had run and explored every inch of the Birthing House after she had been brought here. It was mostly out of her own curiosity, but also Bearn's instruction. He had wanted her to know every inch of the home she would be living in. As it turned out his request had not been in vain.

About halfway down, the corridor forked. One passage led up through a series of crudely cut steps and another continued straightforward. From the noises and smells wafting through the holes, Caz could tell that she was nearing the kitchen.

Taking the steps up, the sounds and smells of the kitchen faded away. For a long while she heard nothing as she ascended the steep stairs. The air grew colder the higher up she went, keeping one hand on the wall to held guide herself as her eyes adjusted to the darkness. The stagnant smell of the dead air began to give way gradually as more holes appeared in the wall.

As the light in the corridor grew, Caz could hear raised voices, but she was still too far away to make out the words. Continuing to move quietly down the corridor, Caz could now hear Eimhir's voice clearly, but there was another voice that she could not place.

Stopping, Caz pressed herself against one of the holes and part of Eimhir's personal quarters came into view. From what she could see there was no sign of Retter. Eimhir seemed to be pacing back and forth as she spoke angrily to the only other figure that Caz could see. She was wearing a long black dress that absorbed all light, color, and even sound as Eimhir paced in front of her. Caz could see Eimhir's face, but only the black-clad woman's back.

The dress clung to the woman's body like a second skin. Long black hair tumbled down her back in gentle waves, her arms crossed in front of her. Caz could not see her face, but there was something about this woman that pulled her in, making it increasingly impossible to look away. Tearing her eyes away, Caz focused on Eimhir who was pacing the room like a mad woman.

"He promised me!" Eimhir shouted, her eyes wild. "He promised me that if I committed my life to him, I would rule all of End! He promised me that I would be the most famous Amesi that End has ever had! He promised that I would have fame and power, and instead I am met with distrust!"

The black-clad woman did not reply as Eimhir continued to pace, her face growing even wilder. Caz pressed closer to the hole, trying to see as much of the room as she could. She still could not see Retter anywhere.

Where are you Commander? Who is she talking about?

"You are unhappy?" The black-clad woman asked. Her sultry voice sent shivers down Caz's spine.

Eimhir spun around.

"Of course I am unhappy!" she exploded. "He broke his promise to me! The Commander suspects something, why else would he constantly disobey me? Every chance he gets, he undermines me, and now this?! He is a thorn in my side. I want him taken care of!"

"And what will you do when his position is vacant?"

"I have someone in mind who can take his place. A fellow Guardian of low rank, but one that I believe will be loyal to me at any cost. I just spoke to him earlier this evening, and he made it known to me that he would do anything as long as it was in the best interest of End. How could serving me not be in the best interest of End?"

Gods. Caz thought as her own words from earlier rang through her mind.

"What about the questions that will come up?"

Eimhir stared at her. "What questions?"

The woman shifted her weight to the other hip.

"You get rid of the Commander without any warning, and there will be questions. If you promote this *nobody*," she hissed, "to his position, there will be even more questions. Do you really think they will be loyal to you after that? Master promised you all of End on a silver platter, but you are becoming increasingly impatient."

Eimhir shoved a finger at the woman. "I am not being impatient! I have bided my time, and I have waited for him to keep his end of the deal, and he has failed me. Nothing has been done to make me stronger or more powerful. If anything I can feel my grip on End slipping away. Your master is a liar, and I was a fool for putting my trust in that snake!"

Caz blinked in surprise. She hadn't seen the woman move, but one moment she was standing in front of Eimhir and the next she had her pinned against the wall with a hand. Eimhir gasped for breath and clawed at her sleeved arm, her feet dangling inches from the floor.

Caz could now see the black-clad woman's profile, her face one of the most beautiful she had ever seen. Everything about her was sculpted perfectly, porcelain skin smooth over her high cheekbones with full lips stained bright red like her nails. Eimhir looked down at her, her eyes now wild with fear instead of anger. Even as the woman held Eimhir against the wall, she did it gracefully.

"I think your attitude is getting a little out of hand, Eimhir. Perhaps you need to be reminded of your place. Perhaps a touch, or a kiss, will remind you of that," she said, pulling Eimhir from the wall so her face was inches from Eimhir's.

"No," Eimhir managed to choke out, trying to shrink away.

Letting go, the woman looked down upon Eimhir who crumpled at her feet. Crouching in front of her, she lifted up the necklace around Eimhir's neck. Eimhir froze as her fingers almost grazed her skin.

"Master was pleased with one thing you did today. Through the stone, he now knows where the girl-child has been hiding. She has been hidden from him for so long, and we have become so weary looking for her. Now we find that she has been right under your nose this entire time. How feeble and easily blinded you humans are."

"What does he want me to do?" Eimhir rasped as the woman let go of her necklace. She shrunk back against the wall, trying to get as far away from her as she could. Eimhir kept her eyes on the floor, trembling when the hem of her dress brushed her knee. Caz had never seen Eimhir afraid of anyone like she was of this woman.

The woman looked down at Eimhir. "He is coming for the girl-child, and he wants you to do nothing."

"Nothing?" Eimhir asked.

An evil smile swept over the woman's face. Eimhir's body went rigid as the woman put one of her long nails under her chin and lifted Eimhir to her feet. Eimhir tried to pull away, but she couldn't. Thin black lines began to appear on her skin where the sharp end of the woman's nail touched her. Her eyes were wide with shock.

"Yes, do nothing, dear girl. Very soon you will get your heart's desire to be the most famous Amesi of all. That is what you want, isn't it?"

"Yes," Eimhir whispered through gritted teeth.

The woman's' smile deepened. "Then what Master is sending to your doorstep will satisfy just that, my dear. All you need to do is be patient. Can you do that?"

Eimhir nodded, her face twisting in pain as the lines thickened.

"Good. Shall we seal that promise then?" the woman asked, leaning closer to Eimhir and planting a soft kiss on her cheek.

Eimhir's eyes opened wide as searing pain exploded from where the woman's lips touched her face. She wanted to scream, pull away, hit the woman to get her off, but pain shut her mind down. The burning spread to her tongue, and down her neck, her throat beginning to constrict. It took her brain a long moment to realize that the sweet smell around her was her own flesh burning.

Pulling her lips away, the woman wiped the corners of her mouth with her fingers, her face a mask of pleasure. She looked coldly down upon Eimhir, who lay at her feet cradling her face and screaming in pain. Caz couldn't seem to pull her eyes away from what she was seeing as Eimhir's screams filled the passageway.

Turning around, the woman in black fixed her eyes on Caz. Caz leaped back as the woman's eye filled the hole Caz was looking through. She ducked as a fist burst through the wall next to her head, raining rock and dust down around Caz. Caz scrambled to her feet, black vapor pouring into the passageway through the hole her fist had made. The black vapor began to collect on the floor, swirling as if it had a life of its own.

Caz didn't look behind her as she ran away, so she didn't see the vapor solidify back into the black-clad woman. She stood in the passageway and watched Caz run, her face expressionless. Caz did not stop until she skidded out from behind the tapestry and back into the Great Hall. Pressing the same stone, Caz released the breath she had been holding only when she heard the passageway close with a sharp click.

In her mind, she could still hear Eimhir screaming.

Chapter Six

Aoire sat on the hill overlooking her valley with her arms circled around her knees. The setting sun painted the sky with vivid splashes of pink, orange, and yellow. As she watched the sun go down, the tall grass around her swayed lazily in the warm breeze. It was always warm here, with everything bathed in a golden hue that turned silvery after the sunset. The place where his boots had been the night before was still burned black.

This was their spot - the special place that she could meet Father and Brother in peace. She could feel Father's presence in everything from the soft soil at her feet to the birds that swirled and danced above her. From here, wide rolling hills and meadows stretched out in front of her, framed by tall mountains and pine trees that rose like sentries from the ground. A large lake lay off in the distance with yellow, white, and purple wildflowers spreading out in colorful clusters.

She always felt safe here. At least, she had. Tonight, things were different. Ever since he had appeared, that feeling of safety was shaken. On top of it, this day had arrived.

Aoire had always known this day was going to come, but

now that it was here she couldn't seem to keep the lump in her throat from getting any bigger. Even though everything was clearer here, she could feel an angry presence pressing at the edges of her mind.

The grass rustled beside her and Aoire brushed away a rogue tear as Brother sat down. He didn't say a word – he didn't have to. Aoire leaned into him, putting her head on his shoulder.

"Everything changes after tonight," she said into the darkening night, breaking the long silence. Up above them, stars began to wake.

"I know," Brother replied, his voice deep and soothing. Aoire breathed him in. Like Father, he smelled like the earth after a rainstorm, a smell that no one in End had ever experienced before.

"What was it like for you?" Aoire asked.

"It hurt a lot. The path was both long and short, but it was the result of what my sacrifice would mean to the world that gave me the strength to do what Father called me to."

"I don't know if I am ready. Were you?"

Brother smiled gently as he looked down on Aoire, his brilliant blue-green eyes sparkling with love. "You are more ready than you think, little one. They may not be ready for you, but after tonight they will have to be."

Aoire felt him slip a strong arm around her shoulders, his white robes soft as they rustled against her skin. She nestled in even closer to him. "He's looking for me."

Brother's body stiffened for a moment, his arms tightening protectively. "I know."

"Who is he?" Aoire asked. "Father has kept him hidden from my memories, but I know that I know him. He is so familiar, and yet I cannot place him. He vanishes like vapor any time I try to remember."

Brother placed a finger against her forehead, tracing an invisible symbol into her skin. Immediately memories and feelings flooded Aoire's mind, as the door that had been locked, shattered. She felt overwhelmed by the weight of the knowledge that Brother had unlocked.

Head spinning, she collapsed into him, and he wrapped his arms gently around her as she sobbed. Millennia of pain, sacrifice, and loss, hit her body in waves as the memories kept coming. It felt like a lifetime passed before the memories settled into place and she was able to regain control over her mind.

"I see," Aoire said, her voice shaky. "It's definitely time then."

Brother nodded. "The final battle for the world. You are no longer hidden from him, nor he from you. You know who your nemesis is, the same one we have had since the beginning, and he has the Tree. You must get it back from him if this war is to be finished."

"Did your task feel this daunting?"

Brother smiled gently, his eyes taking a far-off look. "At the time yes, but I had my friends around me to help along the way. You will have your own support in your journey too, and they will at times help you find the strength to carry on. While in the end you will be alone, as I was in my final journey, use your love for them and their love for you as fuel."

Taking a deep breath, Aoire watched as the last light of the sun vanished and the rest of the sleeping stars woke. Starlight twinkled in her eyes, the same blue-green as Brother's and Father's. Brother stayed silently by her side, watching the stars with her. They didn't say a word to each other as they sat on her hill, Brother allowing her to be alone with her thoughts.

"Happy birthday, little sister," Brother said to Aoire, and then he was gone.

"Happy twenty-second to me," Aoire replied softly.

The meadow around Aoire slowly melted away and she was back in her cell, lying in a ball on the hard bed, staring up into the darkness. The thin mattress was cold under her body. The silence of the room and the hallway outside was suffocating.

Sitting up and swinging her feet to the floor, Aoire crossed the small room to the window. She reached a hand up and ran her fingers through the pale light of the morning filtering in from the algae blooms on the cavern wall outside. She closed her eyes, trying to go back to the meadow, but couldn't. Ever since Caz had put her in the cell the angry presence had grown, making even that short visit extremely hard. She could feel the raw anger in the room, deep sadness layered underneath immense rage.

Hearing the bolt shift in the cell door, Aoire blinked as dim light from the hallway spilled in. She finally made out a figure in the doorway once her eyes adjusted.

"Ahearn?" Aoire asked, staring at the silhouette in the door.

"Again, that's not my name," Caz said, grabbing her by the arm. Aoire could hear an edge of fear to her voice.

Caz's grip tightened on her arm painfully as she pulled Aoire into the hallway, and slammed the bolt into the wall. Dust covered her black leathers.

Aoire jumped as she felt the presence in the room throw

itself against the door. "Why are you releasing me, Ahearn? What has changed?"

Caz didn't seem to notice the presence. She toke Aoire by the elbow and lead her away. "Someone is coming for you, someone or…something. Commander didn't want you out of his sight and he tried to stop me, but I didn't listen. He was right as usual, there is no way that you can stay here. After what I witnessed tonight, I am not leaving you here to be butchered."

"What did you see?" Aoire asked.

Caz didn't reply at first so Aoire grabbed her wrist. "Ahearn, what did you see?"

Caz's bottom lip trembled slightly, but her voice remained strong. "A woman was in Amesi's chambers. They were talking about the Commander, about you, and about End. Then she just…attacked. I have never seen anyone like her before. She was terrifying, but beautiful. Her touch had an effect on Amesi, burning her somehow."

"You saw this? You were in Eimhir's quarters?"

"Not exactly *in* her room. There are seven hidden corridors throughout all of the Birthing House. I was ordered to find out where the Commander is and I was in one of the hidden corridors when I saw it happen."

"Did you end up finding out where Retter is?" Aoire asked.

Caz peered into the Grand Hall once they ascended the staircase, stopping at where the hallway joined the Grand Hall. From where they stood she could see everything from the arched balcony to a portion of the Grand Hall beyond. It was eerily quiet at this early hour, the only movement coming from a few servants carrying out their tasks.

"Not yet," Caz replied. "But I may know a way how. I

imprisoned you in the cells, and by the rules of our order only I can allow you back out again. I can get you to a safer room without her even knowing you had been let out of the cells. Eimhir suspects that I am on her side; if I question her about the Commander, she may be willing to tell me where he is."

Aoire put a gentle hand on Caz's arm. She could hear Father whispering to her as she stood with Caz. "No."

"No?" Caz asked, looking down at her.

Aoire shook her head. "No. I know where they put Retter."

Caz's eyebrows shot up. "How could you possibly know where he is?"

"I was told. We need to get him out and back to the Guardians before Eimhir asks to see me. You need to tell them what you saw." Aoire replied.

Caz planted her fists on her hips, her face darkening. "What aren't you telling me? There is no one that could have told you where the Commander is, because no one knows except for Eimhir."

Aoire looked at Caz, her voice steady and clear. "Caz, I promise that I have nothing to do with either Eimhir or the woman that you saw, Narcissa. I am given my knowledge by the one that created me, and I only know what he tells me. The two of them serve a great evil, one I am called to defeat, but for now we need to get to Retter. If you can trust me as far as that, I promise everything I am telling you now will ring true."

Caz stared at her. Aoire spoke with such authority, much more than her small stature and young age would suggest. As it did the moment she had seen her in the hall, something stirred deep within Caz. She knew Aoire spoke the truth.

"That woman's name is Narcissa?" Caz asked slowly, looking sideways at Aoire.

"Yes."

"What was she? I have never seen anyone with that kind of strength or speed, or anyone that could vanish like that." Caz said.

"She is a Basher and one of the original Seven. She is the leader of the Lefeela and if he sent her here..." Aoire trailed off, her hand absently fiddling with the cloth that wound around her burnt wrist.

"A Lefeela? Here? In End?" Caz asked, her face going pale. Fire danced in her mind's eye again.

Aoire looked at Caz and saw that she was lost in memory. Stepping in front of her so that her body filled Caz's field of vision, Aoire lightly touched her hand. "Ahearn, I need you to focus. We have to get to Retter. We have to warn the Guardians."

"But I don't know where he is," Caz said, blinking as Aoire's touch pulled her from her memories.

"I do, remember? You said you knew this place better than anyone else, at least the hidden hallways. Can we get to the Southern Tower without being seen?"

Caz shook her head. "There isn't a secret hallway that leads up there. The only way is to go up the main staircase, but there is a Guardian at every hallway entrance. We will be completely in the open."

"No Guardian is stationed at this entrance?" Aoire asked.

Caz hesitated. "No one guards these hallways anymore."

"Why?"

Caz shifted her weight uncomfortably. "Because no one

has used them since their inhabitants went mad and died. If we go to the Southern Tower, we will be seen."

"No, we won't. I can shield us."

"How?" Caz asked.

Aoire smiled at her and Caz frowned. "You make absolutely no sense to me."

Aoire continued to smile. "I know."

Taking Caz's hands, Aoire closed her eyes and focused on the blue veined root surrounding the ball of energy behind her navel. It shifted and turned the ball of fire blue, sending a current of energy coursing through her entire body and into Caz. Caz felt all the hair on her body stand on end as electricity and heat coursed through her veins. All her senses heightened in ways that no Guardian training could teach.

"Dleihs," Aoire said, her eyes snapping open. Caz took a half a step back. Aoire's grey eyes were now bright blue, rimmed in darker blue. The air around them thickened, blue lighting radiated around them both.

"What is the name of End is this?" Caz asked, reaching a hand out to try and touch the lightning. It moved with her arm, never touching her, but sparking above her skin. Without replying, Aoire left the hallway.

"Hey! Aoire! Someone will see you!" Caz shouted, running after her.

"No one can see or hear us now," Aoire replied, waving away Caz's comment.

Aoire moved towards the spiral staircase that led to the top of the Birthing House. Sighing, Caz fell in step beside her, her eyes still darting around. She steeled herself as a maid came out from one of the hallways that branched off from the grand hall, but Aoire did not slow down or change course as the maid drew near.

Taking a deep breath, Caz was sure the maid would see them. Her brow wrinkled as she passed by them, feeling the warmth of the lightning. She paused to look around, but eventually shrugged and then continued off towards the kitchen.

"How?" Caz asked, staring at her hands and the lighting around them. The maid had been so close that Caz could have touched her if she wanted to.

"It's called Shield Magic, a derivative of Blue Magic. The spell I use is simple, but one that I can bend to my will. Whatever I imagine, I can create," Aoire replied.

"That word you used, that's a spell?" Caz asked.

Aoire nodded.

"Are all spells spoken?"

Aoire shook her head. "No, not all. Some are only thoughts."

Caz gritted her teeth as they ascended the staircase and passed a Guardian on the first level. His body flexed as he sensed their presence, but he did not come after them.

Relaxing, Caz eyed Aoire. "Are you a Sihir?"

"No, Ahearn. I am not a Sihir," Aoire replied with a small chuckle.

"Then what are you? I thought only Sihir women could bend magic to their will."

Aoire looked off into the distance. "I am something else entirely."

"And what is that? You mentioned that you were created, did your Father create you?"

"This way," Aoire said, ignoring her questions. They had reached the very top of the spiral staircase, an intricate glassless window making up the entire top of the roof of the Birthing House. It allowed light to pour down the middle of the staircase, and create a beautiful design on the floor. Caz leaned over the bannister, looking down at an intricate tree design. She had never been this far up before, so she had never seen the design from this view. At the top of the stairs, a single, bare hallway led to an old door.

"He's in there?" Caz asked, peering down the dark hallway.

Aoire nodded. "Does that surprise you?"

"We never put anyone in here. This is where the Amesi come to die after naming the next to succeed her."

Aoire stared down the short, bare hallway to where two beautiful ionaithe lanterns hung on either side of the old door. Ornate algae blooms cast bright light down the hall. She could feel the weight of countless Amesi souls crying out in their dying moments. It felt similar to the presence that had been back in the cell Caz had put her in, but less angry and aggressive. In the midst of it all she could feel Retter's presence.

"He's definitely in there," Aoire replied.

Starting down the hall, she threw an arm out at her side. All the air and lightning from around her and Caz leaped from their bodies. The air swept down the hallway in a rush, exposing ancient lanterns hanging on the wall under layers of dust. Faded carpet on the floor appeared as the dust was blown away.

The lightning followed, striking the lanterns. They blazed to life, illuminating the hall with a bright blue glow. The air seemed to not only uncover the lanterns and carpets that had been covered in dust, but for a moment Caz saw them as they had originally been – ornate, beautiful, and delicate.

Reaching the door, Caz ran a hand over the ionaithe locks. They were complicated, three sets of three locks that intersected and wove together in intricate knots.

"I've never seen locks like these before. I am not sure we will be able to open the door without a key," she paused, leaning closer. "Is there even a keyhole in here?"

"No, there won't be one. These are called Eternity Locks. When locked, they have no beginning or end. Without knowing the proper way of opening them, they will stay locked forever. You could hide anything behind this door and it would never be able to leave," Aoire replied.

"Then how do we open it? Neither of us brought a key."

Aoire pointed to the stone border that ran around the arched doorway. Faded writing in a language Caz had never seen before was carved into the stone.

eerf ti stes traeh fo erup eht emit eht litnu emit lla

rof neddih eb lliw ereh ni decalp si hcihw taht

"That's the key."

Caz looked at the words. "How? Is the key hidden within them? Can you even read them?"

Aoire gently stroked the faded words with reverence. "It says, '*That which is placed in here will be hidden for all time until the time the pure of heart sets it free.*'"

"What language is this?" Caz asked, still gazing at the carved words.

"It's the language of my father."

"Your father? How? It sounds very ancient."

"It is," Aoire replied, pressing the palm of her hand against the middle set of locks. A symbol of a fish within a triangle began to glow in the middle of the arch. As it did, the locks began to uncurl themselves with a soft click. They straightened out into three straight bars and then disappeared into the wall. Once the locks were gone, the door vanished from view, plank by plank, to reveal a dark room. It was circular in shape and devoid of any windows.

Pulling a lantern off the wall, Caz and Aoire stepped into the room. Light from the lantern spilled around the room. There was not a single piece of furniture inside. Through the think layer of dust on the floor, Caz could see the thin outline of a circle carved into the floor in the middle of the room.

"It's empty. Are you sure he is in here?" Caz asked.

Aoire nodded. "He's here. He's simply hidden. Remember when I told you that you could hide anything in this room and it wouldn't be able to escape unless set free? The locks aren't the only way to keep someone or something trapped in here."

Aoire stepped into the center of the circle carving. Kneeling down, she placed the palm of her hand against the floor. Closing her eyes, Aoire began to whisper in the same language she had spoken when reading the words on the door.

Aoire's eyes snapped open. "He's here."

"Right here?" Caz asked, pointing to the floor. Aoire nodded.

Caz pinched the bridge of her nose, squeezing her eyes shut and sighing. "Well, where then, Aoire? I don't know about you, but I don't see him anywhere in here."

"Laever," Aoire commanded, her eyes turning pure white.

A bright white glow began under the palm of her hand and then a ripple of air came from her body, blowing away the dust and carrying with it the smell of the earth after a rain. The white light spread out from her hand like trails of water, illuminating an intricate geometric design etched into the floor.

As the lines of the design lit up, seven smaller circles within the bigger circle became visible. Each had their own symbol in the middle, slowly turning as the white light filled them. As they turned, a thick white line spread all around the outer circle. Once it became one continuous line, white vines began to sprout up from the floor, weaving together to take the shape of a man.

Concentrating, Aoire felt beads of sweat begin to form on her forehead, pressure building within her as more of the male figure took shape. She could feel the strain on her body as her *opari* worked to release him. Powerful magic had put him here and it took even more to release him.

Once the vines had created a fully formed man, Aoire pulled her hand from the floor. The white light immediately vanished, leaving only the light from Caz's lantern glowing dully in the sudden darkness.

"Aoire?" Caz called out, her eyes still adjusting.

"She's here," Retter replied.

"Commander!" Caz blurted. Her eyes finally adjusted and she could see him standing next to Aoire. His arm was around her hip, supporting her. Her eyes were back to their light grey color, the smell of earth after a rain lingering subtly.

"I told you he was only hidden," Aoire said weakly, leaning on Retter's strong arm.

"Are you okay, Aoire?" Caz asked.

"I will recover." Aoire replied. A small smile played at the edge of her lips. "Do you trust me now, Caz?"

Caz didn't reply, but flashed Aoire a quick wink.

Retter studied the exhaustion on Aoire's face. "Perhaps you should rest before we leave."

Aoire shook her head. "I will be fine."

"I am guessing you cannot shield us again for the journey down the staircase from here?" Caz asked.

Aoire shook her head again. "No. Certain spells take more out of me than others. I will need to recover more before attempting to use my gift on more than one person."

Retter looked around the small oval room. "I didn't think Eimhir would go to these lengths to keep me silent."

"Yes, what about Amesi? She is already furious that the Commander does not follow her orders, what do you think she will do when she finds out you both are gone?" Caz asked.

"What is Caz talking about?" Retter asked.

"After I took Aoire from the Grand Hall, Amesi ordered me to put her in the old cells. The ones the first Birthers were imprisoned in when they lost their minds," Caz stated.

Retter put up a hand. "Wait, she told you to take Aoire to the cells and not to a Prospects chamber?"

Caz nodded.

"She is growing increasingly brash," Retter said softly, his eyes distant.

Caz hesitated a moment before speaking. "There's more that you should know, Commander. After I took Aoire to the cells, I was sent by Major General Tol and Major General Mannix to find you. No one had heard from you, or seen you, since the scene in the Grand Hall. I instead found Amesi talking to a Lefeela in her private quarters."

Retter's face darkened. "She's in league with a Basher."

"It appears so, but I am not sure it's mutual. From what I saw the Lefeela seemed to be in charge," Caz replied.

Retter sighed, "It explains a lot - her change in character over the years and her growing thirst for power. Especially if it's a Lefeela she is working with. They are nothing but pride and it is the pride in others that they hunt and consume."

"We can't worry about that now. You two have a story to report," Aoire said.

"But how will we get back down without being seen?" Caz asked.

"Now that I am back, no Guardian will dare stop us. Eimhir's reach does not yet extend past me and she knows that," Retter replied. "Besides, the ones not loyal to the Guardians will continue to reveal themselves and be dealt with accordingly."

"Who was it that placed you in here?" Aoire asked.

"Major Cayden," Retter replied. He rubbed a hand on the back of his head. "At least, I think it was him. Shortly after he and I left the Grand Hall everything went dark."

Caz nodded. "Major Generals Tol and Mannix also told me it was Cayden that took Retter here."

"He must also be in league with Eimhir and Narcissa. Or at least Eimhir," Aoire stated.

"Narcissa?" Retter asked.

"That's the Lefeela that was in Amesi's room," Caz said.

Retter shook his head sadly. "Cayden may not be the only one. Where there is one, there are two. Now that we know how far up this evil has spread, we need to find a way to rid ourselves, and our home, of it. This place and its people are our sacred duty to protect. If things are starting to shift, we need to find a way to take control again," Retter said.

"What do you suggest, Commander?"

"We need to get back to Major Generals Tol and Mannix. They need to hear what we all have seen. They can be trusted, and they can help us come up with a plan," Retter replied.

As they left the room, Aoire touched a small ionaithe stone set into the wall near one of the lanterns. Slat by slat the wooden door reappeared and fell into place. Once they had fallen back into place, the Eternity Locks slid out from the wall and wound around each other, stopping once they were exactly as they had been. The last lock rang crisply as it fell into place. It looked as if no one had been there at all.

Walking away from the door, all the light from the lanterns formed into small balls and one by one, flew into Aoire's open hand. She closed her hand around the balls of light, lifting her fist to her lips.

"Nedrah," Aoire whispered, blowing gently into her hand. Her *opari* turned from white to orange, and from her mouth came a small trail of orange light. It entered her hand and surrounded the light balls. Opening her hand, the balls of light were now bright blue glass marbles. Smiling to Retter and Caz, Aoire handed each of them one.

"How?" Retter asked, holding the marble in the palm of his hand. He had seen glass currency before, but never anything this large or pure before.

"Don't ask. She won't explain it in a way you can understand anyway," Caz replied, tucking her marble into the small black satchel on the small of her back.

"Let's just call them a gift for now," Aoire replied. She dropped the others into the pocket of her trousers. "Never take for granted a gift freely given. You may never know when you may need to use it."

"See?" Caz grumbled as they left the hall and descended down the staircase. The only light left behind them was from the two ornate lanterns on either side of the door at the end of the hall. There was no sign that anyone had been there.

Chapter Seven

Major General Tol's eyes darkened as Caz and Retter took turns sharing their story. It was the early hours of the morning after Collection Day, just a day since Aoire had appeared to everyone, and most of End was still asleep. They were all meeting in Tol's private quarters, as it was the only place that could promise them complete privacy. Caz knew that no hallways ran behind any of the Guardian quarters.

The Guardians quarters were below the Birther's rooms, taking up the first four levels of the Birthing House. The high-ranking officers' quarters were on each of the first floor hallways, the rest of the Guardians quarters on the second, third, and fourth floors. Above the fourth floor, hallways began branching off to the north and south from the spiral staircase, these hallways and every floor above housing the Birthers and Seeders. All Guardians of the same house stayed on the same floor, allowing for deeper unity within their ranks.

The northern room were where the Birthers lived and learned, ending their years with bringing the first of their children into the world. The southern chambers were where the Seeders lived when not performing their duty.

Amesi's quarters took up the entire Northern fifth floor so that she was above the Guardians and below her charges.

Caz and Retter stood in the middle of Tol's room, their backs straight with their hands clasped behind them. Tol was seated behind his writing desk with Mannix at his shoulder, leaning back with one hand resting lightly on the arm of his chair as he listened. His other hand gently rubbed the edge of his mustache, his eyes bright as he listened.

Aoire stood behind Caz and Retter, leaning against the wall. Mannix's eyes never left her, his arms crossed over his chest and his legs shoulder-width apart. Even Tol felt his eyes drawn to Aoire time and time again. There was something about her that felt familiar.

"And you believe some sort of attack is coming soon?" Tol asked, gesturing for Aoire to step forward.

Aoire straightened her back. "Yes."

"From who? Bashers? This Narcissa woman?" Tol asked.

Aoire stepped forward. "The attack will come from Bashers, but I do not yet know what kind. Vyad, at least that is what he is calling himself now, rules the Bashers. He is hundreds of thousands of years old and he has gained a lot of power over that time."

"This Vyad is going to attack us? Why?" Tol asked.

"Not him personally, but he will send an attack. He is looking for me. He has been for years and now that he knows that I am here, he will let nothing stop him."

"What makes you so sure it's you he wants?" Mannix asked.

Aoire calmly unwound the strips of cloth so they could all see the webbed scar that wrapped around her wrist. Thin black lines had appeared, outlining the finger marks and spreading towards her elbow.

"He gave me this two nights ago, along with the promise that he was coming for me. Father, my father, has kept me hidden from him - protected - my whole life. Now that I am twenty-two though, that protection has lifted. It is no secret anymore that I am residing in end, so it is safe to say that Vyad will send someone for me. Perhaps his top General, Narcissa, will come. Vyad does not like to loose, so you can be sure he will send a powerful force after me," Aoire said. She wrapped the strips of cloth around her wrist again, wincing as she did.

"Why wouldn't he come himself? If he is so powerful, couldn't he get to you any time he wants?" Mannix asked.

Aoire looked at him steadily. "Does a General go himself into a place he has never attacked when he can send others ahead of himself? No. Vyad will send someone disposable."

"Are you sure he controls the Bashers? From what we have seen and know of them, while they may work in some kind of unit when they attack, their attacks seem random and no two are alike," Tol asked.

"Millennia ago Vyad created them. He's the only one they obey," Aoire replied.

"How is it that you know so much about this Vyad, his future actions, and the Bashers?" Mannix demanded putting his hands on his hips. "Could it be that you are working with him too?"

Aoire fixed Mannix with an icy stare. Her face which had been serene was now drawn tight, her eyes stormy. Electricity crackled around her as the air grew cold.

"I hope you are not implying, Mannix Lightfoot, that I would ever be in league with that murderous snake. My family has been attacked and hunted by him and his horde of soulless monsters for longer than you can even fathom!

As far as how I know what he will do next, I know this because he is unimaginative. He feeds off of the pain and fear of others, trapping them into a life of torment. It is this fear and pain that Father and I work to destroy. If you need more evidence as to how this creature works, I would be happy to share with you the countless memories I carry of the pain he has caused," Aoire replied, her voice hard.

Mannix opened his mouth to reply, his face an odd mixture of anger and shock. No one had ever spoken to him like that before. He snapped his mouth shut in the end, an odd sensation of respect for Aoire washing over him.

Tol uncurled his hands once the tension in the room had ebbed. "Mannix does bring up a good point, however. Someone else must be working with Vyad. What is it about you that would merit this kind of attack?"

"I come from a family that is even more powerful than he is. My very existence is a threat to him. In fact it's the *only* threat to him. He has been searching for me my whole life, utilizing his vast network of spies to try and find me." Aoire replied.

"If he has spies everywhere, how did he not know you were here?" Mannix asked.

"Father has kept me hidden. Not just from Vyad, but from everyone so that he could prepare me for the final battle," Aoire replied.

"Twenty-two. Your father did a good job hiding you if you are past the age of processing and we are just now meeting you. Your entrance last night caused quite a stir," Tol said.

Aoire defiantly stuck out her chin. "It is not Father's intent for me to live a life of slavery."

Tol tilted his head slightly, gazing at her with gentle

eyes. "Are you sure about that, Aoire? It seems that while you may not have been born into the life of a Birther or an Unborn, you are still a slave. To live a life where you have to defeat a great evil, was this your choice or your father's?"

Aoire placed her hands on Tol's writing desk and leaned forward. "Let me speak plainly. You may not understand this, Major General, but it has always been my calling to do this. This was both my choice and Father's - one that we made together. I do not consider this life to be one of slavery, but of sacrifice. I believe the Guardians know a little something of sacrifice? How many of your men have been lost in their duty to the Birthers? How many here in End have died to save the ones they love? It is no different for me. Slaves are not given a choice what life they are forced into, but I chose to fight."

"Spoken like a true Guardian," Retter said.

"I agree," Tol said, pushing his chair back and getting to his feet. "It seems to me that wherever you are going, you will need all the support that you can get. May I make a suggestion?"

Aoire nodded.

"Stay hidden for now. Vyad knows you are here, but Eimhir believes you are still housed in the cells. If we do not yet know when this attack will come, allow us the time to devise a way to smuggle you out of End safely and quietly," Tol said.

"I will need to take Caz and Retter with me when I leave," Aoire said.

"Absolutely not!" Mannix exploded. "If this attack is as bad as you say it will be, we will need all available Guardians here to help protect the city."

"Mannix," Tol said, turning to face his friend.

"We can't possibly be talking about this?" Mannix interrupted. "Retter may be the Commander, but he still reports to us. If she is going on this crusade, and takes two of our strongest Guardians with her and we are attacked, that could mean the difference between victory and defeat. A Guardians duty is to the Birthing House and the Birthers within, not to run off on an adventure!"

"Mannix!" Tol's voice was sharper.

Mannix didn't seem to hear, but instead zeroed in on Caz, moving out from behind Tol's desk. "First Lieutenant, your father - the former Commander - gave his life to protect you and this Birthing House. Are you really going to dishonor his memory by running away and disavowing your duty, when we know there is an attack coming? If it hadn't been for him, you wouldn't have even survived. You have already shown that your loyalties may not be to the Guardians. If you leave now, you will be branded a traitor."

"Major General Mannix!" Tol barked. Caz's face was blank as she stared straight ahead - her Guardian mask firmly on her face.

"Sir?" Mannix said turning around.

"You will stay here after they leave. I wish to speak to you in private. The rest of you may go. Aoire, we will speak about your request at a later time, but for now, Guardian Caz can show you to more comfortable quarters. I believe the room next to Caz's is empty."

Tol turned his eyes to Retter. "Commander, there are some Guardians and new recruits who are awaiting to receive their orders. It would do them well to see you back. Dismissed."

As the door closed behind them, Tol turned back to Mannix. He began to speak to him in hushed tones. Just before the door closed, Aoire could see the anger and frustration on Mannix's face and then they were cut off from sight.

* * * * *

Caz didn't speak a word as they left Tol's chamber, even when Retter departed. Aoire fell silently in step beside her, this time willingly. They silently moved up the stairway to the second floor where the hand-to-hand combat Guardians stayed. As they walked, Aoire could see respect for Caz in the eyes of her fellow Guardians, but Caz was absorbed in her thoughts.

"Place your hand here," Caz said, stopping before one of the simple doors that lined the hall, and pointing to a small square panel set halfway up the door. There was no door handle.

Pressing her palm against the panel, Aoire could feel warmth collect under it, and then a sharp stab to each of her fingers. A sixth followed on her palm. Breathing in sharply, Aoire pulled her hand away. Six small dots of purple-red blood on her hand mimicked the dots on the panel. Aoire watched as her blood was absorbed, and then a click came from within the wall.

"What was that?" Aoire asked, rubbing her hand.

"Some sort of sensor. All the doors here have them. In fact, all the doors in End have something similar to this. This room is yours now, and no one else may enter without your permission until your death. At that time, it becomes available for the next person who claims it," Caz explained.

"Parting gift from LiquiTech I see," Aoire muttered, pushing open her door.

"LiquiTech?" Caz asked. She stood in the doorway while

Aoire looked around her new room. It was furnished in the same simple way as Caz's. Caz watched Aoire run her fingers gently across the furniture. Eimhir had looked down her nose at the furnishings, whereas Aoire seemed to delight in them.

"You can come in, Ahearn. LiquiTech was an old company, from a time long forgotten. Every door in End has a sensor because LiquiTech are the ones that found and built this city," Aoire explained, her fingers lingering on the frame of her bed.

Caz stepped into the room, closing the door behind her. "All those things you said to the Major Generals, and all the things that you seem to know...are you...I mean..."

Aoire clasped her hands in front of herself and gazed patiently at Caz. "It's alright Ahearn, ask what is on your mind."

Caz looked at her from under her eyebrows. "Why do I feel like you already know what I am going to ask?"

Aoire laughed. "I may, but you won't know until you ask. It does the curious ones no good to keep their questions unanswered."

"Fine. Are you a Seer?"

"You mean can I see into the future and the past?"

"Yes."

Aoire shrugged a shoulder. "In a way, yes. If Seer is the term that you are most comfortable with then, yes, you may think of me as a Seer. It is true that I can see the past as well as the future, but it is much more than that. I see the past because I have lived the past, and I see the future because I have lived the future as well. I exist in the present because the present is where I am needed most."

"That makes no sense," Caz replied. "There has to be a

reason that you know all that you know. Saying that your father tells you makes no sense either."

"I understand all of this can be hard for you to wrap your head around Ahearn-"

"Caz," Caz interrupted sharply.

Aoire's eyes twinkled, but she pressed on. "I understand that this is hard for you to wrap your head around, because your life here in End has been so concrete. At the start of every day you know exactly what your duty for that day entails, but now you are being presented with something abstract."

Caz lifted her eyebrows and crossed her arms over her chest. "You know how hard this is for me to understand? Do you really?"

Aoire gazed gently at her. Looking at her, Caz had never realized how impossibly old her eyes were. They were old and wise, far older than the youthful face that held them.

"What is it that is most confusing for you, Ahearn? Perhaps we start there," Aoire replied.

Caz pinched the bridge of her nose, sighing. "I don't know. How about this father of yours? You say you have one, and yet you were obviously not born here in the Birthing House, or End. So you can't possibly have a Birther mother or a Seeder father."

Aoire sat on her bed and grew quiet. She finally spoke softly. "Would you like to meet him?"

"Who?" Caz asked.

"Father." Aoire replied.

When Caz did not reply, Aoire continued. "You are more intelligent and discerning than others think you are, Ahearn. I get the sense that you are searching for something, and have been searching for a long time - ever since your parents died in the attack that burned down your house and left you scarred. Commander Bearn, your foster father, took you in after finding you in the streets, didn't he?"

"How do you know that?" Caz whispered, staring at Aoire.

Aoire smiled wistfully. "Father. He knows everything about you, Ahearn, and he tells me all that I need to know. Bearn was the one who taught you to hide your gender as a woman, and taught you how to protect yourself - becoming a safe haven for you and giving you a family. But he also died, just a few short years later in another Basher attack. Is that why they frighten you so much?"

Caz swallowed hard, her voice barely above a whisper. "Yes."

"No one else here knows that you are a woman, do they?"

Caz shook her head. "No. Bearn kept it a secret from everyone, even changing my name to Caz."

"Ahearn, the longer you keep your identity a secret, the harder it is going to become. Being a woman is not something to be ashamed of, or to fear. Not even in a place like End."

Caz scoffed. "How is that even possible when being a woman is essentially the same as being a slave?"

"Because no one can enslave one that is free."

"How is it that you talk of freedom so easily?" Caz asked. "Even within the Guardians they are not free to have a family of their own, and I must hide myself at all times. Freedom is not something easily experienced in End."

"It will not be that way forever."

"How do you know that?" Caz asked, putting up a hand

as Aoire opened her mouth to speak. "Because of your father. I get it."

Taking a deep breath, Caz paced the room with her hands on her hips. Turning around, Caz finally spoke. "Nothing that has happened since the Commander brought you to the Birthing House has made any sense. You talk about your father, a great evil you must defeat, and you seem to know intimate details about everything."

"But?" Aoire asked.

Caz sighed, throwing her hands up in the air. "It all seems to make perfect sense! I have felt the growing darkness here in the Birthing House and know that this life cannot be the only one young women, and men, are subjected to. We force our young girls to bear children generation after generation, discarding those that are unable to satisfy our intentions for them, and then when the ones that do can no longer carry children, they are thrown away as well. This may be our way of life, but I have to believe that it isn't the only way."

Caz took a deep breath. "If this father of yours has a better way, then yes, I would like to meet him. After all, what could I possibly have to loose?"

"Then come sit." Aoire said.

"What?" Caz asked, blinking in surprise.

"You said you wanted to meet Father."

"Here?"

Aoire chuckled and nodded. "Right here, right now."

Sinking to the floor, Caz sat cross-legged across from Aoire. Aoire took her hands in hers, her palms cupping Caz's hands.

"Close your eyes and take a few deep breaths. Try to calm your mind and I will do the rest," Aoire ordered.

"This is really going to work?" Caz asked, opening one of her eyes to look at Aoire.

"Close your eyes, Ahearn," Aoire replied, tightening her grip. Caz could feel the same rush of heat and electricity run through her body as earlier, and at that same moment, everything around them went quiet.

Open your eyes, Ahearn.

A deep voice drifted around her, surrounding her and enveloping her like a warm blanket. She could feel gentle warmth on her face. From behind her closed lids something bright glowed.

Caz opened her eyes, blinking against the sudden sunlight. As her eyes adjusted, her hands flew to her mouth. Stretched out before her was a vast ocean as far as she could see - the water a brilliant blue-green. Waves rolled lazily over one another in slow succession, white foam capping their tops and covering the sand near her toes. Her boots were gone.

The sun was warm on her body as she stared out at the ocean before her, sunlight sparkling off the water like millions of tiny diamonds. It was so bright and clear, so different than the light given off by the algae lanterns in End. The color of the ocean was more vivid and alive than the light in End.

Caz had never seen the ocean. She had never heard the sound of waves crashing over one another. She had never felt the sun on her skin before in her life. No one in End had ever seen an ocean or sunlight, and yet she knew this was what was in front of her.

She looked up when a seagull swooped overhead and gave a shrill cry as it dove through the air. Extending its wings at the last minute, it landed gently on top of the waves. Bobbing lazily on the rolling water, it fixed her with beady black eyes. Digging her toes into the warm sand, Caz closed her eyes and turned her face up to the sun.

Putting her arms out at her side, Caz drank it all in. She had never felt warmth like this before in her life. A content smile spread across her face.

"I could stay here forever," she murmured out loud.

"You should," the deep voice said from next to her.

Caz's eyes snapped open in surprise and she looked at the tall figure standing next to her. Blue-green eyes flecked with gold looked back at her warmly. Thick hair that matched the full beard on his face fell around his shoulders, his bare feet poking out from underneath the hem of his robes. She could tell that he was very old and very wise, but he carried himself with the same youthful vigor that she had.

Caz looked up and down the beach for any sign of where he had come from. No footprints lead up to her.

"It's you," Caz said, reaching a hand up to touch his face. Deep lines appeared at the edges of his eyes as he smiled at her. Her hand caressed his cheek and his own reached up to cup over hers. As soon as he touched her, a jolt ran through her body.

"I have waited for you to come to this place for a long time, Ahearn," he said, his hand dropping to his side with her fingers intertwined within his. His hand seemed to envelop all of hers, calming her and making her feel at peace. His grip was strong, but soothing, and he made her feel like she was the only person in the world that he wanted by his side.

"What is this place?" Caz asked, her eyes pulled back to the ocean.

He looked out upon the rolling waves with her. "Do you like it? This is a place that only you and I are meant to share."

"It's beautiful," Caz breathed.

"It's only because of the heart that desired it," he replied and Caz could feel tears spring to her eyes.

"I don't deserve this."

"Why?"

"What could I possibly have done for all this?"

He laughed gently. "Child, there is nothing you could have done. A father wants nothing more than to love his children."

Caz's eyebrows knit together. "What do you mean? I thought you were Aoire's father? I have a father, actually, I had two."

"Yes, I am Aoire's father but I am also Father to all those who truly believe in me. I created this for you," he motioned to the ocean, "and you can come back here anytime you wish. I will claim you as my own, but only if you desire it. He cannot hurt you if you are mine."

"You mean Vyad."

"Yes, I mean Vyad. He is very old and very evil. He has terrible plans for all my children."

"Like that woman, Narcissa?"

"Narcissa is simply a peon to him, a creature to send out to do his evil bidding. What you saw is a fraction of his power."

Caz shuddered. She relaxed as she felt his fingers tighten over hers.

"If that is only a fraction of his power, how is it that anyone could be safe from him?" Caz asked.

"I protect my own. The fate that Vyad wants for everyone is not the one that was ever meant to pass."

Caz looked silently out over the waves as they continued to curl over one another. The seagull was still sitting on the surface of the water, watching them both, every now and again dipping his head under the water to wet his feathers. Water lapped lazily against her ankles as the tide started to come in. She could feel the pull of the current around her feet.

"My fathers, where are they?"

"Safe. In life they both had creideamh, which allowed them to live on forever. They wanted the same for you, but accepting creideamh is a willing choice."

Caz bit her bottom lip, thinking. She had heard a few in End speak of those that held creideamh - an ancient faith in only one deity, vastly different than the polytheistic faith that many in End held. These few believed that their one deity could do everything, and more, than all the other deities in End combined.

Caz had lived most of her life by only being able to trust herself, especially after Bearn had died. She had seen the zealousness in which others ostracized the few with creideamh, but being an outsider wasn't foreign to her. She wanted to see her fathers again so badly, and she had never felt so accepted, at peace, or loved as she did now holding his hand. She seemed to fit right in with him, and that was a feeling she had never experienced except for with Bearn. If this was what creideamh meant, Caz could accept this.

"What would I have to do?" Caz finally asked. The sun had begun to set, washing the sky with purple and gold.

"Accept me. Be a part of my family. Then aid Aoire."

"That's it?"

"One more thing, you can no longer be known as Caz. Your given name is Ahearn Lionheart, and that is whom you need to embrace once you leave End. Caz was a name given to protect you, but you no longer need it."

The idea of finally revealing herself terrified Ahearn, even though his words rang true in her heart.

Taking a deep breath, Ahearn nodded. "I have always wondered what gave those that held creideamh such peace, and if it comes from you, I can see why. Nothing right now makes any sense to me, least of all Aoire, but if nothing makes sense, then I choose what will give me solace."

With a light chuckle, he pulled her close to his chest and kissed her forehead. "Welcome home, my child."

Warmth and joy spread throughout Ahearn's body as he held her, watching the sun dip behind the ocean together. As soon as the sky fully darkened and the stars came out, he left as quietly and suddenly as he had arrived. Ahearn sat alone on the beach, listening to the roll of the waves.

Time to wake up, Ahearn.

His voice drifted on the wind, echoing inside of her mind and heart. She took one last deep breath of the sweet, salty air, and then her eyes snapped open.

She was back in Aoire's room and for a moment she felt disoriented. Her chest felt warm and she could still feel his lips on her forehead, sealing their time together, but the harshness of End in contrast to the warmth of the beach was disarming.

Everything on the beach had been bathed in hues of gold, brimming with life. She could feel the warmth of the beach slipping away, replaced by the cold reality of End. Aoire looked at her, smiling deeply. Her eyes were the same green-blue with golden flecks as his had been.

"What just happened?" Ahearn asked. She stared at Aoire. "Your eyes. I have seen eyes like that before. They are exactly like his!"

Aoire blinked, her eyes turning back to grey.

"How do you do that?" Ahearn asked.

"Welcome to the family," Aoire replied, ignoring her question.

"Family," Ahearn repeated, the word feeling strange on her lips. "I have not had a family in a very long time."

"Aren't the Guardians a kind of family?"

Ahearn shrugged. "Yes, but not one that I chose. They were chosen for me. I was seven when my parents died. Commander Bearn found me in the street, half dead from my burns, and he took me in. He had always wanted a child, so he raised me."

"How was it that Bearn could keep you?"

Ahearn smiled wistfully. "He was different from any other Commander. It was actually a golden time for the Birthing House with him in charge. He was able to keep me because he was a man of such integrity that everyone respected and trusted him. His name still carries weight here, even though he died over ten years ago."

"You were how old when you came here?" Aoire asked.

"Seven. Bearn died when I was nine," Ahearn replied.

"You were named a Guardian with only a few years of training?"

"Rules never seemed to stop him. Bearn saw that I was naturally skilled, even though I was two years past the age of branding for a Guardian," Ahearn replied, pulling up her sleeve. The outline of a sword was seared into her forearm, a starburst at the tip of the blade near the inner bend of her elbow.

"And the fact that you are a woman?"

"Bearn told me that no one could ever know that and began calling me Caz. No Guardian has ever been female and I took his warnings seriously. I wanted to make the man who had saved my life, and loved me, proud. After losing him, I swore that I would continue to uphold his wish for me and stay a Guardian. If they found out that I am a woman...I don't know what they would do, but next year I will be the age of processing. If they found out now..." she trailed off.

"They could make you a Birther."

"Yes. Bearn did not want that life for me, so he did the only thing he could think of. I can't dishonor his memory like that."

"What did Father ask you to do?"

"He told me to follow you wherever you go, and after we leave End I am no longer to be known as Caz," Ahearn replied.

Aoire nodded. "Father knows if you reveal yourself before we leave, your life could be in danger."

"Or worse," Ahearn said looking away.

"Or worse," Aoire agreed. "Father is not going to put you in that kind of danger. Are you sure no one else here knows?"

Ahearn's eyebrows knit together. "Positive. Someone would have said something by now. Eimhir has hinted that she may know, but if she really did, why wouldn't she expose me? Why would she take such an interest in me, or want to make me the next Commander, if she knows me to be a liar?"

Aoire nodded in agreement, but her eyes were no longer focused on Ahearn or the room. In front of her, she could see all the threads of secrets that ran through the whole of End. They were laid out in front of her like a large, intricately woven knot, but she couldn't see how the knot would unravel when one of the threads were pulled. There were too many similar outcomes for Aoire to know what would really happen.

When she spoke, Aoire's voice was distant. "I am sure you are right. For now, nothing has changed as far as the Guardians and the rest of End knows. Things are shifting more rapidly, but right now we need to wait and see how the dust settles. Get some rest Ahearn, the time to act may come faster than anticipated."

Getting to her feet, Ahearn left Aoire's room and went straight next door to hers. Undressing quietly, she slipped into her bed, Aoire's words echoing in her mind - *nothing has changed.*

Everything has changed. Ahearn thought to herself a moment before slipping off into a dreamless sleep.

Chapter Eight

"How long has it been since Caz and Retter brought Aoire and their story to us?" Tol asked Mannix who stood next to him, overseeing a group of young Guardians in training.

"Nearly a week," Mannix replied. "Do we really believe their account?"

"I do not take threats upon my city lightly and neither should you," Tol replied.

"I don't like waiting," Mannix scowled, looking out over the recruits. His arms were locked tight across his chest. "Is this attack really happening or not?"

Tol smiled slightly. "It almost sounds as if you want it to happen."

"Of course not," Mannix said. "I would never want any harm to come to anyone in End, but it seems to me that knowing an attack is coming and have it not happen yet, is almost worse than not knowing."

"It seems to me that we have been given a gift. By knowing in advance, we can better prepare. End has never been prepared for an attack of any kind from the Bashers, but now we are on alert. The more time that passes simply means more time to prepare."

Mannix's eyes moved to the south end of the city where the outer wall was still being repaired. They had lost many good men, Guardians and Protectors alike, in that attack.

"Part of the wall is still down, Tol. How fortified are we if it isn't repairs aren't done in time?"

"We will be as prepared as we can be, my friend. The Protectors have been alerted to the situation and they have doubled their patrol. More Guardians are on duty during their rounds, and even the Sihir have been told of the situation. We have done all that we can do. Now we just hope that our training does not fail us at the time it's needed," Tol said.

"All this activity means that Eimhir has probably noticed," Mannix said.

Tol's eyes darkened. "Let her notice. If she is going to put End in danger then we have every right to try and save it."

"So you still think the girl-child was telling the truth?" Mannix asked.

"Would I have reason to otherwise?"

Mannix shrugged. "Her story seemed like a bit of a stretch to me."

"Remember, my friend, that the strangest stories are often the truest. There is symmetry in the odd. Her story was too complex to be a lie, plus there is no need to hide behind the truth."

Mannix grunted. "Something that your one-god religion taught you?"

Tol nodded. "You may have reason to need many gods, my friend, but I have need for only one. No, that is not just something my religion has taught me, but something our old friend Commander Bearn often told me."

"Where is Caz?" Mannix asked, his thoughts turning at the mention of Commander Bearn.

"I assigned him to be the personal Guardian to Aoire. It was the only way to satisfy the Commander and keep him at his post. Plus, I wanted to keep Caz out of view of Eimhir. I don't like the sound of this extra attention she has taken in our young brother," Tol said.

"Aoire seems to have had quite the effect on both Caz and the Commander."

"She is rather exquisite and I too have noticed that. However, it's not just those two that have been affected by her. Apparently, many of our youngest recruits are besotted with her as well. There is something about her that makes people feel at ease. I do not blame Retter for his feelings towards her, but he is a man of principal. He knows his duty and he will not ignore it, not even for her," Tol said.

"Major Generals," a cold voice said from behind them.

Tol and Mannix turned to see Eimhir. Her eyes were cold and hard, full of fury and pain. Half of her face was covered with thick bandages, dark blood and yellow stains seeping through the white linen. The skin around the bandages was bright red and blackened in places.

"Amesi," Tol and Mannix said in unison, nodding to her.

"How are you feeling Amesi?" Mannix asked, his eyes lingering on her bandages. "No one has seen you for a week."

"I have been preoccupied," Eimhir replied icily. "These are the rising Guardians?"

Tol looked back at the young boys taking a break. They were of various ages, most about nine or ten, but some were younger.

"Yes. The training program seems to be suiting them

well. Guardians learn the value of discipline at a very young age. It's one of the most valuable lessons we teach them."

"Discipline," Eimhir repeated, her mouth twisting as if the word had a sour taste to it. "What has discipline taught you, Major General Tol?"

Tol looked at her with the same expression Mannix had seen him adopt when a young recruit was testing him. "That in the end, it is my duty to uphold the ideology of the principles taught to me by my Guardian family. It is not up to me to make decisions based off of my own selfish desires, but to put the lives of my brothers and the people I am called to protect, above my own."

"I see," Eimhir said, her cold gaze sweeping over the young boys. "Send them all home."

"What?" Mannix asked, blinking in surprise.

Eimhir turned her empty eyes back to Mannix. They were so devoid of emotion that he felt his skin crawl. "Did I stutter, Major General? Send them all home. There is no need for them here anymore. I am effectively ending the Guardianship program, bringing in Protectors to guard over the Birthing House."

"You can't do that!" Mannix said.

"Actually I can, and I have. The Birthing House and everything that goes on inside it and around is my responsibility. The Guardians no longer have a need here. It would be cruel to keep these boys from their families any longer than they already have been," Eimhir replied.

Tol took a step closer to her. "You forget your place, Eimhir. We all took an oath to protect the Birthing House and those within until our dying breath. The Guardians have been around since the first Birthers and the first Amesi."

Eimhir drew herself up, staring at him with a sneer. "No, Guardian, *you* forget your place. Without the original Amesi, the Guardians never would have existed. I have spent the last week looking over the original texts, and it seems that once any Guardian breaks his sacred oath, all other Guardians are held liable. Your unity is your greatest asset, and also your greatest downfall. A Guardian did break his oath recently, and it wasn't just any Guardian. It was the Commander."

Eimhir's eyes twinkled with delight. "Since it was the Commander who broke the oath, the one that handpicks the recruits, inducts them, trains and oversees them - how can I trust that other Guardians have not been corrupted as well? How can I entrust the safety of my girls to a group of men who could be betraying their duty? There is no way to see how far the poison of his disobedience to me, and to his duty, has spread."

"His poison? What about *your* poison?" Mannix asked.

"Mannix," Tol warned, watching as Eimhir absently twirled the bead around her neck.

The more she touched the stone, the colder her demeanor became - something that troubled Tol. There was something about the stone around her neck that was changing her. Aoire's warning about Vyad's vast network of spies echoed in his mind.

"My poison?" Eimhir asked, her voice odd. It was hallow, as devoid of emotion as her face was.

"We all have seen the way you have entrapped Cayden and have gotten him to do your bidding. And the way in which you have focused your attention on Caz," Mannix said.

Eimhir cocked her head to the side, a smile spreading

across her lips, never reaching her eyes. "How is my dear Caz? I haven't seen him around lately and I usually find him lurking in a corner, or in hidden corridors behind walls. He should be more careful, those corridors are very old and have never been repaired or tended to. It's a wonder they haven't collapsed yet, crushing someone within."

A shiver went down Tol's spine. He shared a look with Mannix.

"We sent him on an errand," Tol replied. "Commanders orders."

"Ah," Eimhir replied, the smile melting from her face. "I am sure it was. Never you mind, I will find Caz eventually and deal with him. He may need to be reminded of his place with the Guardians, or the place that he truly belongs. I have informed all of you of your uselessness. I expect everyone to be gone by the end of the day."

"You do not have the power to do this, Eimhir," Tol said.

"It's *Amesi* to you Guardian," Eimhir snapped, her eyes flashing, "and as I have already explained, I do. What I didn't have to do was to tell you. I could have had you thrown out on the streets like an Unborn. You can choose to leave on your own accord or be cast out. I suggest you take the former."

Without waiting for a reply she left the training center, her dress swirling around her ankles.

"Are we really going to leave?" Mannix asked once she was gone.

Tol scoffed. "Of course not. The entire Protector force could not win against even a fraction of our youngest Guardians. Eimhir believed she was showing us her strength in playing this hand, but what she doesn't realize is that she gave away something else entirely."

"What?"

"She has revealed when the attack is going to happen. It will happen sometime tomorrow, most likely in the early hours of the morning when much of End is still asleep. Why else would she order the Guardians to leave the Birthing House tonight?"

Realization washed over Mannix's face. "She wants the house to be less protected when the Bashers come for Aoire."

Tol nodded. "This Vyad must have a strange power over her if he has persuaded her to allow those she has sworn to protect be attacked and killed. The only reason he must be targeting the Birthing House is that he knows that Aoire is here – not just in End, but actually here in this building."

"What are your orders?" Mannix asked.

"Go gather the Commander and the rest of the high ranking officers and bring them to my chambers. I have an idea and they should all hear it. It will only work if they all agree. Make sure Cayden is with them as well. If he is working with Eimhir then we will feed him all the information he needs," Tol said.

Nodding in salute, Mannix spun on his heel and left.

Grant me the wisdom to lead with the strength that you have given me. Tol prayed as he left the training grounds and walked back towards the Birthing House. He felt creideamh wash over him and his thoughts narrowed, solidifying into a plan.

* * * * *

"What in the?" Ahearn asked as she and Aoire walked into the main courtyard of the Birthing House.

It was a bustle of activity and from up on a balcony,

Eimhir watched over all of it with an expressionless stare, one hand on the bead around her neck. Birthers stood in small groups, watching as servants rushed in and out of the Birthing House with the Guardians' possessions.

Everything was strewn about, chests and personal belongings being shuffled out of the Birthing House and pilled in the backs of carts. It was a steady stream of activity that was drawing the attention of Endians who had begun to collect outside of the courtyard.

Aoire felt Eimhir's eyes on her as soon as they entered the courtyard. Looking up at the balcony, Aoire locked eyes with Eimhir as she pointed at Aoire, whispering into Cayden's ear. Half of her face was covered with bandages. A wave of evil washed over Aoire, making her stumble in her steps momentarily.

"Come on," Ahearn said, taking Aoire gently by the elbow. "We need to get you to the Commander."

Weaving in and out through the chaos, Ahearn and Aoire picked their way to the Guardian Tower. Pushing through the opening in the wall that led from the main courtyard, they were met with a very different type of chaos.

Major General Tol was standing in the middle of a throng of angry Guardians, all of who were shouting at once. The newest recruits were standing in a large group off to the side, looking completely lost. Servants were running in and out of the training chambers, taking whatever tools were set inside out with them and throwing them in haphazard piles in the middle of the courtyard. The sound of metal-on-metal was almost loud enough to drown out the sound of angry Guardians.

"Caz!" Retter's voice rose above the shouting. He quickly made his way over to them, falling in next to Aoire.

"Commander, what is going on?" Ahearn demanded.

"Let's get inside. It will be easier to explain someplace quieter and more private," Retter replied.

Leading them into the hand-to-hand training chamber, they pushed through the activity within to the back where no one was. The edges of torn parchment were left on the walls and the sparring circle was no longer groomed, but covered with the boot prints of countless feet. The noise from outside was reduced to a bearable rumble this far back. From here they could still see if anyone tried to come near them. Their training chamber was the only one that was built in the shape of a large oval, allowing full view of everything from anywhere you stood within.

"What is going on?" Ahearn demanded again.

"It's Eimhir, isn't it?" Aoire asked. "She had something to do with this."

Retter nodded. "Her or that creature she serves, Vyad. All we know is that this morning she effectively disbanded the Guardians and is moving the Protectors into the Birthing House."

"What?!" Ahearn said. "How can she do that?"

"It has to do with the old laws and my decision to leave on Collection Day. Apparently, I broke my oath by leaving my post on the most sacred day of our year. The Guardian program was built on complete and total unity, and if one Guardian breaks their oath, then all are forfeit. Because of my act, she now has the power to dismantle our entire way of life," Retter said, his eyes brooding.

"So we are being thrown out?" Ahearn asked, putting her hands on her hips.

Retter nodded. "Yes."

"Why tonight?" Ahearn asked. "I mean, why the rush? Why not give the us a week to get our affairs in order?"

"Vyad is attacking tonight or tomorrow," Aoire said. Her quiet voice cut through their conversation.

"Of course," Ahearn said, realization dawning on her face. "Of course he is. If Eimhir can get rid of the most powerful fighting unit in all of End, then she can increase the chances of Bashers finding Aoire and giving her over to Vyad."

For a brief moment, fear crashed over Aoire like a wave. She clenched her hands together into small fists, digging her fingernails into the palm of her hands to keep herself from screaming.

"We have to leave. Tonight. If I am not here, then Vyad has no reason to attack and hundreds of lives can be spared," Aoire said.

Retter's large hand gently enveloped hers. "We have a plan Aoire. We are not going to let you get taken, but we can't possibly get you out when all of this is going on. Eimhir needs to think that she has won this small victory so her guard will be down and we can get you out safely.

"Right now, the other leaders are gathering up their men and the recruits, and we are all going to make a show of leaving the Birthing House as one unified force. You will stay behind because you have no reason to leave. Most likely Eimhir is going to order your arrest as soon as the Protectors arrive, but what she won't know is that a small group of us will be coming back dressed as Protectors. We are expecting the attack will happen shortly after the changing of the guard, but we can't know the exact moment when. The change over should happen quickly enough, so Aoire you should only be alone for about an hour."

"And me," Ahearn said.

"What?" Retter asked.

"And me. I will be staying with her," Ahearn clarified.

Retter shook his head. "No."

"No?" Ahearn asked, arching one eyebrow.

"We need something else from you, something equally as important. You have explored the secret tunnels that run in the walls of the Birthing House ever since you came to live here, yes?"

Ahearn nodded. "Yes."

"Well Eimhir knows about them too. She threatened to collapse them, but I know for a fact that she doesn't know about the ones that run under the Birthing House."

"What tunnels? No tunnels run under the Birthing House, only the sewers run there."

Retter nodded. "That is what everyone believes, because only Commanders are given this information. Bearn could not share it with you unless you had aspirations to become Commander. The tunnel that connects to the sewers is hidden under the fireplace in the kitchens and if you didn't know about that one, I would bet that Eimhir doesn't as well. The sewers will give us a clear way out of End, one that I bet even Bashers wouldn't willingly follow us through. Caz, I need you to stay hidden by the main entrance to this tunnel, and protect it. That way when we can make a quick exit."

"It's a good plan," Ahearn said. "But I still don't like the idea of leaving Aoire alone inside the Birthing House."

Aoire bit her bottom lip, not wanting to let her concern show, but she agreed with Ahearn. It was a simple plan and one that could work well, but it hinged on them being able to get to her and then to the sewers. The pain in her wrist spiked every time Vyad's name, or the Bashers were mentioned, and Aoire had no idea of knowing how her wrist would react during a full-fledged attack. Not to mention if she would even be able to use her *opari* amidst the pain.

"It's the best plan we have right now. Did Eimhir see you when you came back?" Retter asked.

Ahearn nodded. "She was watching everything from her balcony. Cayden was with her."

Retter scowled, spitting to the side. "Chances are he will stay behind. Eimhir seems to have him in her pocket. He may even be the one she sends for Aoire. Aoire, we should get you back inside and into your room. No one can gain entry unless you open the door, and welcome them in. It will give you another level of protection, and this way when we come for you, we know exactly where you are."

Aoire took a deep breath. Opening her mouth to speak, she was cut off by a low horn letting out three short blasts. A sudden hush fell over all of End. Everything stopped.

After what felt like ages, the horn sounded another three short blasts, this time faster and more urgent. Before the last note faded away, the ground beneath them began to rumble, and then shook violently.

Chapter Nine

Eimhir gripped the stone bannister as the ground shook violently. A crack appeared under her feet, splitting the balcony in two. Below her, everyone tried to regain their balance, the horns in the distance still crying out. They stopped as a black shadow erupted from the entrance to the cavern, enormous cracks appearing in the walls. A shrill scream accompanied it, terrifying and piercing. Stumbling back with her hands over her ears, Eimhir manages to enter the Birthing House.

Chaos had erupted inside as well. Servants, Birthers, and new recruits ran in every direction. Pushing her way through the throng, she could see the wild fear in their eyes, cracks appearing on the walls and the floors of the Birthing House.

Coming into the Grand Hall, Eimhir grabbed onto a pillar as the ground pitched. A shrill scream rang out and then was silenced as a chunk of the spiral staircase fell and crushed those beneath it. No one seemed to notice she was there.

Gripping the glass bead around her neck, she slipped down a side corridor before anyone saw her. Eimhir knew what was coming for End, and she knew what would then come to aid End. She also know she couldn't allow anyone in to help.

Moving down the corridor as fast as she could, Eimhir kept a hand on the wall to steady herself. She felt the smooth walls give way to rougher rock. The walls here were older, sturdier, and so the tremors were less violent. There was only one group of women who ever used this corridor, and Eimhir had no desire to let them in.

Thrown against the wall as an enormous tremor shook the Birthing House, Eimhir scrambled to get her footing. Pushing herself away from the wall, she hurried faster as the muffled screams from above grew. Death had begun to weave its voice into the tumult, like a dark thread on a tapestry of white.

Turning another corner, Eimhir halted. An ornate, round, wooden door was at the end of the corridor. Eight symbols were carved into it, behind her a short staircase led up towards the Grand Hall. This was the main corridor from the hall to the door, but she had chosen the way that allowed her not to be seen. The side corridor she had exited from was cut exactly like the rest of the walls, so when she took a step forward it seemed to disappear from sight.

The sound of screaming was louder here, spilling down the open stairs and echoing all around her. Pulling a black orb from her pocket, she stepped towards the door. The orb was such a rich black that all color and light around it was absorbed. Cold heat radiated from the orb in waves. The heat didn't affect her hand, but instead it started to melt the handle and the stone around the door.

Just as she was about to touch the handle with the orb, the door swung out to reveal a large group of women dressed in colored robes of red, orange, and yellow. The robes were cut simply, but made of the finest material. A silken cord of braided rope the same color as their robes was tied around their waists, and their eyes were the same color as the robes they wore. The air around them hummed with power.

Stumbling backward to feign surprise, Eimhir slipped the orb back into her pocket before any of them could see it. "Thank the gods you are here Sisters of the Sihir! End, it is under attack!"

A tall woman in front, dressed in yellow robes, stepped forward. Waves of black hair cascaded down her back, her large, yellow eyes set in olive skin. The cord at her waist gathered her robes around her and showed off her wide hips. She was nearly a head taller than any of the other women with her and had a commanding presence.

"Amesi," she said, nodding to Eimhir. Yellow sparks danced around her fingertips as a blood-curdling scream rose behind them.

Eimhir flattened herself against the wall, her face ashen. "Save them please, Sihir. Save my city, and my girls."

"Very well, Amesi," she said more curtly, her eyes flicking for a moment to Eimhir's pocket. Eimhir's fingers tightened protectively around the orb, wondering if the woman had seen it. The woman's eyes rose to meet Eimhir's, one eyebrow raised slightly.

Without another word, the Yellow Sihir led the throng of Sihir women behind her towards the stairs. Once the last had left the room, Eimhir waited until they were gone from sight, and then kicked the door so hard it slammed shut with a loud rattle. Cursing to herself under her breath, Eimhir raced back down the hallway she had come from. If she couldn't stop the reinforcements, she would get to the one he wanted.

* * * * *

Aoire's eyes opened wide as her left arm straightened violently at the same time the horns blasted. Her wrist began to twist backwards, every joint straining to stay attached. Pain drove her to her knees, black dots clouding her vision. Through her blurred vision she watched as her wrist nearly twisted around completely.

Aoire barely felt Retter scoop her up, his arm supporting the weight of her body as the ground pitched beneath them. They could hear screams coming from outside the training center. A large crack ran up the side of the center and across the ceiling, raining dust and rocks down upon them. Retter half-carried Aoire out of the room, Ahearn glued to his side.

Entering the training courtyard, Aoire blinked through the pain and tried to make sense of what was happening around them. People ran in every direction. Plumes of dirt rose into the air as numerous enormous cracks split across the ground. She could hear orders being barked and saw Guardians falling into ranks. Outside of the courtyard, screams were rising up from the city, and every now and again a horn would sound.

With a shrill howl that sounded like thousands of voices screaming in unison, a dark shadow burst out of the cavern entrance. It appeared with such force that it seemed like an explosion had gone off. The cavern wall cracked up to the ceiling and enormous piece broke off, crushing the walkway that had led down to End.

Still howling, the shadow form expanded until it stretched over the entire city. Everyone pressed their hands against their ears as its howl rattled their teeth, sending fear straight to their hearts.

As the creature grew, Aoire felt every muscle in her body twist and seize. She felt a deep, cold, dread spread through her amidst the pain, turning her blood to ice. Her wrist twisted violently one last time and a series of sharp pops filled her ears.

Loosing all feeling from her elbow down, Aoire's arm dangled uselessly by her side. Retter grimaced from the sound of the howling shadow, but kept his grip firmly around Aoire's waist to support her. He looked upwards to try and get a better look.

As Retter watched, the shadow creature began to become more defined. It took the form of a faceless creature with long, spindly arms and legs. Its limbs stretched across the entire ceiling of the cavern, its face devoid of a nose, ears, or mouth. Long fingers with sharp nails dug into the cavern, keeping the figure attached to the ceiling.

As suddenly as they began, the shrill scream and tremors stopped. Pulling their hands from their ears, Retter and Ahearn shared a look. Helping the people closest to her back to their feet, Ahearn looked up. Her eyes grew as the creature opened its mouth, widening until it was as large as the city. Everyone fell to their knees with their hands over their ears as it screamed again, louder and more painfully shrill than before. The buildings of End shook, cracking as the noise reverberated through the entire city.

Pain exploded behind Ahearn's eyes, her skull feeling like it was going to shatter. She could feel every bone in her body reverberate as the scream filled her, disorienting her. She felt warm blood begin to seep from her ears.

The creature pulled its limbs in and dove head first

towards them, pulling chunks of the ceiling down with it. It collided with End, its mouth swallowing the city whole and plunging End into darkness as shadows surrounded them like a thick fog. Ahearn, Retter, and Aoire gagged, the air around them thick and suffocating.

Trying to see in the darkness, they were nearly thrown down as the ground beneath them shook again. A great crack split down the middle of End and into the Birthing House, ripping the city in two. The shadowy fog was sucked into the great crack, allowing them to take a deep breath. For a split second everything was silent, and then a new scream rose up.

"Khalefo!" The word was almost drowned out by the screams rising up across End. Great plumes of smoke erupted in multiple areas of the city at once, the sound of houses collapsing and bloody screams filling the cavern.

"Get away from the cracks!" A Protector yelled, racing out of the Birthing House.

Looking at a crack in front of them, Ahearn jumped back as a dark figure crawled out of the earth. At first, it looked similar to the shadow creature, and then its body began to shit into the form of a muscular man with black hair. Its face was human, multiple sharp objects pierced into its face and shoulders.

"Khalefo," Ahearn whispered.

She moved backward as the Basher lurched at her with incredible speed, a sickening sneer stretched across its face. Her feet were fast and light on the ground, luring the Basher into a dance.

As it advanced, the Basher pulled one of the sharp objects from its shoulder. A serrated knife slid from its body, no blood on the blade or its skin. Dodging each one of its attacks, Ahearn flicked her wrist. A small, straight blade, with a cluster of five small dots on the hilt, appeared in her hand.

Ducking under one of its attacks, Ahearn spun into its body. She drove the blade up into the underside of its chin, piercing it through the mouth. The black dots illuminated for a moment, black light spilling out from where the blade had pierced its skin.

As the creature screamed, the black light filled its eyes. Twisting the blade, the black light poured out of its body and flowed into the dots. As it did, its body went rigid and its skin turned grey. Ahearn yanked her blade free, tucking it back up her sleeve. She put her boot on its chest and pushed, turning away as the Khalefo disintegrated into dust before its body ever touched the ground.

All around them, the same kind of Bashers were pulling themselves out of the ground, engaging Protector and Guardian alike in battle. The only sound louder was the inured and dying screams of Endians. End had, in moments, become a butchering field.

"We need to get her inside and away from this," Retter said as the battle raged around them. With one movement, he pulled out one of the twin blades that lay crossed over one another on his back, and took off the head of an approaching Khalefo.

As if to reply, Aoire's head rolled slightly and she moaned. Sweat glistened on her whole body. She convulsed as a new wave of pain swept over her. Every time a Basher came close, new waves of pain rocked her, tossing her about amidst fire and ice.

"Can you cut us a path through?" Retter asked, tossing his sword to Ahearn.

With a glare, Ahearn snatched his sword out of the air and gripped it tightly. She impaled an approaching Basher to the ground, pushing her boot against its chest to pull the blade free. Walking over its fallen body towards the Birthing House, Ahearn didn't slow as she continued to carve through incoming Bashers. Retter followed closely behind her, Aoire cradled in his arms.

"We have to get to the kitchen!" Retter shouted as soon as they entered the main hall. The fissure that ran through the middle of End had also split the Grand Hall in half, multitudes of Bashers spilling out. They climbed up the walls like ants and descended upon anyone they could find with a shrill cry. The floor was slick with blood.

Hearing the whistle of metal through the air, Ahearn side stepped as a Basher swung his sword at her. Stepping backwards and parrying his attacks, she lured him into another intricate dance. Cringing as his sword bit deeply into her shoulder, Ahearn used the momentum of his attack against him. Spinning away, she used the flat of her sword to block his next attack and then flipped backwards. Kicking out, she relieved him of his weapon. Twisting up from the floor, Ahearn cut him in half. Surprise was frozen on its face as she stepped over its body.

The sound of an explosion came from behind them.

"Sihir!" Ahearn breathed, spinning around.

The robed women from the corridor now spilled out of the eastern hallway and into the Grand Hall. Power crackled in the air; fire, lightning, and waves of heat, swirled around them. They were beautifully powerful and terrifying all at once. In unison, the Bashers let out a bone-chilling battle cry and swarmed towards the Sihir.

Time seemed to slow.

As Retter and Ahearn watched, a long whip of fire came from one of the red-robed Sihir in the front. Her red eyes flashed with fury, her dark blonde hair gathered into a long braid that hung down her back. The Red twisted her hands intricately in front of her and the whip wrapped around the neck of a Basher across the hall. With a tug she pulled him from the wall.

Once the Basher was down, the whip recoiled, twisting into a ball of flame that engulfed him. It turned him to ash and then transformed into a scaled, winged beast with sharp teeth and a long tail. Bursting from the fallen remains of the Basher, it roared as it flew around the room, engulfing every Basher and creating a wall of fire that contained the battle.

For a moment the battle seemed to turn in favor of End. Lightning blasted from the hands of the yellow Sihir, tearing across the hall and leaving great marks in the walls, ceiling, and floor. A bolt hit one cluster of Bashers and radiated out from where their hearts should have been, connecting them all. They exploded into ash, but another wave of Bashers was right behind them as they continued to pour out of the crack in the middle of the Grand Hall.

Explosions rocked the Birthing House, Retter shielding Aoire as a wave of heat came from an Orange and blasted outwards, turning Bashers into dust. From another Orange came a translucent wall, pushing back every body and Basher it came in contact with. It didn't stop until it collided with the far wall, flattening all of them. Ahearn and Retter could see the strain and exhaustion on the faces of the Sihir as they continued to weave their powerful spells. A few had already collapsed, their power exhausted and all the life gone from their eyes.

"Commander look," Ahearn said, pointing with the sword.

Retter turned to look as Major General Tol and a tall, olive skinned Yellow fell into step next to each other.

Moving through the hall, it was as if they could read each other's thoughts. Her spells were powerful – jagged balls of lightning rolling around the Grand Hall and mowing down any Basher in their way while great burst of lightning took down Bashers by the dozen. He constantly stepped in front of her to fend off any that managed to get close, his sword spinning in expert and intricate attacks.

"Caz," Retter said, dark movement from within the crack drawing his eye. Thick black sludge had begun to seep from it, moving slowly across the hall towards Tol and the Yellow. Ahearn did not reply, her attention on Tol and the Sihir. It seemed as if all attention was now on them.

"Caz," Retter repeated, more urgently as the ooze stopped. It began to fold over itself, rising higher and higher, to take on the crude form of an enormous person.

Once the ooze was tall enough, the form solidified and the oily ooze slid off to reveal a man. He looked exactly like the smaller Khalefo, but had more metal piercings on his body. He stood nearly eight feet tall, his hulking form clothed in shiny black leather that matched his dark hair. He had formed on the side of the fissure closest to Tol and the Yellow, but the beautiful dance of death that they were engaged in had everyone transfixed.

"Caz!" Retter snapped as the new Basher took a step towards Tol and the Sihir, the floor cracking underneath him.

As he moved, smaller versions of him fell from his body and enlarged once they hit the ground. Hearing Retter's voice, the giant turned to look over his shoulder, grinning when he saw Aoire unconscious in Retter's arms.

"Get them," he said, pointing at Retter and Ahearn.

"Caz! Run!" Retter shouted as every Basher in the room leaped down from the walls, or rose from the body they were devouring. They began to rush towards Retter and Ahearn like a tidal wave.

"Protect them at all costs!" Tol ordered.

Ahearn glanced over her shoulder as they raced across the hall to see the large Basher move towards Tol and the Sihir again. Bashers streamed past him towards her and Retter. Gripping Retter's sword even tighter as she ran, Ahearn could hear Bashers exploding as the Sihir did everything they could to help.

Ducking as ashes rained over them, Ahearn looked over her shoulder once more to see a young Orange wink at her. A blast of orange light came from her body, forming into transparent shackles that wrapped around the bodies of every Basher nearest to Ahearn and Retter, pinning them to the ground. She and the other Sihir vanished from view as Retter and Ahearn skidded around a corner.

Ahearn shoved Retter towards a nearby supply closet, diving in behind him. She slammed the door shut before the pursuing Bashers could see where they had gone. The supply closet was littered with old tables, chairs, and broken lanterns amidst other items. Retter propped Aoire up against the wall, her eyelids fluttering.

"We need to move quickly. We don't have long before they figure out where we went," Ahearn said, pilling whatever she could in front of the door.

Using her knee to break an old algae lantern off the top of its ionaithe staff, Ahearn shoved the staff against the top of the door, and the other end into the ground, to keep it barricaded. She lurched back, the door shaking as something threw itself, or was thrown, against the door.

"What are you doing?" Retter asked, kneeling next to Aoire. Ahearn had now started moving tables and chairs away from the edges of the room.

"There used to be an entrance to one of the hidden hallways here. I used it as a child often, but as you can see, this room hasn't been used in years," Ahearn replied. The door rattled again.

"You're sure it was in here?" Retter asked. He moved a table and a bunch of old tapestries that had been stacked behind it fell. Shoving the tapestries aside, the door shook more violently. On the other side of the door, they could hear a female speaking to the Bashers.

"I sort of have to be, don't I?" Ahearn snapped, looking at the door.

Pulling an old rug away from the corner, Ahearn's face brightened as an old wooden door with a rusted ionaithe hinge appeared. She kicked at the hinge as something even heavier was slammed against the door, nearly ripping it from the wall. Kicking the hinge as hard as she could, it snapped in half.

Kneeling down, Ahearn flung the door open to reveal a dark hole. "See! I knew it was still here."

"We need to go," Retter said, the door shaking violently again. It began to split at the hinges, and they could hear a hissing sound rise up from behind the door. Retter handed Aoire down to Ahearn just as the door exploded.

Fragments and shards of the door flew everywhere. A large piece sliced Retter's neck, smaller ones cutting his hands. Once the dust settled, Retter could see Eimhir standing on the other side, surrounded by Bashers. The bandages had partly fallen away from her face, revealing a burn that splashed across half her face. The edge of her mouth wouldn't open, her lips now melted together. Thick blood and pus had begun to ooze down the side of her neck, but she didn't seem to notice.

In her right hand, she gripped a black orb that absorbed all light and color around it. She was holding it where the door had exploded inward. Eimhir had no magic that he knew of, so Retter knew the orb had to hold powerful magic.

"Get them! Bring her to me!" Eimhir screeched and pointed at Retter as he dropped into the hole, slamming the door shut over his head.

Shoving a piece of wood into the crack to wedge the door shut, Retter could hear the screams of the Bashers as they threw themselves against the door. Black smoke began to filter through the cracks, swirling around he and Ahearn.

"Run! Go!" Retter shouted as the smoke thickened around their legs. Hands grabbed their ankles in the darkness. Straining, they pulled free and raced down the hall. From behind them, they could hear the Bashers scrambling over one another in their bloodlust.

Ahearn took a sharp left as the corridor forked and shifted Aoire in her arms, lowering her shoulder to push through a wall of packed earth. She gasped as she felt her shoulder pop, but the wall gave way. She and Retter spilled out near the kitchen, jumping and stumbling over bodies.

Skidding into the kitchen, Retter slammed the double doors shut behind them. He unsheathed the second blade on his back, shoving it through the handles of the doors.

Ahearn lay Aoire down on a table near the fireplace as Retter began pushing anything he could in front of the door.

"You said the entrance to the sewers was in here?" Ahearn asked, looking around. Broken pottery and tools were mixed with the dead.

"The fireplace. It's the lowest point in the kitchen, and the easiest to hide," Retter replied.

Crouching in front of the fireplace, Ahearn could see a small corner of stone with the grain going in the opposite direction as all the rest, underneath layers of soot and ash. It had been exposed as a scullery maid fell. Ahearn dragged her finger through the ash, mapping the outline of the rock. It took up nearly the entire floor of the fireplace, a great metal grill set on top of it.

"Commander, help me move this," Ahearn said, ducking into the six-foot tall fireplace and pressing her back against the wall. Propping her foot against the grill, Ahearn pushed with all her strength while Retter pulled. Slowly, the grill scraped across the floor, dragging a line through the blood-spattered ash.

"I need something solid," Ahearn said, reaching out a hand without looking up.

"Here," Retter replied, handing her the hilt of a broken sword.

Ahearn began striking at the stone, every strike jarring her injuries. She could feel fatigue and pain creeping in on the edges of the adrenaline that pounded in her ears. A dull ache had begun in her shoulder, coupled with the sharp sting of where the Basher blade had split open her shoulder. Ahearn grimaced as she continued to work, sweat collecting on her brow.

"We should see to your shoulder," Retter said, watching her.

Ahearn glanced at her limp arm as she worked on the stone. Both she and Retter were covered with dried blood and dust, but had no way to know how much of the blood was their own. Ahearn knew she could not think about that right now, she had to find them a way out of End.

"It can wait," Ahearn replied, turning back to the stone.

"Guardian Caz," Retter commanded. Ahearn looked up, pain creeping into her eyes.

"Let me see it," Retter said a little more gently.

Sighing, Ahearn straightened up. Stepping out of the fireplace, she grimaced as his fingers ran over her injured shoulder, the sharp pain making her head spin. Tearing a long strip of cloth off the shirt of a dead cook, Retter bound her shoulder tightly.

"That's the best I can do right now," Retter said.

Ahearn nodded, some of the color coming back to her face. Retter couldn't remember the last time he had been this close to Caz, and there was something he had never noticed before, but it was impossible. It was against the Guardian code and Bearn would have never broken the code, not in this way.

"What?" Ahearn asked, pulling back.

Retter shook his head, blinking. "Nothing. Nothing at all."

Looking at him sideways, Ahearn moved back to the fireplace and took to striking the stone again as Retter moved to Aoire's side. The sounds of the fighting in the Birthing House had ended, an eerie silence settling in. The sound of the sword striking stone rang out sharply.

Soon, the stone began to crack. With a final strike, the

stone cracked across the middle, caving in slightly. Hearing a sound outside of the kitchen, Ahearn struck each half of the stone as quickly as she could. Small pieces fell away at first, and then larger chunks cracked off. Finally, the stone split completely. They heard the sound of stone hitting shallow water as the smell of stale air and human excrement rose to meet them.

Ahearn and Retter's heads snapped up as a hissing sound came from the doors. Black smoke began billowing in through the bottom and edges of the door. As it did, it began to collect into a pillar. Everything around it turned black and began to melt – stone, wood, and ionaithe fixtures alike. Ahearn felt her stomach turn as she recognized the black smoke.

"We need to go," Ahearn said. The pillar began to take the shape of a tall, voluptuous woman.

"Is that her?" Retter asked, lifting Aoire from the table. She moaned as he moved her.

"Yes! It's time to go!" Ahearn shouted, pushing him towards the hole. The pillar was nearly formed.

Lowering herself into the sewer after Retter and Aoire, Ahearn caught sight of Narcissa's porcelain face as the smoke dissipated to reveal her standing in the front of the door. A patient smile was painted across her blood red lips as she watched them slip into the sewers. The wood of the door behind Narcissa had melted away, an impossible multitude of Bashers standing on the other side. Their eyes moved between Narcissa and the kitchen, but none of them dared to move past her.

Whispering a goodbye to the place that had once been her home, Ahearn dropped into the sewers. The kitchen and Narcissa's languid smile vanished from sight.

Chapter Ten

Narcissa stepped nimbly around the bodies of the dead as she walked the quiet city. The early-morning light of the algae blooms cast long shadows around her, the hem of her black dress heavy with blood. It made no sound as she walked through

Broken bodies and buildings littered the streets. Some of the homes were still smoking. All around her she could see the paths the souls of the dead left behind, mapping out the last moments of their lives. Some ended where their body had fallen, others were cut off suddenly as a piece of rubble fell on its victim.

It was Narcissa's ability as a Lefeela that allowed her to see these soul paths. Tracking her victims by their souls was how every Lefeela hunted. In her mind, Narcissa could hear the dying cries of the entire city. A smile played on her lips.

In the distance smoke rose from where the blacksmiths' forges had broken, their fires slowly burning through the city. The Birthing House rose behind Narcissa, its regal façade only a shattered remnant.

Narcissa's thoughts turned to Aoire. When last she had seen her, she was being carried out of the Birthing

House through the sewers. There was no way that Narcissa was going to step foot in those sewers, that was for a far lesser Basher than she. If she needed, she would go the long way around. She was not concerned - there was only one way out of End now that the path to the world above was reduced to rubble.

There was no rush. All three of them were injured and Aoire was next to useless. Without her, the other two would be an easy addition to Narcissa's collection. For a moment she looked wistfully at the body of a child lying on her back. Hunger for the soul that no longer lived inside of the body grew within her.

Continuing her stroll around the city, Narcissa didn't slow as Khalefo came from the shadows and fell in step beside her. They merged together into the giant Khalefo that had appeared during the attack. Every time one of his shadowy Khalefo merged with him, he seemed to grow a bit bigger, another metal piercing appearing on his body.

"Fearg," Narcissa said once he had fully formed.

"Narcissa," Fearg replied. His smooth voice was a stark contrast to his savage appearance.

"Did your minions leave anyone alive?" Narcissa asked, lifting her skirt to step over a piece of rubble.

His face darkened at the thought. "Just that Amesi woman."

Narcissa's eyebrows arched. "Really? Are you sure, Fearg?"

"What are you implying, Narcissa?" Fearg demanded.

"I am not implying anything. I am simply stating that some managed to get away," Narcissa replied.

"And how could you possibly know that?" Fearg asked, anger flashing in his eyes.

"You only see on one level, Fearg. It's what makes you such a good battering ram, but you forget that I see far more than you ever will. I can see the trails that every soul leaves behind and I am telling you that some have escaped."

"Not my fault if some got away," Fearg grumbled, jamming a thumb over his shoulder in the direction of the Birthing House. "Maybe that Amesi woman is the one to blame. She was the one that was supposed to keep those accursed Sihir witches out of here, and failed. Last I saw of her, she was holed up in her chambers. She ran off as soon as you arrived."

"I see," Narcissa said. Her eyes were drawn back to the Birthing House.

"Did you see the one Master wants?"

Narcissa nodded, turning around to walk back towards the Birthing House. "They left through the sewers. When I saw them last, she was unconscious. Masters poison did its trick."

"And you just let them go?" Fearg asked.

"Go? Go where? They have no place *to go*, Fearg. There is only one other way out of the cavern, if they can even find it, and it's a three days journey from here. I am far faster than any of them. I will find and deal with them as Master has instructed me to," Narcissa replied.

"Then what are we doing heading back to the Birthing House? Shouldn't you be going after them?" Fear asked.

"In time. Right now I think Eimhir needs company," Narcissa replied.

Entering the courtyard of the Birthing House, steam was still rising from the great cracks that ran in every direction. The Birthing House was barely still standing, great parts of the walls and ceiling broken off. As they walked, pieces of ground and bodies fell into the cracks. Steam rose up with a sharp hiss from within the cracks. Narcissa met the empty eyes of a young Birther, hunger grumbling within her again.

"Apparently you don't discriminate," Narcissa said, looking back at the city behind her.

"Do you?" Fearg asked. Picking up a piece of shattered wood, he used it to pick something out of his teeth. "Why would I, anyway? Killing is easy. Keeping my brethren at bay to allow someone to live is the hard part."

"I can see why Master named you leader of the Khalefo. Only a brute in life could create this kind of carnage," Narcissa said, stepping around a large pile of rock at the entrance to the Birthing House.

Fearg bristled. "And what about you, Narcissa? What did you do in life to become leader of the Lefeela?"

Narcissa smiled wickedly to Fearg and turned away, ignoring his question. She had been the first of the Seven that Vyad named, and she had seen each of the other six Basher Generals named. Including Fearg. Before the Generals had been chosen, she had had many years alone with Vyad. She was the one he relied on most, the one that he gave the toughest tasks to, and the hardest conquests. Fearg has always been beneath her. She felt no need to satisfy him with a response.

Looking around, Narcissa had to admit – at least to herself – that Fearg was powerful. She could it in the carnage and destruction around her, but he lacked imagination.

Anyone can kill, what Narcissa did was so much more. What she did was intimate. She learned what made her victims tick and used that to grow close to them before striking, instead of bursting in and ripping everything to shreds as Fearg did time and time again. Shows of violence and strength were not always symbols of power and might.

"Eimhir is in her room?" Narcissa asked.

"Sure is. As soon as you showed up, she bolted. I placed one of my Khalefo outside her door and she hasn't emerged since," Fearg replied.

Narcissa smiled. "She must be terrified. We should go see how we can alleviate some of that fear."

Narcissa vanished from the Grand Hall and reappeared in front of Eimhir's door. Fearg appeared next to her, solidifying from his smoke form. The Khalefo outside of the door merged with his body, and from behind the door they could hear the sound of furniture shattering.

Pressing her hand against the door, the wood began to warp. A black mark spread out to cover the whole door, the wood smoking. Once enough of it had burned away, Narcissa stepped through the still smoking door.

Eimhir stood in the middle of her room, shattered furniture all around her. She held a piece of her broken chair over her head, ready to strike whoever it was trying to get through her door. Her face paled the moment she saw Fearg and Narcissa. She dropped the chair and clasped her hands in front of her, trying to regain some sort of composure.

"Narcissa..." Eimhir started, her voice cracking. She licked her lips nervously, her eyes darting between Narcissa and Fearg. Her pale skin made the burn on her face stand out even more and her body began to tremble as Narcissa drew near.

"Care to explain what happened, Eimhir?" Narcissa asked.

Eimhir's hands nervously smoothed the skirt of her

dress. "The attack happened like planned but the girl had help. Two Guardians, Caz and Retter, they got her out."

"I know. I saw," Narcissa said.

"You...you did?" Eimhir asked quietly.

"I thought you put the Commander in the NeverEver. If you did, how is it that he was around to get the girl-child out?" Narcissa asked, walking around Eimhir. She lightly trailed her fingers across Eimhir's back, making Eimhir shudder.

"The girl got him out somehow, there was nothing I could do!" Eimhir replied, her eyes wild.

Narcissa raised an eyebrow, stopping in front of Eimhir. "And Caz? I thought you expected to name him Commander so that he would be under your thumb like," she snapped her fingers a few times, "what was the name of the other one you turned to your side?"

"Cayden," Eimhir said quietly.

"Ah yes. Cayden. Wasn't he one of the first to die?" Narcissa asked, looking at Fearg.

Fearg grinned, his head brushing the ceiling. "Yes. I dropped a balcony on him."

"Aoire must have gotten to Caz somehow! It's the only explanation!" Eimhir cried desperately.

"Or the only explanation is that you have failed again," Narcissa's voice cut right through Eimhir.

"It wasn't my fault!" Eimhir argued, but her voice was small and deflated.

She took a step towards Narcissa, wringing her hands together. "Please, Narcissa, none of this is my fault. I did everything as you instructed, but everything got out of hand so quickly! All my plans evaporated when the Sihir showed up. I couldn't do anything! I tried, I really tried, I promise! You have to believe me, please."

Fearg snorted. "Obviously you didn't. You even had my help and the help of my Khalefo, and still you failed."

Eimhir opened her mouth to reply, but her mind was blank. She stood trembling in the middle of the room.

Narcissa nodded. "Fearg is right, Eimhir. You've failed us more than once this night and this is not the first time you have failed. You weren't able to keep the Commander hidden away, Vyad told you to wait and be patient, and when Fearg showed up, you rushed in to aid him instead of obeying. Fearg could very easily have gotten her, but now because of your actions the girl-child is on the run. With help."

"But I-" Eimhir started, and then cut off as Narcissa stepped closer. She gently lifted up the black bead around Eimhir's neck, her fingers barely brushing Eimhir's neck. Immediately red burns rose up like stripes on her pale skin. Eimhir tasted blood in her mouth as she bit down on her cheek to keep from crying out.

"I do not believe you deserve to wear this anymore. There are no more excuses that can help you now. Master Vyad is very disappointed. He has given you plenty of chances and you have failed every time," Narcissa said.

Eimhir closed her eyes, her whole body trembling. A single tear rolled down her cheek and traced a path through her burn. Narcissa's hand closed around the bead and with a tug, she pulled it from her neck.

"Now, because of your incompetence, he is sending me to intercept them and bring the girl-child to where she belongs. You no longer serve a purpose, Eimhir."

Eimhir's eyes snapped open as Narcissa pressed her lips

against Eimhir's, her hands holding Eimhir's face tightly. Her body stiffened and then began to writhe as black veins radiated out from her lips. She clawed at Narcissa's hands frantically, but eventually her arms fell by her sides.

A ball of pale light appeared in Eimhir's chest, illuminating her from within. It rose up through her body, passing from her and into Narcissa through her mouth. Eimhir's skin turned grey as her soul left her body, her eyes the last to turn ashen. All breath left her lungs and her body went completely limp.

Narcissa pulled away, sucking in the last of Eimhir's soul. The light of her soul traveled down her throat to where it settled underneath her ribcage, and then radiated throughout her entire body. Letting go, Narcissa sighed contentedly as Eimhir crumpled at her feet. The light of Eimhir's soul vanished as it was absorbed into Narcissa's body.

Looking at Eimhir's lifeless heap on the floor, Fearg smiled wickedly. "You've really made it an art form of killing your victims, haven't you?"

Standing a little taller, Narcissa wiped the edges of her mouth with a finger. Her skin was smoother, and her lips and nails were a deeper shade of red, almost black. Any signs of age had vanished from her face.

Deep inside, Narcissa could hear Eimhir screaming and pounding against Narcissa to let her out. All of Eimhir's memories and emotions were now a part of Narcissa, joined by the countless memories and emotions of everyone she had slain with her kiss.

Narcissa could always hear them, thousands of voices inside of her head. She knew that eventually Eimhir would calm, as the realization that she was trapped inside of

Narcissa set in. Now, with Eimhir's soul inside of her, Narcissa would be just a little stronger, just a little faster, and would live longer. It was the way that all Lefeela lived – the souls of the ones they took adding to their lifespan and strength, making them more powerful.

"It's time for us to leave. I have a girl-child to find," Narcissa said, the hem of her dress barely brushing Eimhir's grey hand as she turned to leave. Eimhir's empty eyes stared after them as she and Fearg walked away.

Chapter Eleven

"Your wounds need tending to," Retter said.

Ahearn shook her head, looking out over the lake at End. "Later."

"Caz, you can barely lift your arm," Retter replied.

In the sewers, they had been followed by a small group of Bashers that had nearly overtaken them, but Retter had managed to collapse part of the tunnel and cutting them off. From there, it had taken nearly a day for them to make it through the rest of the sewers and out into the hidden tunnels.

Aoire slowly regained more color and control over her breathing the further away from End they moved. Coming to an impasse in the tunnels, Retter led them down the only path that was clear and they emerged near the far end of the cavern, tucked away in a small outlet. Here, a cluster of Dhunni trees and the shape of the cavern hid them from view of End and anything that may be left alive.

Breathing in the fresher air, Ahearn moved down by the water's edge and thrust Retter's sword into the soft earth, quietly gazing back at her fallen city. Retter laid Aoire in the roots of a nearby tree before walking down to stand next to Ahearn. The roots shifted to cradle her body, creating a smooth nest for her. A look of peace washed over Aoire.

"I'll be fine," Ahearn replied, setting her jaw stubbornly. Blood had stopped flowing from the cut on her shoulder, but she still could not move her arm.

A memory filled Retter's mind. "Go into the water."

"What? Why?" Ahearn asked.

"The water. I saw Aoire put her wrist in the lake the day I first met her and it seemed to help her somehow. She also told me that the original use of this lake had been hidden from us. Perhaps it can help you," Retter replied.

"But she's different from me. Maybe it only helps her kind," Ahearn said, looking back at Aoire.

Retter shrugged. "Only one way to find out."

"Then why don't you do it?" Ahearn snapped.

"My injuries are not as serious as yours are," Retter replied.

Ahearn glared at him, but eventually conceded. She was exhausted physically and mentally, and the sharp pain she felt every time she moved made her head spin. Even breathing triggered pain in her body.

Eyeing the lake warily, Ahearn slowly entered the water. She was surprised by how warm and thick it was around her. Once she was far enough in, she lowered herself until the water touched her chin.

A small current pushed against her legs, sweeping her feet out from under her, but Ahearn didn't sink. Floating in the water, Ahearn felt other small currents come around her. She felt the warmth of it slip under her leathers and into her skin, growing hotter as it surrounded what was broken inside of her.

Thin trails of white smoke began to seep out from under

her leathers, the pain flowing away with the smoke. It felt as if someone was tugging at her wounds, pulling the injury out of her. She could feel strength slowly return to her body and feeling return to her shoulder.

Looking at her shoulder when she felt a particularly strong tug, Ahearn could see the white of her bone where the Bashers blade had bit into her flesh. It was a deep cut, deep enough to have cleaved through skin and muscle. Beneath the trails of smoke she could see her skin beginning to knit together, the trails thinning out and then vanishing once the wound was closed. Ahearn felt another current come behind her and push her back into a standing position. Rising out of the water, she was completely dry.

"The pain's gone," Ahearn said, rotating her shoulder. Her jacket was still torn where she had been cut, but a thin white scar now covered the wound. It had a slight opalescent shine when the light caught it.

"That's exactly what I was hoping for," Retter said, turning around and rushing to Aoire's side.

Pulling Aoire's cloak from around her shoulders, he gently lifted her out of the nest of roots. During the frenzy in End, Retter hadn't noticed how light she was, even in her unconscious state. Carrying her into the lake, Retter slowly submerged her into the water.

Retter was also surprised by how warm and thick the water felt, not cold and thin as he expected. The water seemed to surround her body and support it - even Retter felt weightless. A rainbow of color spread out from Aoire's body and then arced, turning back and settling on top of her like a second skin.

When the colors touched her, the water around her began to bubble and foam. A stark hissing sound rose from the water, and her wrist began to thrash about, as if trying to get out of the water as quickly as possible.

The colors intensified and then thinned out to create a multitude of shinning threads that wrapped around her wrist. They strained to pull it under the surface of the water. Some of the threads snapped and her wrist popped above the surface. Retter grabbed onto Aoire and held her wrist under the surface with all his strength until the threads could gain control.

With a grunt, Retter was thrown backward when Aoire's hand lashed out once more and punched him in the chest. For a moment Aoire's back arched and then the threads erupted from the water and snapped around her arm, pulling it back under.

Black ooze began to seep out from in-between the colored threads. Some threads unraveled from her body, wrapping around the ooze to imprison it as the others held onto her until all the ooze was pulled from her. It twisted, trying to get away from the threads and back to Aoire as a current of water pushed it away. Finally the ooze was enveloped and devoured by the threads, dissipating into the lake. The surface of the lake stilled, as if nothing had happened. Aoire's body relaxed and her eyes slowly fluttered open.

"Retter?" Aoire asked weakly.

Retter breathed a sigh of relief, a small smile lighting up his weary eyes. "Welcome back. You gave us quite a scare."

"What happened? Why aren't we in End?" Aoire asked as she stood up. Her hair and clothes were completely dry, as were Retter's.

Retter lifted her wrist from the water, marveling at it. Vyad's burn was still there, but it had turned to glass. He ran his fingers over the hard scar and Aoire shook her head as if to say it didn't hurt anymore.

"End is gone," Ahearn said from the shore.

"Gone? What do you mean?" Aoire demanded, she and Retter wading out of the lake.

"You don't remember?" Retter asked.

"I remember us speaking in the training yard, then nothing but pain and darkness," Aoire replied, absently rubbing her left wrist. She had no feeling where the burn was.

"Bashers attacked yesterday while we were talking, and when they did you lost consciousness. We got you out, but everyone else..." Ahearn trailed off, handing Aoire's cloak to her. Aoire wrapped it around her shoulders, the roots uncurling from the shape of her small nest and returning to their original state.

"They died," Aoire finished.

Retter looked at her. "You really don't remember any of this?"

Aoire shook her head. "I remember the ground shaking like End was experiencing an earthquake, and then I woke up here in the lake. Which Bashers attacked?"

"Khalefo," Retter replied.

Aoire took a deep breath, closing her eyes in sorrow. "Wrath," she whispered. "Did anyone survive?"

"We don't know. The Sihir showed up to help and that gave us time to escape, but we didn't have the chance to see if anyone else got out," Ahearn replied.

"Vyad," Aoire said through clenched teeth. Her face darkened as she looked back across the lake at the silent city of End. "He really is capable of going to great and terrible lengths to find me. We should go before he figures out where we went."

"Leave?" Ahearn asked, "And go where, Aoire? End is the only home I have ever known."

"There are other cities," Aoire replied.

"What?" Retter asked. "I have only heard of the city the Sihir come from, much less multiple other cities."

"End was not the only city that humans populated after the world above – Earth, as your ancestors knew it - ended. There are five sanctuary cities where people found solace," Aoire said.

"Five?" Retter asked, running a hand through his hair. "How is it that we did not know this?"

"There is much that has been hidden for far too long. In the beginning, the elders thought they were keeping the locations of the cities safe from the Bashers, not knowing that Vyad would know where every city was located." Aoire replied.

"And if the location of End was never a secret, the other locations won't be either," Ahearn said.

Aoire nodded.

"You told us that Vyad has been looking for you your whole life, but Bashers have been attacking us far before you were born. If we are to go with you, then we need some sort of explanation to all of this," Retter said.

"Many hundreds of years ago, Vyad entrapped a great symbol. A Tree. It is this Tree that is the cornerstone to his destruction. I am called to set it free, the only one who can, and he knows that. By trying to destroy each city, Vyad believed that he could prevent my birth," Aoire said.

"If Vyad knows the location of every city and is looking

for you, how is it that we will get to one of them safely?" Ahearn asked.

"We will take the ancient tunnels that connect and protect each city," Aoire said.

"Tunnels cannot protect a city," Retter fired off.

"These do. Any Basher caught within them will burn up," Aoire replied. "It is not easy for them to enter any of the cities, which is why they cannot attack quickly."

"They seemed to enter our home easily enough," Ahearn spat bitterly.

Aoire nodded, pulling her knees to her chest. "Eimhir's collusion with Vyad is concerning, and most likely the main reason they could attack with such force. The Amesi's main job was keeping the Birthing House safe. It is a symbol of life, one that all of End once hinged on. If Eimhir was no longer keeping the Birthing House as her top priority, then the safety of End was already forfeit before the attack."

"So what do we do?" Ahearn asked. "If people can be so easily corrupted, how do we fight an evil like that?"

"The fact that people's hearts can be easily changed, in the end, works in our favor. Wherever there is evil, there is always light. Even the smallest amount of light can be enough to ignite a wildfire," Aoire said.

"And how exactly is this wildfire going to be ignited?" Retter asked, adding, "And what is a wildfire?"

Aoire looked at him. Too much had changed in such a short time, not been passed down through the generations. There was so much that she wanted to tell them both, but she could see the exhaustion on their faces.

"You both should get some rest. The Dhunni trees will protect you as you sleep tonight. Tomorrow morning, we will begin our journey to the next sanctuary city - City of

Truth," Aoire said. Not waiting for an answer, she vanished into the forest.

Walking aimlessly through the forest, Aoire disappeared into her thoughts. Time moved differently here, one could get lost in the forest for what felt like days and only a few minutes would have passed. Aoire could feel Father's presence in the trees around her, growing stronger the further into the forest she moved.

Gradually, the trees began to thin and then opened up into a wide clearing with a floor of thick moss. Five Dhuuni trees rose out of the center of the clearing, their silver trunks twisting together in a spiral to create one enormous tree. Their thick roots braided together as they rose out of the ground, part of them arching gracefully to form a small opening. Warm golden light came from within, the subtle smell of earth after the rain wafting out and filling Aoire's nostrils.

Slipping inside, the warm light welcomed her in. The top of the tree cave rose to immense heights, the roof invisible no matter how far back Aoire craned her neck to see. Beautiful golden flowers with three petals grew out of the tree trunks, white orbs of soft light floating in the air around Aoire.

Out of the middle of the cave, four slender, silver trees rose from of the mossy ground. They connected seamlessly to form an intricate roof of thin, ornately woven branches. Moss covered the top of the roof, the same three petaled flowers growing from here as well. Stepping underneath, Aoire looked up at a delicate chandelier with three bright lights that hung down from the middle of the roof. Beautiful, thin, silvery-green vines were draped around the chandelier. They stretched out and wound around the pillars, the gentle scent of honey filling Aoire's nose as she breathed in deeply.

Underneath the chandelier, a long wooden table was laden with food of every color and size. Great baskets of fruit and meat spilled out amidst enormous loaves of bread. At the end of the table, a beautiful fountain of golden liquid was bubbling. A long, purple, table-runner with gold trim ran the length of the table, matching the golden cutlery and dishes that were set for her. Breathing in the decadent scents, Aoire hadn't realized how hungry she was until now.

"Eat," a deep voice said from behind her. Aoire spun, seeing a tall figure standing in front of where the opening to the cave had been. The wall was now smooth, no trace that an opening had ever been there.

"Father!" Aoire cried, throwing her arms around his neck. He wrapped his strong arms around her, his thick hair smelling of earth and rain. Aoire felt hot tears stream down her cheeks. He held her until she stopped shaking.

"I want you to tell me everything," Father said once she had calmed, sitting on the bench beside her, "but first I want you to eat."

Aoire nodded, grabbing everything she could reach and devouring it. Once she was full enough, Aoire told her Father everything from Vyad invading her dream and burning her wrist to the moment she woke in the lake.

Running his fingers over the glass scar on her wrist, Father frowned. She waited for him to speak, studying his face.

"It is concerning to me not that he was able to touch you, but that he could leave a mark like this. Vyad has always been able to come into our presence, even to approach the throne, but this level of contact has never happened before," Father said.

"It seems he is getting more bold. Or more desperate," Aoire said.

"It would make sense that he would. He has control over the Tree, but knows that his time is coming to an end. It would make sense that he would escalate his attempts on your life," Father said.

"Is that why would it hurt so badly when I used my *opari* or when the Bashers appeared?" Aoire asked, watching Father trace the outline of Vyad's fingers on her slender wrist.

Father's blue-green eyes were studious. "When Retter placed you in the lake, your wrist tried to escape. It had to have been the poison Vyad left within you trying to escape the healing abilities of the lake."

"Poison?"

"Yes. When evil comes in contact with something – anything – it leaves a mark. Because Vyad came in contact with you for a prolonged period of time, and because he is pure evil, he left a poisonous piece of himself in you. Since the Bashers are his creation, many of them his own progeny, anything of him will try to get back to itself. The more Bashers there are, the stronger the pull. Remember Daughter, even though you may be part celestial, the body you inhabit is human. It has its limits."

"Great," Aoire replied, pulling her wrist close to her chest and glowering. "So he left a piece of himself in me? How do we get it out?"

"It's out. The lake did as it was designed to do, but there could be lingering effects."

"Such as?" Aoire asked.

"The scar is there as a reminder of your trials. My son still holds the marks of his, but those were ultimately used for the greatest good possible," Father replied.

Aoire put her face in her hands. "Well I don't like it. That pain was like nothing I have ever experienced before, and it made me useless. I could have used my *opari* to help save some of the souls in End, or-"

Aoire cut off as a sob threatened to escape. Tears filled her eyes.

Father laid a hand over hers. "I know, Daughter. I feel the same pain that you are feeling. This is merely the beginning. This journey will be filled with many hardships. I know that I am asking a lot of you, and that this may not all make sense, but you were created to do this. Only you can."

Laying her head on Father's lap, Aoire allowed the tears to flow. She didn't know for how long she cried, but Father stroked her hair as she sobbed. Eventually, sleep took her, and when she woke the tree cave was bare.

Aoire lay in the soft moss for a few more moments before pushing herself up. A leather satchel was lying near her head, made of beautiful chestnut-brown leather with golden words inscribed on the strap. An ornate golden buckle latched the top of the satchel closed. She could feel the hum of power radiate from it as she slipped it over her head.

"Thank you, Father," Aoire said.

Pressing her fingers to her lips, she kissed them and softly pressed them on the bark by the arched doorway. The same symbol from the entrance to the NeverEver appeared at the top of the doorway, glowing brightly. Aoire stepped out of the tree cave into the clearing, feeling rested for the first time in days. She barely noticed the bag nestled against her hip.

Starting back towards the beach, the trees behind Aoire began to shimmer and then they vanished. Aoire could still feel Father's presence in the forest around her as it closed in behind her and blocked the clearing from view.

Chapter Twelve

Standing near the water's edge, Aoire reached out with her *opari* and before her eyes End City transformed. Now, Aoire saw the fallen as dots of bright light. Portions of the city were brighter than others, and in others the lights were more spread out. Scanning the city with her eyes, Aoire's brows furrowed.

A dark spot had appeared in the woods. It troubled her because she could not see its source, nor feel anything about it. It seemed to be shielded from her the same way Vyad had been, and it was moving towards them quickly. Turning away, Aoire kept a small thread of *opari* open within her. She now knew where the dark spot was at all times, even when she wasn't looking directly at it.

"It's time to go," Aoire said, laying a gentle hand on Retter's shoulder.

Retter woke immediately, his back straight against the trunk of a tree. Ahearn was nestled in the branches of the same tree, but she awoke as well. She flipped down from her sleeping perch and landed in the soft sand next to Retter.

Warriors. Aoire thought, smiling to herself.

"How far away is City of Truth?" Ahearn asked.

"A few weeks journey," Aoire replied.

"Then we need to find fresh water, food, and a way to carry it all, before we leave. I am guessing that there is no Trading Post on the way to Truth," Retter said.

Aoire saw his eyes dart towards End and she patted the bag at her hip. "I have everything we need right here."

"In that tiny thing?" Ahearn asked, eying the small satchel. "How is that even possible?"

Aoire opened her mouth to reply, but a cold breeze spread across the lake, rustling the trees around them. Her eyes scanned the forest, the hair on the back of her neck standing up.

"It's time to go," Aoire said, widening the thread of *opari* to encompass Retter and Ahearn in a protective field. She could see the black spot was hovering at the edge of the forest near their beach. She couldn't see anyone in the woods, but didn't want to wait to find out who belonged with the black spot.

Leading Ahearn and Retter into the forest, Aoire breathed a little easier as the trees closed in around them. She could feel Father all around her, strengthening her while the trees shielded them. Even Retter and Ahearn seemed to walk a little taller.

Looking behind her, the black spot was still on the edge of Aoire's field of vision. She could feel a chill in the woods, the black spot hovering back at the beach. She could also feel the forest thickening around them, folding them into it's own protective embrace, trying to prevent the black spot from growing any closer.

* * * * *

From behind branches, Narcissa watched as Aoire, Retter, and Ahearn vanished into the forest. Moving carefully between the trees so that she wouldn't touch any of them, Narcissa emerged onto the beach where they had been moments before. Her way had gotten increasingly difficult as the trees thickened around her. She could feel the purity of the soft sand under her feet, hot through the soles of her boots.

Following them into the trees, the branches and roots tightened around her. Falling forward when a root appeared in front of her suddenly, she grabbed onto a nearby branch to steady herself. Hissing sharply as the bark burned her hands, Narcissa pulled herself backward.

"If I could, I would burn you all down," Narcissa said, smoke rising from her hands. The trees creaked as if in reply, and Narcissa could swear that even more appeared in the spaces between the others. She felt frustration and anger bubble up within her, seeing that her pursuit of Aoire was being forcibly slowed.

Scowling, she pulled herself up straighter and continued to pick her way slowly through the forest, being as careful as she could not to touch any more of the bark. Even through her dress, she could feel the purity of the trees burning her if she drew too close to one of them.

Cursing loudly as the trees continued to encroach even more around her, black lines began forming at the edges of her eyes. Cold heat radiated off of Narcissa in waves, blackening the trees around her. They shriveled up, the leaves turning to ash and falling off.

A low howl, like a creature in pain, rose up from the trees as more of them blackened, delight dancing in Narcissa's eyes. Reaching out a slender hand to touch one of the afflicted trunks, Narcissa grinned when it did not burn her. It was ice cold.

Turning her eyes back to the path in front of her, Narcissa smirked as the trees pulled away from her as quickly as they could. Able to move freely, she wasted no time. Behind her she could hear the trees weeping for their fallen brothers as she swiftly resumed her pursuit of her prey.

* * * * *

"What is this place?" Retter asked, a cluster of thick branches opening to reveal a small clearing.

It was similar to the one that Aoire had been in the night before, but instead of five trees twisting together, the trunks of these five were bent away from each other in a graceful arch, their branches vanishing into the ground. In the middle of them, a sixth tree grew straight, much taller than the rest.

Small buds grew from each branch. Drawing closer, the buds opened up to reveal seven bright yellow petals fading into white at the ends. Millions of tiny orbs of light spilled out every time the buds opened, floating and twisting gently in the air. A low humming sound filled the clearing.

"This is a sacred place. These six Dhunni trees are the original tress, the ones that all other Dhunni are birthed from. They are Dhuuni in the purest form, virgin trees untouched by evil of any kind," Aoire replied.

Ahearn smiled as hundreds of orbs surrounded her, hovering a hairs breadth above her body. "What are these? They're beautiful."

Aoire lifted a hand, a small cluster of orbs collecting over her palm. "Dhunni seeds. They will gather in groups of thousands to create just one tree," she giggled as the lights caressed her cheek, and then floated off over the forest canopy.

"This is how the Dhunni trees are grown?" Retter asked, even his normal stoicism replaced by reverent awe.

Aoire nodded, watching the orbs float off. "Yes. These trees will never stop and they can create as many seeds as are needed."

"Where are they going?" Ahearn asked.

"To End," Aoire replied softly.

"Why?" Retter asked, his eyes turning back towards the city they could no longer see.

Aoire laid a hand on one of the trunks and smiled sadly as one of the flowers pressed itself against her cheek. More seeds drifted out of it and swirled around Aoire before rising above the canopy.

"Their main purpose is purification. They will plant where there needs to be a cleansing," Aoire said.

"What will happen when the seeds get there?" Ahearn asked.

Aoire shrugged. "Who can say? Such horrific tragedy took place in End and these trees will do what they are designed to do – to purify."

"What do you think will happen?" Ahearn asked again.

"I think the trees will take the city back, and whatever happens it will be beautiful. It is not in the nature of the Dhunni to create something ugly," Aoire replied. She cupped her hands and a cluster of seeds collected above them, taking the form of a shinning Dhunni sapling before dissipating and floating off into the distance.

Retter's head snapped up as a shrill wail rose up in the distance behind them. He could see a thin trail of smoke curling above the canopy. "Something's coming. We should go."

"In a moment," Aoire said, opening her satchel.

Reaching inside, she pulled out a glass ball with a golden seal. Swinging open the seal, Aoire held it underneath one of the flowers. Aoire waited until it was filled to the brim with seeds and then snapped the seal shut. Striping a nearby branch of all of its leaves and one flower, Aoire dropped them into her bag with the glass ball. They all spun around as a deafening crack came from behind them.

Narcissa stood across the clearing from them, black smoke swirling around her sultry form. The trees closest to her had been blown away, completely uprooted. Even from across the clearing they could feel fury radiating off of her in waves. Retter and Ahearn moved to step in front of Aoire, but she shook her head to stop them.

"You must be Aoire," Narcissa said, the smoke settling around her ankles and then vanishing into her dress. Seeing Aoire now, Narcissa felt curiosity rise up within her. She could feel the purity of the power within Aoire, pulling her in. Deep within her heart she felt a rare longing to know more about Aoire, followed by Besit's cold grip tightening painfully around her heart. The longing vanished as her heart hardened again. All she saw now was a skinny, red-haired, girl-child. She had taken down much more intimidating foes.

"You aren't much to look at are you girl-child? Even so, perhaps you can answer something for me. Apparently, you are supposed to be so powerful that my master wants you captured, but not destroyed – he is planning to do that himself. Yet, upon looking at you, I don't see what would merit such a request or even such devotion from your two Guardians. What is it about you that causes such a reaction?" Narcissa asked, stepping into the clearing.

Aoire lifted her chin. "You have no business here, Narcissa."

Narcissa frowned, the authority in Aoire's voice a mild surprise. Keeping her eyes on them, she began to pace. "Actually, I do. My business is with you, Aoire, whether you come to accept it or not. I do not fail. Ever. It's why Master has sent me. After the inexcusable failure of Eimhir to keep you captive in End, Master wanted to make sure that the job was completed properly this time."

"What did you do to Eimhir?" Ahearn demanded.

Narcissa put a hip out and crossed her arms under her breasts, placing a single finger on her chin. "What did I do to her? Simply what she deserved. Don't tell me that you are actually concerned about the woman that betrayed the whole of End?"

A sly smile spread across Narcissa's face, looking Ahearn up and down. "At least she took your secret to the grave, my dear."

Ahearn's hands clenched into fists and she ground her back heel into the ground. Aoire grabbed her wrist and shook her head. "Don't. She is trying to bait you. You cannot touch her, or she will kill you."

Ahearn clenched her jaw, but relaxed enough to reassure Aoire she wouldn't attack.

"Tsk-tsk, did I hit a nerve?" Narcissa asked, smiling.

"I will say this one more time, Narcissa – you have no business here. This is sacred ground, and you should leave before you are forced to leave," Aoire repeated.

Aoire's *opari* roared inside of her, the ball of fire burning bright green. Her eyes now green, energy flowed from her and into the ground. All across the clearing tiny light orbs began to drift up from the algae at their feet, hovering close to the ground.

"What are you going to do?" Narcissa scoffed. "Do you really think a skinny little creature such as yourself can defeat me with some light?"

Aoire shook her head. "No, I don't need to defeat you. I only need to distract you."

Flicking her wrist toward Narcissa, Aoire focused her *opari* on Narcissa. The light orbs flew across the clearing with immense speed, slamming into Narcissa with such force that she stumbled back a few steps with all the orbs attached to her. As they covered her, she began to scream both in pain and anger. Everywhere they touched, they burned. Narcissa clawed at herself, trying to get them off of her.

Grabbing ahold of one of Retter and Ahearn's hands, Aoire knew she wouldn't have much time to act. Tapping into her *opari* again, the ball of fire and her eyes changed from green to blue. The moment they did, the light orbs fell from Narcissa's body and vanished into the ground.

With a snarl, Narcissa launched herself at them. Time seemed to slow as she approached, and for a moment Narcissa was certain she would reach them before they could get away.

A clap like thunder rang out along with a flash of blue light. Narcissa hurtled through the air where they had been only milliseconds before, and sprawled on the ground. Getting to her knees, she threw back her head and howled in anger, the ground around her turning black.

Chapter Thirteen

Laur gasped for air as her head broke the surface of the still pool. Pulling herself out, she sat by the water's edge and drank in the air in great gulps. No water dripped from her clothing or hair, and it took a moment for her eyes to adjust to the dim light.

She was sitting in a small cavern, lit by twenty-two algae torches with ionaithe poles, half of them barely emitting any light. Most of the light came from the pool, which glowed faintly. Anytime she moved her legs, ripples of white light extended out, then faded away as the surface of the water stilled.

Next to her a small ionaithe pillar rose out of the ground. A large stone, called the taisteal, was in the center of it. Threads of brilliant color swirled around inside it - yellow, orange, red, green, blue, purple, black, and white swirls, all moving on their own. They intersected and bisected each other in splashed of color.

Laur could see the purple thread shinning brightest before it faded back to the same brilliance as the others. A large section of the taisteal had cracked off, lying on the floor with a thick layer of dust over top of it. Picking it off the ground, Laur could see there were threads within. She slipped it into a pouch hidden in the folds of her worn jacket, where it rested with other artifacts she had collected.

Pushing herself back until she hit the cave wall, her feet hung slightly over the edge of the pool. It was tiny, the surface completely still. There was no sign of the swirling whirlpool that had brought her here from an identical pool in City of Truth. Laur could still feel the tingling effects of the violent tug and the stomach-dropping rush that had transported her here.

Colors had surrounded her as soon as she had dove into the pool in Truth, rushing by in vibrant swirls. It had been harder to breathe in this portal, almost like traveling through sand instead of water, and Laur wondered if the intensity of this trip had to do with the cracked taisteal.

Looking around her, Laur attempted to get her bearings. She had never come through this portal before, but she thought she might be in End by the color of the cave. A worn staircase was cut into the cave wall across from Laur, the only way in or out.

Pulling her left leg close to her chest, Laur grimaced in pain. Her heavy breathing echoed as she tugged at her boot. It resisted, but finally came free. Looking down, Laur could see that her foot had swollen to nearly twice its normal size. It hung limply, a deep gash running down from her ankle to the middle of her foot. Dried blood had collected around the wound, her skin beginning to turn various shades of blue and purple. The white of her bone stood out starkly through the dried blood and mangled skin. Laur tried to wiggle her toes, but they barely moved.

Grabbing the hem of her jacket, Laur tore off a long strip with her teeth and began wrapping it tightly around her ankle. Her breath caught in her throat as pain shot up her leg, sending the cave spinning.

Tying off the ends of the cloth, Laur collapsed back against the wall. Her chest heaved and tears streamed freely down her face. She waited until the cave stopped spinning before trying to move again. Grabbing her boot, Laur steeled herself and then yanked it on in one swift movement. Screaming in pain, she leaned over and retched, running the back of her hand across her mouth when done.

Gripping the wall, Laur hoisted herself to her feet. Pushing her curly hair out of her face, she grabbed the closest lantern to her and swung it down against a sharp outcropping, snapping it off. Gripping the shaft tightly, she glanced nervously back at the pool before hobbling up the stairs.

She knew the ones hunting her would find where she had gone and come for her. Even though they would not be able to come through the portal she had used, Laur knew they would find another way. They always found another way.

She was still surprised that she had been able to come through this portal with the taisteal as damaged as it was. It was obvious this portal hadn't been used in many years, and Laur suspected she had stumbled upon it by mistake. Or perhaps it had been provision from someone or something else.

Keeping a hand on the wall as she hobbled up the narrow staircase, Laur's nose began to twitch. End had a distinct smell to it, but now it was coated with a sickly sweetness. In the darkness, Laur felt the old wooden door before she saw it. The sweet smell was stronger here, and it didn't take Laur long to figure out what it belonged to.

Laur's nimble fingers ran lightly over the door, feeling the deep grooves of age in the thick wood. Light filtered through where the door connected to the wall and where age had eaten away at the wood. Wedging her staff underneath the top hinge, Laur bore down. With a long groan, the hinge broke away. Doing the same to the bottom hinge off, Laur gently pushed the door. It hit the ground with a loud thud, a plume of dust rising up.

Gripping her staff tightly with both hands, Laur hobbled out of the hallway. Torches lit the walls around her, everything eerily still. There was no sound other than Laur's breathing echoing loudly around her.

Shuffling down the hallway towards the only opening she could see, Laur exited into a larger hallway identical to the one she had just been in. Behind her, another doorway sat, rounded with eight symbols carved into it. Two ornate lanterns hung on the wall, spaced evenly around the door. Laur knew through there another portal lay in wait. She had seen Sihir travel to the other cities through portals behind doors just like this. Scowling, Laur turned her back to the door.

Sihir, Sisters of the Order. They were the ones who were sworn to protect every living creature, but when her power manifested itself in her, the Sihir turned their backs on her. Laur had been thirteen when the purple magic within her emerged and the Hunters had showed up, killing her parents. She had come to the Sihir for help, but they took one look at her now purple eyes and told her that her power was an abomination. They told her it should be cut from her and then they slammed the door to their temple in her face. That had been nearly eight years ago. Laur had been on the run from Hunters ever since.

Growing up, she had always been a quick study and an incredibly bright child, two attributes that served her well now. She had been forced to learn how to be even faster than the Hunters chasing her, how to be smarter than them, and how to defend herself at all costs. Laur studied all she could, and she grew stronger in every way that she knew how.

Laur hated her power. What good was power if it was the very thing that got her parents killed, turning her into a fugitive? She did everything she could to hide the fact that she was a Purple, even going to such lengths as drinking a tea that colored her eyes from purple to grey, but even that didn't last. Over that last few years she had to drink it more frequently, always afraid of being found out. Laur found it ironic that it was her power as a Purple that allowed her the travel freely between cities by way of the portals, but also marked her for death - only a Sihir could use the portals.

Hobbling as fast as she could, Laur followed the stench. Her body ached from being on the run all the time, and all she wanted was to sleep. Laur gasped as her foot caught on the edge of a piece of rubble, stumbling a bit. She could barely put any weight on her injured foot anymore, dragging it as she walked.

Laur had been hiding in the library at Truth when the Hunters finally caught up with her. This newest group was a particularly vicious one. Laur had barely been able to activate the taisteal and dive into the portal, before her foot was nearly severed from a flying dagger. Once in the portal, her only thought amidst the pain was to get someplace safe. She had emerged in End.

"Dear heaven," Laur breathed, coming to the top of the stairs.

Entering the Grand Hall, Laur felt tears sting her eyes. Dried blood was splattered on the floor and walls, pooling in some areas. Everywhere she looked, bodies were strewn about.

Tiny light orbs floated in the air and between the fallen, but that was the only movement. The bodies of Guardians lay next to Protectors, Birthers, and Seeders alike. Even the colored robes of Sihir dotted the hall. A great crack ran down the middle of the Grand Hall, splitting the great structure in half. Thin smoke still curled lazily from within. A few orbs of light landed on some of the bodies and vanished within them. Laur left the Birthing House as quickly as she could, the smell of blood overwhelming.

Stepping into the main streets of End, Laur felt tears running freely down her cheeks. It wasn't any better out here. Carnage was all around her. The last time she had been in End, it had been a bustling metropolis of life and prosperity, but now the whole city was shattered. Black smoke rose to the ceiling of the cavern, and every now and again a piece of rock fell to the ground. The silence was deafening.

Laur could only think of one creature that could do something this heinous. She had heard stories of the Khalefo, but she had never seen the after affects of a Khalefo attack with her own eyes before. Shivers ran down her spine as she picked her way through the city, empty eyes watching her in return.

Moving slowly through End, Laur heard faint sounds in the distance.

"Hello?" Laur called out, her voice shaking.

Silence replied and then she heard the sound of three

familiar voices. They were raised and the moment she heard them, Laur felt fear run through her.

Swinging her legs over the broken wall of a home, Laur cringed as her boots landed on a ceramic pot. The sound of the breaking pot rang sharply throughout End.

Hearing the voices shout, Laur dropped down and pressed her body as tightly against the broken wall as she could. The top of the wall just covered her head, part of it low enough that she could see around the wall without giving herself away. The voices drew near to her and Laur was certain they would be able to hear the pounding of her heart. Soon, she could hear all three voices of the Hunters distinctly.

"She came here? Why?" a deep, gravelly voice drawled. Laur called this one Accent. She had begun giving them nicknames, never knowing their real names because Hunters never used them.

"She most likely thought that she would lose us with that little trick of hers. Or maybe she thought she could hide away here like the rat that she is. Her kind isn't welcome anywhere," a second voice replied, higher pitched with a slight slur. Laur called him Fists.

"Regardless of why she came here, this place is a graveyard. It'll make our job much easier, especially since she is injured. She can't have gone far, but make sure that you are covered. Remember what happened to the last Hunter party sent after her?" a third voice said. He was the leader of them. Laur had named him Blade, and it had been his dagger that had sliced her foot open.

"Witch won't control me, no sir. I'm lookin' to add her to my collection," Accent replied. Laur could hear the glee in his voice.

Gripping her staff tightly, she called upon her power and felt it course through her. It was always there, but she could only feel it when she focused on it. The pain in her ankle doubled as her senses were heightened and then dulled as her power coursed through her veins, calming her. She hated using her power, but she refused to be a Hunters prize.

Turning her head to look around the wall, Laur ducked back quickly as she caught sight of them.

Hunters were vicious mercenaries for hire. These particular ones had been chasing her for over a year now, sent after the last group succumbed to her Touch, which she called *ukitu*. Laur had had even fewer times to rest with this group than any of the others. Somehow, they always knew where she was. Somehow, they were always a half step behind her.

Hearing one of the Hunters approach her hiding spot, Laur slide behind a taller wall. Closing her eyes, she pushed herself to her feet, swaying against the sharp waves of pain. Gritting her teeth and balancing herself, Laur waited until the Hunter came into view and then spun out from behind the wall, striking quickly.

She hit Fists in the groin with the butt of her staff, and then swung it upwards so that it cracked into his chin, snapping his head backward. Blood began to flow from his split chin. Grabbing his wrist as he stumbled back, she called upon her *ukitu* and everything around them slowed. Their eyes locked and she felt their heartbeats slow, become one. With a jolt, her power coursed into Fists. His eyes turned from pale brown to bright purple and then back again. All intensity left his face and he stared at Laur with quiet awe.

Pressing a finger to her lips, they sunk to their knees.

He watched her silently as she looked around the corner of the house, leaning forward to grab her hand as she moved to leave. Turning back, she placed a hand out.

"Stay," she mouthed. Fists shot her a pleading look, but shrunk back against the wall. He watched her with a pained expression as she vanished from sight.

Creeping up behind Accent, Laur slipped her staff over his head and pinned it against his throat. He grabbed onto the staff and tried to pull her over his head, but Laur pushed her boot against the back of his leg, tightening her grip on him.

Spinning so her back was pressed against Fists, Laur gathered all her strength and hurled him over her head into a wall. His body dropped to the ground, and Laur was on top of him before he could gather his senses. She pressed a knee under his chin and her other boot on top of his wrist. As his eyes fluttered open, Laur touched his throat with two of her fingers and his eyes flashed purple, and then back to medium grey a moment later.

"Where is the last one?" Laur hissed through pain and gritted teeth, grabbing Fists by the hair.

"Right here, girl," Blade said from behind her. Laur felt the sharp prick of his dagger-tip in the small of her back, forcing her to slowly rise off of Fists. Once she was up, she felt the sharp end of Blade's dagger leave.

Turning around slowly to look him in the eye, Laur put the end of her staff down and gripped it tightly. Her power was still coursing through her body, but she could feel the pain in her ankle growing. Fists had not moved from his position on the ground. He looked up at her with a strained expression, his eyes darting between her and Blade. He and Accent would not move unless she gave them a direct order.

"That is an interesting ability that you posses. I can see why your kind is feared and hunted," Blade said.

He was a man of average height with a long scar that ran down the side of his face. His eye was milky white where the scar pierced through it, the other eye deep grey. Rows of silver knives were attached to his belt, another row rising from the top of his boots. He was wiry in stature, but Laur knew he was deceptively strong – it took a lot of strength to be able to hurl those daggers with such force and accuracy, even with one blind eye.

"It comes in handy when I am being hunted by rats like you," Laur replied, her bottom lip trembling slightly.

A dagger appeared in his hand, making it absently dance between his fingers. "Just doing my job darlin'. It makes no difference to me whom I hunt, all that matters is the price being paid," he pointed the dagger at her, "and the bounty on *your* head is the largest in all of Hunter history. Perhaps it's that dark magic that you hold within you, perhaps not. It makes no matter to me. I simply intend to collect you and then my bounty."

"Collect me?" Laur asked. This had been the first time she had heard that she was wanted alive.

Blade whistled. "Oh yes darlin'. The bounty on your head used to be dead or alive, but after your little stunt in Rarities, you have been upgraded to alive only."

"I had nothing to do with that," Laur said. The faces of those she had affected flashed in her mind.

"I heard otherwise, and so have others. You gave quite the show of power back there, one that caught the attention of the benefactor of my benefactor. They want you alive so they can study you. Figure out how that darkness within you works," Blade said.

"I will be no one's slave to study," Laur said, tightening her grip on her staff.

Who is hunting me? Laur thought desperately.

In her mind, she could see a running list of the most powerful houses in each city, but she could not discern which of those would be powerful enough to have hunted her for this long. Hunters did not come cheap and this was the sixth group sent after her in eight years.

Blade sat on the edge of a broken wall, fiddling with his dagger. Laur kept her eyes on him, watching his every move. She had never encountered someone as swift as he, in the blink of an eye everything could change, and she would not be caught off-guard by him again.

"We Hunters have been chasing you down for a while, haven't we? How long has it been?" Blade finally asked.

"Nearly eight years," Laur scowled. "Your kind killed my parents."

"Eight years," he whistled, tapping the flat of his blade against his knee. "You must be exhausted, child. Wouldn't it just be easier to come with 'my kind' than to continue to fight us?"

Laur's eyes flashed. "I will never come with you, Blade. You will have to kill me first."

Blade rose from his perch. "I will not kill you, but whether I bring you back walking or in pieces, it makes no difference to me. I will have that bounty on your head. I have already taken a slice out of you, it shouldn't be hard to take more."

Laur took a sharp breath as his hand flexed and she jerked to the side. Shrieking as one of his knives flew past her, it embedded itself in the wall behind her. Laur reached up to wipe away a trickle of blood on her plump cheek. She had managed to move out of the way enough so that the knife only cut her cheek. It stung sharply.

Spinning her staff in her hands, she deflected his blades as he threw them at her with lightning speed. Walking towards him slowly, Laur waited until he ran out of blades on his wrists and reached for the ones around the top of his boots before she struck.

Pressing off her feet, Laur launched herself at Blade and slid across the ground as he lunged at her with a long, serrated knife. Spinning her staff above her head as she slid under him, Laur felt it connect with the inside of his leg. Rotating her staff, Laur flipped him into the air. Blade landed on his back with a grunt, twisting his body immediately to get into a crouched position.

Laur was just a little faster.

Jamming her staff into his neck, his body went rigid as pain and lack of air paralyzed him. Striking him across the temple, Laur sent Blade rolling across the ground. Before he could gain his bearings, she was on top of him, pressing her knee into the small of his back.

Laur grabbed a fistful of his hair, yanking his head back so that his eyes were forced to roll up to look at her. Blood and sweat glistened on her swollen cheek as she stared down at him in fury, her purple eyes bright from the power that coursed through her veins. Setting her staff down, Laur leaned her face close to his.

"I have been running from *your kind* for ages. What makes you think that I have not learned how to defend myself? How to be faster, how to be stronger, and how to be smarter, than you lot? I think you have underestimated me for the last time. Maybe this will finally teach you, and your benefactors, to leave me alone!" Laur said.

Blade grinned up at her, his ear bleeding from where Laur's staff had hit him. "He will only send more. Hunters even more skilled than me."

Laur yanked, digging her knee even further into his back so that his chest was completely off the ground. "I have done nothing to deserve this!"

He began to chuckle between gasps of air. "You were born. That is enough."

Snarling, Laur slammed his head down on the ground, his nose cracking loudly. Before he could react, she pressed a hand against him and felt his whole body go slack. Standing up, Laur stared down at him.

"Roll over," she commanded. He immediately flipped over, his face a broken, bloody mess. He looked up at her.

"Stand up."

Scrambling to his feet, Blade stared at her eagerly through the blood.

"This is what you are going to do. You are going to report back to your benefactor, or superior, or whomever it is that you report to, and tell them that I am dead. That you succeeded in killing me. I want this to end," Laur commanded.

He nodded earnestly. "Yes, my Lady. Anything you wish."

"Good. You will take those other two with you as well. They will collaborate your story, but before you go, you will tell me everything you know about your benefactor," Laur said.

Distress entered his eyes as he began to dry wash his hands. "My Lady, I-I would, but Hunters never know who it is that hire them. That is part of the deal. We are not told anything other than our mark and where we are to leave the evidence, and then we get paid. I could not tell you who hired us even though I want nothing more than to do just that."

"So I have been hunted for the past eight years and I still don't get to know by who?" Laur asked.

Blade nodded, frustrated tears springing into his eyes. "I am so sorry, my Lady, please forgive me," he pleaded.

Anger flared within Laur, but as she looked at him she felt it dissipate as quickly as it rose up. Using her *ukitu* left the ones she touched completely in her control until the moment she died. There was no way to release them.

She only used *ukitu* to protect herself, but had never stuck around to see its effects. Just how powerful it was began to sink in. Blade and all the others she had ever touched were now hers, wanting nothing more than to please her. How could she be angry with someone who was reduced to a shell of his former self?

No, she found she couldn't. She hated herself for having done this to him, even in a moment of self-preservation, but perhaps she could turn this around to redeem herself and them.

Thinking quickly, Laur snapped her fingers. "Fists! Accent! Come here!"

The other two Hunters popped up from where she had left them and quickly ran to her.

"My Lady?" they said in unison.

"You three are going to be my spies. I want you to return to wherever you report to, and find out everything that you can about the one chasing me. Anything you find out that you believe is relevant, you will report back to me by using these," Laur said, pulling out three golden rings set with deep purple-blue stones.

They were simple in design, four prongs holding the stone in place. The prongs faded to silver as they curled around the edges of the stone. They all matched the more ornate gold and silver ring that Laur wore on the second finger of her right hand.

"You will wear these at all times. Any information that you find out, any at all, you will tell me by rubbing the gem. It will allow you to communicate with me no matter how close, or how far, we are from one another," Laur said, handing a ring to each of them. They slipped them on their fingers, the rings expanding to fit perfectly.

Looking at the three of them in front of her, Laur felt her heart break again for the life she had forced them in. She decided she would find a way to release them from this curse.

"That is all. You have your orders," Laur said. Nodding vigorously to her, the Hunters turned and ran back towards the Birthing House.

Twisting the ring on her finger, she waited until they vanished before she sank to the ground. Closing herself off from her power, pain and fatigue crashed over her like a tidal wave. Slumping back against the wall, Laur's vision blurred.

Barely able to hold her head up any longer, Laur figured she had bought herself a few days. Darkness crept in on the edges of her vision and finally, she allowed herself to sleep. This time, for the first time in years, she closed both eyes.

Chapter Fourteen

Laur's eyes fluttered open, the sound of a man and woman talking piercing her slumber. She had no idea how long she had been asleep, but could see the light orbs floating in the air had nearly tripled.

Pushing herself to her knees, Laur crawled around the broken wall, and peered out the empty doorway. From her vantage point, she could see an impossibly tall man clad all in black leather with sharp objects all over his body, and a slightly shorter woman in a long black dress. They made no attempt to keep their voices down, most likely because they thought everyone in the city was dead. Laur could sense evil all around them.

"Where do you think they will go next?" the man asked, his deep voice harsh and demanding.

"They left through the sewers. The only other way out of the cavern is through the old tunnels. Especially since you destroyed the only other way out."

Survivors? Laur's brows knit together as she listened.

"That way leads to the surface. I thought it was still uninhabitable," he said.

The woman looked at him. "Feel free to go up and let us know what you find out."

He glared at her, but changed the subject. "You'll intercept them at the lake then?"

"If I have to. I plan to reach them before they get that far. They can't be moving fast with the girl-child in the state she is in," the woman replied, pushing her long hair off her shoulder. Laur caught a glimpse of her porcelain smooth skin and bright red nails.

"Be careful of those trees. Purity burns our kind."

The woman scoffed, scowling at him. "I know what those trees can do, Fearg."

"I was only trying to help," Fearg said.

"Then you should be carrying out your orders if you really want to help. I can handle myself and do not need anyone's help. Much less from a Khalefo like you," she snapped.

"As you proved," Fearg said, motioning towards the Birthing House. Laur caught a glimpse of his face. It was handsome, but had sharp metal lining his cheekbones.

"Let that be a lesson for you not to cross me. How about you get along and return back to Vyad to report what happened here? I have a girl-child to collect and you bore me," the woman said, her voice sharp.

Fearg's eyes glowered and his hands clenched, but he dipped his head low in a kind of bow. Judging by the woman's body language, Laur could tell it wasn't a sign of respect.

As he lifted his head back up, his body evaporated into a million shadow forms that swirled around with a blood-chilling scream. They enveloped the woman in black, who made no effort to move out of their way, and then burst up from the ground. Screeching, they flowed out of the cavern through the opening to the surface, cracking off more pieces of the cavern wall. The woman's dress and hair billowed around her as they left, but her body remained still.

Laur breathed out sharply once he was gone, not realizing she had been holding her breath. Clapping a hand over her mouth, Laur darted back from the doorway as the woman's head snapped around.

Laur caught a glimpse of her face, and from what she could see the woman was breathtakingly beautiful with a long, graceful neck and porcelain skin. It was her eyes that struck Laur the most – beautiful, almond-shaped black eyes with power and fury swirling within them. She was flawless.

Holding her breath again, Laur listened for any sound of the woman. Nervously fiddling with the ring on her right hand, the purple stone began to glow. From inside the ring, she could feel the strength of the women in her bloodline calming her and helping her focus. The ring had been passed down from daughter to daughter, eventually coming to Laur. It was the last thing her mother had ever given her before she died and the only thing Laur had left of either of her parents.

After a while, Laur heard the swish of her dress as the woman moved away, breathing more easily once it faded. Hearing nothing for a while, Laur gripped the wall behind her and pulled herself gingerly to her feet. What little rest she had gotten had helped to take the edge off the pain in her foot, but every muscle in her body ached for more. She could barely feel her foot anymore, and whenever she tried to put weight on it, the hot pain made the world around her spin.

The battle with the Hunters had intensified the

discomfort she was already feeling. From the warmth pooling in her boot, she could tell that the wound had opened up again. Any Healing Houses that had been in End would have been destroyed along with the rest of the city and without the air of Healers, Laur knew nothing could be done right now. Laur had read the Healing texts but it had all been gibberish to her. Only Healers were taught how to decipher the texts to know what herbs and salves worked in unison to heal a wide array of maladies.

Not seeing any sign of the woman in black anywhere, Laur moved slowly towards the wall, leaning heavily on her staff. Parts of the wall was still intact, a large section by the Birthing House that had crumbled away when part of the house had fallen on it. She could see the Dhunni forest spread out into the rest of the cavern.

Laur had studied many of the texts about the five sanctuary cities during her travels. Being a fugitive, Laur had found other ways to alleviate the aching loneliness inside. Books had been one of those ways, and she had found a strange sort of comradery with them. Books did not betray her.

Only one city, Truth, held books of any kind - books about everything and anything. It had been in Truth that Laur had gorged herself on the vast storehouses of knowledge built underneath the city. It was here that she learned the awful truth behind why the Five were built and what made each unique. It was also here that Blade and his comrades had found her.

Pulling herself up onto what was left of the roof of a nearby home, she scanned the horizon, spotting the woman's dark form entering the Dhunni forest. She could also see the bright blue haze within the forest, given off by the lake. From here she could see multitudes more of the tiny orbs of light floating towards End above the canopy. They now made a long path that connected End to the forest. Looking out upon the forest, a page from *A Codex of Five* appeared in her mind.

> While each Five has its own attribute that makes the city unique, it's the crystal blue lake that lies in each cavern that connects the Five together from across the miles that separate them. These lakes hold properties that are unique and useful to their host city alone, and like a living creature, they seem to want to offer up their attributes on an altar to the city they protect. We have been to each of the Five, and we have done all we can to record our findings here in this Codex, with the hopes that it can aid those that will come after us. No name has been given to the lakes, but perhaps we should name them for posterities sake. I would call the lake at End, Ar Shiul, because of its

ABILITY TO HEAL ANY MALADY, ILLNESS, OR EVEN REVERSE THE FINAL GRIPS OF DEATH, BUT MY COMRADES DO NOT WANT TO GIVE NAME TO ANYTHING OTHER THAN THE CITY. THOSE COMING TO LIVE HERE MUST BE ABLE TO MAKE A NEW LIFE FOR THEMSELVES WITHOUT OUR MEDDLING. IT PAINS ME TO SAY THAT WE HAVE ALREADY MEDDLED TOO MUCH IN THE AFFAIRS OF MAN. THAT IS A JOB FOR ONE OF THE GODS OR PERHAPS FOR THE ONE GOD. MAYBE ALL THAT IS HAPPENING TRULY IS OUR FAULT...

- R. SAOIRSE, YR. 3073

Laur's foot began to tingle in anticipation as she read the words *Ar Shiul* in her mind. She hoped she would be able to see if the words written by Saoirse's hand were true. Crawling down from the roof, Laur paused as a large group of orbs swirled around her, softly caressing her skin before floating away. Laur rubbed her cheek where they had touched her, her skin slightly warm.

In astonishment she rubbed harder – the cut on her cheek was gone. She turned to watch more orbs float into the city, gaping when a body in front of her vanished. Tree roots grew from their empty clothing, expanding out to cover the blood-soaked ground.

Stepping into the forest, the evil presence of the

woman was heavy in the air. The trees that were clustered thickly in front of Laur began to shift apart. She had never seen Dhunni trees before, but she had read about them. Marveling at them now, she realized no text could do justice to the beauty of the trees in front of her.

Moving slowly through the silver trunked forest, Laur felt a ripple of power move through the trees alongside her. The white leaves rustled in the windless air and she heard a voice inside of her head.

Find her. Help her.

With a jolt, Laur realized she had heard that voice many times before. As it spoke, the trees opened up in front of her, allowing her to move through the forest unimpeded. She could see the glow of the lake more brilliantly now.

Following the path as it curved through the forest, the trees around her began to blacken. The smell of burnt wood began to replace the clean smell of earth as the blackened trunks around her multiplied. Laur felt a wave of sadness ripple through her, making her stall in her steps. It didn't feel like she herself was sad, but instead was feeling the grief of the Dhunni for their fallen brethren. Exiting the forest where the path ended by the lake, Laur saw that it reappeared off to the side, leading her back into the forest. A thin trail of smoke rose above the canopy.

Pausing at the lakeside, she could see four sets of distinct footprints in the soft sand. Looking at the water longingly, Laur wanted nothing more than to dip her foot in and see if the texts were true. Another soft wave of power ruffled her hair and she reluctantly turned her eyes back to the forest, as the voice repeated itself in her head.

Find her. Help her.

Walking into the trees again, Laur could feel the

disparity of the forest thick around her. Almost all the trees here were burned and as she moved along the path, the sound of voices filled the air. A trail of orbs floated over the trees above her, denser here than in End.

A sudden explosion pulled her attention away from the orbs.

Scurrying forward, Laur stopped behind a blacked trunk. A small clearing was in front of her and it was from here that the voices were coming. The woman in black had her back to Laur, standing in the middle of a circle of uprooted trees.

Across the clearing three figures stood, two dressed in black and in between them stood a girl with flaming red hair. Waves of power radiated off of her, matching the power coming from the woman in black. Smoke curled around the black-clad woman's body as she stared the others down.

Chapter Fifteen

"You have no business here, Narcissa," the red-haired girl said. Even from across the clearing, Laur could see she was wise beyond her years, and spoke with an authority that could not possibly be her own. The power that Laur felt coming from her felt just like the power that had led Laur here.

The woman in the black dress – Narcissa – began to pace. "Actually, I do. My business is with you, Aoire, whether you come to accept it or not. I do not fail. Ever. It's why my master has sent me after you. After the inexcusable failure of Eimhir to keep you captive in End, Master wanted to make sure that the job was completed properly this time."

One of the black-clad figures behind Aoire, spoke up. "What did you do to Eimhir?"

Narcissa shifted her weight to one foot, her hip jutting out. "What did I do to her? Simply what she deserved. Don't tell me that you are actually concerned about the woman who betrayed the whole of End?"

"At least she took your secret to the grave, my dear," Narcissa added.

Laur was sure that the Guardian was going to launch forward and attack Narcissa, but Aoire grabbed their wrist, shaking her head slightly. She whispered something to the Guardian and Laur saw them relax, their eyes remaining stormy.

"Tsk, tsk, did I hit a nerve?" Laur could hear the joy in Narcissa's voice.

"I will say this one more time, Narcissa - you have no business here. This is sacred ground, and you should leave before you are forced to leave," Aoire repeated.

Laur could feel stronger waves of power coming from Aoire, overpowering the strength of Narcissa's power. All around the clearing orbs of light drifted up from the ground and hovered.

"What are you going to do?" Narcissa scoffed. "Do you really think a skinny little creature such as yourself could defeat me with some light?"

Aoire shook her head. "No, I don't need to defeat you. I only need to distract you."

Laur's eyes widened as Aoire flicked a wrist toward Narcissa and all the orbs rushed at her. They slammed into Narcissa with such force that she stumbled backward, covering her with a layer of light.

Narcissa clawed at her body, trying to get the orbs off, screaming in pain and anger. At the same time, Aoire grabbed the hands of the two Guardians behind her. The orbs fell off Narcissa as a bright flash of blue light filled the clearing, and a loud concussion of air accompanied it. Once the light faded, Laur blinked in disbelief.

Narcissa was now across the clearing where the three of them had stood. They were gone. Throwing back her head, the sound that came out sent shivers down Laur's spine. Without looking back, Laur dashed away from the clearing.

Crawling through branches and scrambling over roots, Laur tried to put as much distance between her and the clearing as possible. She could still hear Narcissa howling in anger behind her. A blast of air hit her from behind, slamming Laur forward into a branch.

Gasping, Laur looked over her shoulder. Whole trees uprooted and flew into the air, crashing into the forest. Narcissa stormed past her, her eyes sparking. Laur could feel waves of cold heat coming off of Narcissa as she moved past.

Slipping behind a tree, Laur squeezed her eyes shut. Trying to control her breathing, she could still hear trees being torn from the ground and flung into the air. She opened her eyes once the sound moved far enough away.

Letting out a deep sigh, Laur ran a hand through her curly hair. Hobbling into the clearing, Laur looked around in disbelief. Just moments before Aoire had stood with her two companions and faced off against Narcissa, a woman who made Laur feel nothing but fear. Now there was no sign that anyone had been there other than a small ring burned into the ground. Kneeling down, Laur gently touched the ring. The dark circle was warm under her fingers.

A twin flash of blue light appeared in the distance, pulling Laur's eyes to the cavern wall. Behind her, the sound of crashing trees stopped. The floor of the cavern began to shake, a black pillar of smoke swirling into the air. Gripping her staff tightly, Laur hobbled as quickly as she could towards the light.

* * * * *

Ahearn and Retter gasped for air, the three of them reappearing in the mouth of an enormous tunnel. Letting go of their hands, Aoire slouched against the wall to steady herself.

"How did we get here?" Ahearn asked, her hands on her knees.

"Transportation," Aoire replied. Her cheeks were flushed.

"Where are we?" Retter asked.

"Not far from the clearing," Aoire said. Behind them, a thin curtain of algae vines covered the entrance to the tunnel. Some algae had begun to grow into the tunnel, stopping when it came into contact with deep designs imbedded in the hard earth of the tunnel. What little light from the cavern that entered the tunnel was tinged green from the vines.

"What are these?" Ahearn asked, running her hands over the symbols carved into the smooth walls of the tunnel.

Deeply carved swirls and patterns covered the walls, ceiling, and floor, creating beautifully intricate patterns. The tunnel was mammoth, large enough for ten people to stand abreast and still move around easily. The walls were made of hard earth, as if cut right into the side of the cavern and then petrified over millions of years. The tunnel dipped and curved in every direction, stretching back as far as they could see. Other tunnels branched off in different directions.

"These symbols will help to show us the way to Truth. These tunnels run under the surface of the entire earth, leading anywhere and everywhere," Aoire replied.

"How will we be able to see where we are going, or even be able to know in which direction to go?" Ahearn asked.

Touching a swirl in the wall next to her, Aoire pointed

down the tunnel as the symbols lit up with a bright blue-green light that extended down and curved off to the left. When it reached a tunnel that intersected the one they were in, that tunnel stayed dark. "That's how."

"Here," Aoire added, unbuckling the top of her satchel and pulling out two small brown leather pouches sealed with a large golden tree. She tossed one to each of them. "These are for you."

Breaking the seal, the pouches fell open in their hands. Inside lay a thin, creamy white wafer edged in golden brown. They were wrapped in a Dhunni leaf.

"What are these?" Retter asked.

"Food. One wafer will keep you sustained for a day, but no more. They will reappear at the start of each day and will give you exactly what you need," Aoire replied.

"Why just a day? Won't it take us longer than that to get to Truth?" Retter asked.

Aoire nodded, "It will, but Father only gives what is needed, nothing more or less."

Retter bit the edge of his wafers, a delicate sweetness filling his mouth. The wafer dissolved on his tongue.

"Honey," he breathed. He could feel warmth and strength spreading through his body as his hunger ebbed.

"What's honey?" Ahearn asked.

Retter shrugged. "I have no idea, but I know this is what it tastes like. It's definitely better than any of the algae foods we ate in End."

Taking a bite of hers, her eyes lit up.

"Good?" Aoire asked.

"Very," she replied.

"What about you, Aoire? Where is yours?" Retter asked.

Aoire rested her hand on her bag. "I have mine here,

along with some other things we will need along the way. Another gift from Father."

"I would like to meet this father of yours one day," Retter said, tucking the pouch into his belt.

Aoire smiled. "You will. Everyone does in due time."

"I met him," Ahearn said, tucking her pouch into the bag on the small of her back.

"You did? When could you possibly have?" Retter asked, looking at her with disbelief.

"He found a way to meet me where I was at." Ahearn replied.

Retter grunted. "Now you are starting to sound like Aoire."

Aoire laughed lightly. "Don't be impatient, Retter. Father will meet you soon."

"Well, what if I am ready now?" Retter demanded.

Aoire patted him on the shoulder. "Soon, Retter. I promise it will be soon."

Turning away as a scowl settled onto Retter's face, Aoire fell in step beside Ahearn. They started down the tunnel, following the blue-green symbols. Moving deeper into the tunnel, more symbols came to life, guiding them as they passed other openings. Back at the entrance, the symbols had already gone dark. No sign they had passed this way could be seen.

"He doesn't like not knowing. It's what made him such a good Commander. He always knew what was happening in End, the Birthing House, and in the lives of his men. Not knowing makes him feel uneasy," Ahearn explained. Retter wasn't far behind her and Aoire, brooding in silence.

"Knowing what was going on in the lives of his men, he never suspected your secret?" Aoire asked softly.

Ahearn shook her head. "No. Bearn trained me well. I didn't think anyone knew, but perhaps I was wrong. Eimhir knew something and so does that witch, Narcissa. Maybe I am not as good at hiding my secret as I thought."

Aoire looked at her, realization filling her eyes. "You're afraid."

Ahearn snorted. "Of course I am! Aoire, do you realize that I have been living with this secret, and keeping it hidden from those closest to me, for most of my life? Guardians are effective in what we do because we trust each other completely. We don't keep secrets, big or small, from each other because secrets cause division. If we can't be one unit in life, how can we be one unit in battle? For the Commander to find out that I am a woman," she said dropping her voice low, "then it would completely shatter his trust in me. Not to mention that no Guardian has ever been a woman before and for good reason."

"Like what?" Aoire asked.

"Guardians do not take wives, because our lives are devoted to serving and protecting others. Having a family of our own would divide our attention and could get us killed, or worse, one of our brothers killed. What would he think, knowing that a woman has been hidden within his ranks all this time?"

"Bearn managed to go against the Guardian order and have you as family."

Ahearn's face darkened. "And it was his love for me that in the end got him killed. It was my fault he died. If I had died in the attack that had killed my parents, then Bearn would still be alive and Retter would not be faced with losing his trust in me."

"You can't think like that. Bearn gave you a chance at a second life. You can't take that for granted."

"He died for nothing then. The one thing he asked me to do, I may not be able to do anymore," Ahearn said.

"Father asked you to reveal yourself, didn't he?"

Ahearn took a deep breath. "Yes he did."

"And?"

"And what?"

"Will you tell Retter?"

Ahearn trailed her fingers lightly along the wall as she walked. "Eventually," she replied, her face absorbing into her Guardian mask. Walking silently next to Ahearn, Aoire could tell that their conversation was over.

Aoire stopped suddenly, turning back towards the way they had come. There was now another presence in the tunnels with them, a weak one that was growing weaker. It was a presence she had not felt draw near to them, she had been so focused on getting Ahearn and Retter to safety. Within her *opari,* she could tell this one needed help badly.

"Aoire?" Retter asked, stopping next to her.

A cool breeze came from behind them, pushing Aoire gently back towards the weakening presence, and Aoire could smell the earth after the rain. Without a word, she dashed back towards the tunnel entrance.

"Aoire!" Retter shouted. Her sudden speed took him by surprise.

"Come on," he said to Ahearn, turning and following after Aoire.

* * * * *

Laur tossed her staff through the algae vines and pulled herself into the mouth of a cavernous tunnel, her heart beating violently within her chest. She had barely been able to see the mouth of the tunnel through the algae vines that hung down the side of the cavern. A cool breeze had ruffled the vines, leading Laur to the tunnel.

Collapsing, Laur flipped herself onto her back and stared at the ceiling. She could no longer feel her left foot from below her calf and the edges of her vision had begun to blur and darken. She knew that Narcissa wasn't far behind, having turned into a terrifying pillar of smoke that was still cutting through the forest towards the tunnel.

Laur was so exhausted that she could barely lift her head. Lying on the floor, the symbols carved into the wall above her started to move. Another cool breeze surrounded and covered her, bringing with it a small semblance of relief.

Laur felt her heart catch in her chest, trying to reach her staff as the sound of running boots came from further inside the tunnel. Aoire appeared in the bend of the tunnel, her eyes intent and piercing. Approaching Laur, she knelt down in front of her. Before long the two Guardians appeared in the bend of the tunnel.

Her fingers curling around her staff weakly, Laur tried to sit up. Aoire slipped her hands under Laur's arms and pulled her effortlessly into a sitting position. Laur looked at her and now that she was seeing Aoire up close, she felt she both understood more about her and at the same time understood nothing.

"How did you find us?" the big one asked, crossing his arms over his chest and staring down at Laur.

"Retter," Aoire said, shooting him a look. "She's injured. How about we deal with that first, before you interrogate her?"

The one she had called Retter said nothing, but Laur saw his eyes soften slightly.

"I saw a flash of blue light right before you vanished, and then another come from up here, so I followed it," Laur replied, matching his stare with one of her own.

Aoire smiled to herself, her nimble fingers working to loosen Laur's boot from around her swollen leg. The dried blood and swelling were making it hard to get her boot off. Laur gasped as it came free with a sickening squelch.

"Retter, come help me with this," Aoire said.

Kneeling down, Retter studied Laur. She was a young thing, with rounded features, and eyes of such a deep grey that they appeared purple. Sweat had matted her curls to her head, glistening on a face twisted with pain. The bandage on her left foot was now various shades of red, heavy with blood. What skin they could see, through the holes in her trousers, had colored from bruising.

"Caz, watch the entrance," Aoire said over her shoulder to the other Guardian. She turned her focus back to Laur. "What happened to you?"

"Hunters," Laur groaned, closing her eyes and leaning her head back against the wall. She swallowed, trying not to lose consciousness. The smell of infected flesh mixed with sweat was heavier now that her boot was off.

"Hunters? How long have they been chasing you?" Retter asked as Aoire began to slowly peel Laur's bandage away. What little color was left in Laur's face drained away. She began to pant as the bandage fought to give way.

"Eight years," she gasped, her knuckles white.

"Gods," Retter swore. "You have evaded them for this long on your own?"

Laur's eyes snapped open, glaring at him. "Yes I have,

Guardian. It's not as if people are lining up to help someone who has a bounty over their head. I have been forced to learn how to defend myself at any cost. If you are curious how I am able to, I would be more than happy to demonstrate."

Retter's eyes softened and he shared a look with Ahearn. He placed a strong hand on Laur's knee and gave it a small squeeze in apology.

"How did this happen?" Aoire asked, the bandage finally giving way.

Laur cried out in pain, the gaping wound in her foot revealed. Fresh blood began to drip from her heel, thick and black. Exposed bone shone starkly in the blue-green light.

"A knife. Blade can throw with amazing speed and accuracy," Laur managed between gasps of air. Her face had turned slightly green. Sweat ran down her face.

"We have to move her," Ahearn said, her eyes still on the cavern outside. She could see the pillar of smoke in the cavern, closing in on them swiftly. Dhunni trees creaked as they split in two, algae dust and orbs of light thrown into the air in Narcissa's wake.

Laur opened her mouth to argue, but snapped it shut as the tunnel spun. Bile rose into her mouth. Moaning weakly, she opted to slump back against the wall.

"There is no way she can move yet, Caz. She can't walk and we can't ask her to. She will need to be tended to here and we will just have to take our chances with Narcissa," Aoire replied.

Retter looked at Aoire. "Do you have anything that can help her?"

"I have just what she needs. Retter, I want you to hold her leg steady. I will need both my hands for this and she isn't strong enough to hold her own leg up," Aoire said, placing a soothing hand on Laur's clammy cheek.

Retter took Laur's injured leg gently in his hands. Laur could feel the rough callouses on the palms of his hands from years of wielding a sword, but they were surprisingly gentle as well.

Aoire focused. Deep within, her *opari* turned white, simultaneously turning her eyes white. Hovering her hands over Laur's injury, Aoire's lips began to move rapidly. A pale white glow appeared under her hands and spread out to envelope Laur's entire leg. As it did, silken threads of glowing white light came from the palms of Aoire's hands and from each of her fingers, wrapping gently around Laur's leg. They entered her wound and began to weave together until it was filled with white light.

The light began to intensify, growing so bright that Retter, Ahearn, and Laur had to close their eyes. Even with their eyes closed, they could see its brilliance. Heat began to spread up Laur's leg as the wound began to close. Aoire could feel a tug behind her navel, where her *opari* rested, begin to grow stronger the longer she was connected with Laur. Memories from Laur's past began to flow into Aoire through their connection, broken images of the life Laur had been forced into by the one thing meant to set her apart. Aoire felt a tear roll down her cheek from the immeasurable pain that accompanied the fragmented memories.

Once the wound was completely closed, Aoire closed off the current of power going into Laur. All the light and threads pulled back into Aoire's hands, also cutting off the jumbled stream of Laur's memories. Aoire's eyes darkened from white to light grey as the light in the tunnel dimmed back to blue-green.

"Look," Aoire said when Laur opened her eyes.

Laur sat up and gaped at the thin white scar on her ankle. All evidence that she had been injured was gone, even down to the dark bruises. Ahearn absently touched the scar on her shoulder, the opalescent sheen on Laur's scar a match to hers.

"How?" Laur asked.

Aoire smiled. "Healing. It's one of my abilities."

"One of?" Laur asked, her fingers running over her new skin.

Aoire ran her arm across her brow, wiping away the sweat that had formed. She could feel the drain the spell had put on her body, the intensity of Laur's memories overwhelming in her weakened state.

"Yes," Aoire replied quietly.

Putting a strong hand under Laur's arm, Retter hoisted her to her feet. Leaning back against the wall, Laur gingerly put her foot on the ground and slowly leaned on it.

She looked at Aoire in shock. "It doesn't hurt at all! I can put my weight on my foot again!"

Handing Laur's boot to her to put back on, Retter looked at Aoire, who was gazing at something unseen, her face paler than normal. Laur's memories were still flooding Aoire's mind in a jumbled mess of emotion and loss. Aoire strained to calm the memories, forcing them away until she could sort through them.

The vines behind them ruffled, drawing even Aoire's attention. The sound of swirling smoke filled the tunnel.

"We need to go," Ahearn warned, her dagger in her hands.

"Laur, you are welcome to continue on the path you have been traveling or you can come with us. It is your choice. If you come with us, we will protect you, no matter what comes through those vines," Aoire said.

Laur bit her lip, feeling tears spring to her eyes. Trust was not an easy concept for her, but she felt drawn to Aoire. Memories of a young girl with curly red hair, an older man whose face she could not see, and a beautiful tree taken captive by a creature with darkness for a soul, flashed in her mind. With them came the same voice that had guided her throughout her whole life.

Go with them.

"We should go then," Laur said, taking her staff from the wall and marching down the tunnel without waiting for any of them to reply.

"Are you sure she should go with us?" Retter asked Aoire as they followed after Laur.

"I know you find it hard to trust others, Retter, but Laur has a significant role to play in all this, just as you and Caz do. There is more going on than any of you can see," Aoire replied, and then fell silent.

She found herself lost in Laur's memories again. The emotion that accompanied them was so strong, that it was taking Aoire longer to disconnect Laur's memories from her own. Some were too hard for Aoire to visit for long, pain and grief so strong that it threatened to suffocate Aoire. The symbols on the wall turned from blue-green to a deep shade of blue-black, casting long shadows all around them.

Far behind them, the pillar of smoke appeared in front of the tunnel opening. It grew smaller until Narcissa's pale hand pushed through the vines and into the dark tunnel.

Chapter Sixteen

Vyad stood in his lavish room, his arms crossed over his broad chest. A crimson shirt stretched across his chest, the sleeves rolled up to his elbows. Black boots rose to his knees, his black pants tight across his strong legs. The shirt was open in the front, his skin a light caramel color. Thick golden brown hair collected on his head in lustrous curls, no beard adorning his chiseled face. Black eyes stared out from beneath his golden eyebrows, matching the seven strips of leather that wound around his wrists. He was an achingly handsome man, angelic and perfect in every way.

Thick red carpets with black trim lay scattered around the large room, covering the black stone floor. A fire raged in a fireplace behind him that took up nearly the entire wall. It cast a red hue to everything in the room, filling it with intense heat. Even amidst the heat, no sweat glistened on his body.

A black crystal bowl sat on the fireplace mantle, filled with apples made of pure gold. Enormous white wings with gold tipped feathers hung on the wall above the bowl. Both the apples and wings echoed the carvings that were hidden all around the room. On each wall hung a large woven tapestry depicting a different battle scene in intense color and detail.

Next to the fireplace stood a long desk made of dark mahogany. It was littered with maps, the wood polished black, and trimmed in bright gold. Behind it was propped a large broadsword of black gold with deep red gemstones set into the hilt. The blade had a serrated edge, sheathed in black leather with intricate designs laid into it. It matched the two knives at Vyad's hip. The ferocity of the weapons only intensified Vyad's allure – he was tall and strong in every aspect.

Opposite the fireplace stood a lavish four-poster bed, with thick red and gold drapes, on top of a matching carpet that covered nearly the entire floor with smaller carpets overlapping it. Similar thick curtains hung all around the room, covering part of the long windows behind them. The sounds of machinery and tortured screams drifted through the windowless windows, but he paid no attention to them. On the ceiling, golden figures were frozen, their faces twisted to echo the screams drifting through the windows.

On the wall next to the bed, a great tree grew out of the floor. The bottom-most branches touched the ceiling, winding between the golden figures. Its roots were spread out across the floor, vanishing into the smooth black marble. The tree was petrified, no leaves or fruit growing from its branches. It was massive; forty men standing with their hands connected would barely encircle the trunk.

Streaks of color painted the tree, muted, but beautiful. They were slowly being engulfed by a black growth spreading from the roots. Only half the trunk was visible, most of the tree vanishing into the ceiling and floor. The same swirling symbols that were on the tunnels in End were also carved into the tree.

Vyad turned to look as he heard the sizzle of lightning. He walked towards a table with a bowl in front of a golden disk, black lightning flashing across the disk. Two figures held the disk on their back, their golden forms twisted unnaturally. Their heads were bent underneath their arms, linking hands at the top and bottom of the disk to hold it in place. A long tail came from each figure and wound around their legs to slither across the tabletop. Their tails twisted together and up, creating the base of the bowl. Glass pillars were attached around the table, filled with millions of black glass beads – just like the one Eimhir had worn.

A short cone rose from the middle of the bowl, the tip flat. On it was one of the round beads. Every now and again, black lightning spread across the surface of the bowl and struck the bead, radiating out to envelop the figures. As it did, their eyes flashed, illuminated black. Slowly, Narcissa's face came into view on the disk, vines and a tunnel appearing faintly behind her.

"Interesting," Vyad said. "So they took the old tunnels?"

"Yes," Narcissa's voice echoed from the disk. Her image shifted and broke apart, as if reflected on the surface of rippling water.

"The tunnels will prove difficult for you, Narcissa. They are far older than you, and they are protected by an ancient power very similar to the Dhunni. The tunnels will hurt far worse than the trees did though," Vyad said. "I want that girl, Narcissa! Do not fail me, as Eimhir did, or you will suffer far worse."

Without waiting for her to reply, Vyad plucked the bead from the bowl and Narcissa's face vanished immediately.

Gripping the bead in his fist, Vyad walked to his writing desk and lifted up a small black box with seven golden symbols carved into the lid.

Inside, on top of satin, were six identical black beads. Vyad placed the one he held in the empty slot, the symbol above it glowing briefly. The same seven symbols that were carved into the lid of the box were inlaid above each stone.

Snapping the lid shut and placing the box down gently, Vyad turned his attention to the maps. He barely started pouring over them when the door to his chambers flew open with a loud crash.

Looking up, Vyad watched as Fearg furiously strode into his chambers. A smaller, more emaciated creature followed after him, his eyes darting around the room. He constantly licked his cracked lips, bones sticking out from under his pale, paper-thin grey skin. His back was curved near the top of his spine and his head jutted out, giving him the visage of a vulture.

No nose adorned his face or ears, both long since rotted away. Long, emaciated legs barely seemed able to hold him up, his arms just as thin. He seemed nothing more than skin and bones. The ends of his dingy tunic and trousers were frayed, but he didn't seem to notice or care. Hunger filled his beady black eyes as he desperately looked around the room for something to eat. Seeing nothing, he looked at Fearg with a pitiful expression.

Vyad looked up from his maps, watching as Fearg stopped in the middle of his room. Both he, and his companion, had already begun to sweat.

"Can I help you?" Vyad asked.

Fearg began to pace, his face still contorted with anger.

The shadow forms of Khalefo appeared around his legs, a swirling mass of limbs.

"That woman..." Fearg paused as he paced, trying to steady his voice. "That woman..."

"Narcissa," Vyad supplied.

"Narcissa," Fearg snarled. "She gave *me* orders. Me! As if I was her lackey!"

Vyad crossed his arms over his chest. "This upsets you?"

"Yes!" Fearg shouted.

"Yes," he repeated as Vyad's eyebrow rose.

"Because?" Vyad asked.

The shadowy Khalefo swirled faster around Fearg as his fury erupted, his body doubling in size. "Because we are the same! We are of the same rank! What gives her the right to order me around?"

Rising towards the ceiling, the golden figures tried to pull as far away from Fearg as they could. The ceiling creaked under the strain of his bulk and in the firelight Fearg's shadow took the form of the faceless Khalefo, extending across the whole ceiling.

Vyad looked up at him, dark clouds entering his eyes. "And who do you think Narcissa gets her orders from?"

Fearg looked down at Vyad, all the color draining from his face. The Khalefo swirled around him as he shrunk back down to normal size, absorbing into his body. When they all finally vanished, Fearg stood in the middle of the room, his eyes staring at the floor.

Vyad slowly walked out from behind his desk, leaning back against it. Fearg kept his eyes on the floor as Vyad stared at him, the grey-skinned creature licking his lips and smiling. Over half its teeth were gone, the ones left inside jagged and cracked.

"So you think you are being treated unfairly?" Vyad asked. Fearg didn't reply, but seemed to shrink even smaller.

Vyad straightened up and walked around Fearg, eyeing him sharply. "Do you know why I have seven Generals? Because each of you had a specific trait or attribute that the others do not. There are things that Narcissa can do that you cannot, and other things that only you are suited for."

Fearg looked up as Vyad stopped in front of him, his eyes eager. Vyad looked him in the eye and placed a hand on his shoulder. "*You,* Fearg, are best at one thing and one thing only – destruction. You lack the intelligence and imagination to do half of what she can do. You were a brute in life and being a brute is all that you will ever be."

Vyad took Fearg's face in his hands as Fearg deflated even more. "Because of this, there shouldn't be a problem if Narcissa, or any other General, gives you orders. Should there?"

Vyad's touch was so hot on his skin that Fearg couldn't answer. He began to squirm.

"Should there?" Vyad asked again, tightening his grip on either side of Fearg's face. It felt like Fearg's skull was about to crack as he nodded his head quickly, his eyes still on the floor. Vyad still didn't let go, waiting for Fearg to answer him verbally. He continued to tighten his grip until Fearg did reply.

"No," Fearg managed as the pain grew too much to bear.

Vyad smiled, patting his face forcibly. "Good boy. And if you ever come in here like that or question me again, I will make sure you join your Khalefo. You are replaceable, Fearg, remember that."

Fearg swallowed, nodding quickly. As Vyad turned back to his maps, the thin creature slunk forward. His eyes darted between Fearg and Vyad, a blackened tongue flicking in and out of his mouth quickly.

"What do you want, Ocras?" Vyad asked, not looking up from his maps.

"Master, I'm hungry," Ocras whined, his hollow voice echoing in his shriveled chest.

Vyad's lips curled into a slight smile as he looked up. "You are always hungry."

Ocras shifted his weight. "I was wondering..."

"What?"

Ocras tongue flicked out again nervously. "I was wondering when I might be able to eat again."

Vyad motioned for Ocras to approach his desk. A large map was spread out over his desk, thousands of crisscrossing lines running across it. The labyrinth of lines connected five symbols – one for each of the Five. A large red mark was slashed through End and right in the middle of the map was a symbol of a large tree. A sixth city with six walls was drawn around the base of the tree. The lines that crisscrossed the map originated from the roots of the tree.

"This is where they will go, Ocras," Vyad said, pointing to City of Truth.

"Are you sure?" Ocras asked, not attempting to hide his excitement.

Vyad nodded. "It seems that you and your brothers may be in for an extra special treat very soon."

"If Narcissa fails," Fearg interjected. Vyad and Ocras turned to look at him.

"Fearg. I forgot you were even still here," Vyad said coolly. "Care to explain?"

Fearg still didn't take his eyes off the floor, but he seemed to have some of his normal fire back. He had grown back to his usual size, still small in comparison to Vyad's quarters.

"You sent Narcissa to find them and bring Aoire back here, but what if Narcissa fails? Would Ocras and his brothers be the second wave of attack?" Fearg asked.

"If Narcissa fails then Ocras' brothers are to devour her before bringing Aoire back here," Vyad replied. "I do not suffer fools who can not carry out a simple command, not even from one of my own Generals. There are plenty of other Bashers that could replace any of you and would do so in an instant. I am sure that a General could keep even a Devorator satiated for a time."

Very few times had Vyad seen joy on a Devorator's face, but Ocras' almost split in two as he smiled. Without waiting to be dismissed, Ocras nearly tripped over himself as he ran from Vyad's room. The idea of having something to eat pushed everything else from his mind.

"And what am I supposed to do?" Fearg asked once Ocras was gone, the normal edge creeping back into his voice.

Vyad stared at Fearg harshly over his desk. "You have already questioned me once today, Fearg. Are you sure you want to do it again?"

Fearg's eyes darted to the figures on the ceiling and his voice wavered a bit, but he pressed on. "Master, I simply want the chance to prove myself. You see me as nothing more than a brute who can only attack and kill, but I believe I can do more."

"And what exactly is it that you would like me to let you do?" Vyad asked.

Fearg took a tentative step forward. "Let me follow Narcissa, not Ocras. Ocras' brothers are already at Truth, they have been for ages, and they know nothing more than their own hunger. If Narcissa fails, how will Ocras be able to control his Devorators from the hunger that will overtake them when they smell Aoire? My troops will not make a move unless I order them too. I am obviously the better choice to send."

Stroking his chin, Vyad looked at Fearg for a long moment before replying. "Very well, Fearg. You can follow Narcissa. If she fails, I want you to make sure that she knows it was me that send you to kill her," he raised a finger. "But you are not to lay a hand on her until you know if she has failed or not. She is to continue to believe that she has my full support until the last possible moment."

Fearg nodded in salute and turned to leave the room, but Vyad called after him, stopping him at the door. "Fearg, I was very impressed by the tenacity and viciousness of your troops when they fell upon End. You have always found a way to express my thirst for battle with the language that best excites me, but if you fail in what you are asking, I will not hesitate to add you to my collection."

Fearg's eyes again flew to the figures on the ceiling and without a word he left Vyad's chambers, his shirt soaked with sweat. This time the door closed behind him with a soft click.

Turning back to the maps, Vyad smiled as a shadow fell across his desk. He watched the shadow take the form of a voluptuous woman with wide hips. Sinking down into the deep chair across from the desk, she crossed one leg over the other. Her body never took solid form, however her features were clear. A petite nose sat on a flawless face, her large eyes empty.

"Are you really going to send that brute after me?" she asked, her voice sounding as if it was coming from far away.

"Only if you fail," Vyad replied, placing his hands on his desk. His eyes twinkled with pride as he looked at her.

The woman looked at her nails, a bored expression on her face. "Have I ever failed you before?"

"You have not, but the human you are trapped within might," Vyad replied.

She wrinkled her nose as if she smelled something rotten. "I hate being trapped inside of that woman. I will never understand why you thought to put me in her."

Vyad shrugged. "She was the vainest woman of her time. She had long ago given her soul up to gain power and wealth. She seemed a fitting vessel for you, Besit."

Besit gazed at the tree. "I will also never understand why you decided to make your home around the base of that tree. Doesn't it remind you of all that you lost?"

Vyad looked at the tree and nodded. "Yes, but it is an even greater reminder of all that I gained when the world above ended. It is a reminder of how powerful my creator is, but an even greater reminder of the power I now hold. The tree is a symbol of my creators' divinity, supernatural might in its purest state, but when the world above ended, the tree weakened. I can now bend it to my will. Once my poison fills the entire tree, it won't be long before I am more powerful than he."

Besit cast a long look at him. "Are you sure that is wise? You lost everything, but your life, the first time you tried to overthrow him. What if he does worse to you?"

Vyad chuckled coldly. "Worse than sentencing me to a life of crawling through the dust? Or being forced to rule this wretched land and all its unholy inhabitants? He gets all the power of the heavens and of all creation, and I get to rule the rejected!"

The room shook as anger radiated from Vyad's body in waves. Besit's body dissipated as a wave hit the chair and then she reappeared.

"I simply wanted to remind you of whom you are dealing with," Besit said putting her hands up. "It was not meant to provoke you. As one of your children, you have my full support as always, but time is running out for me and for the others. These humans whose bodies you gave to us, they are beginning to wake up, to fight back. Something new is rising up and your children do not have the time to wait like you do."

Besit got to her feet, walking through the desk to stand next to him. "This woman you took and put me in, Narcissa, her humanity is fighting back. She is one of the strongest ever that you were able to bring to our side, but I can feel her changing. The souls of the people we have killed are weighing heavily on her. If she changes, it may be a blow to our side that will be hard to recover from."

Vyad put his arm around her shoulders. "Narcissa cannot hold out much longer. Every time she takes a life, her soul weakens and you become stronger. Before long the woman called Narcissa will no longer exist and you, my dear daughter Besit, will be in control. I promised you that I would give you a body again when that damned Gabriel took your original form, and I keep my promises."

Besit shuddered, vanishing for a moment and then reappearing. "Make it quick then. Ever since Aoire was revealed, something in everyone is awakening."

As quickly as she appeared, Besit's form broke apart,

turning back to smoke. Flowing into the fire, the flames turned black and then faded to red again.

Looking at his desk, Vyad lifted up the black box again. Pulling open the lid, his fingers lingered on the black bead that was Narcissa's. Each bead represented one of the Seven Basher Generals in his personal army, and each symbol above the stones represented which child of his Vyad had put in them when the nuclear explosion tore the world above apart.

Overnight, a new era had been ushered in for Vyad. The scales had tipped drastically in his favor, widening the division of power between him and his creator. Vyad had always been lord of the earth, but in one moment his army increased nearly a hundredfold and his creator's army decreased by even more. It put a smile on his face every time he thought about it.

Pouring some wine into a black crystal goblet, Vyad swirled it before taking a long drink. It had been a long time since he had felt more powerful than his creator. The ever-present pain under his shoulder blades and the memory of hurtling through complete darkness before landing on the hard ground was never far from his mind. He could still feel the pain of shattered bone and the burn of torn skin where his wings had once been.

It had been Gabriel that had taken his wings, but Vyad knew his creator had been the one to deal the final blow. He had been the one to order Gabriel to rip Vyad's wings from his back and hurl him into the void. A celestial wound like that would never heal, a reminder of what he used to be and what he had been demoted to. Its why he kept his wings on his wall, to further remind himself of what he was preparing to take control of.

Eden. Perfection.

Vyad could still taste the sweetness of the food and the coolness of the water. He could still feel the warmth of the sun on his face, and the rush of air beneath his wings. He could hear music in the distance, and for a moment his fingers moved with the notes. Amidst the good memories, Vyad also remembered war, pain, and darkness, then waking up to collect his broken wings from the ground next to him.

Placing a hand on the mantle, he lifted his wine glass in salute to the apples and wings. Taking a long drink, he flung the glass into the fire, shattering the crystal. The fire roared.

Vyad curled his top lip back in a silent snarl at the wings and apples before turning away. No matter how much he tried to distract himself with drink and pleasure, nothing seemed to be able to satiate his hatred or anger. Every soul that he won was another knife in his creator's heart, but the satisfaction never lasted long enough for Vyad. The only thing that would satisfy him would be to bend Aoire to his will, make her his own personal trophy for all eternity.

Turning towards the tree, Vyad stepped as close as he could get. Power radiated from the tree, subtle but strong, creating a protective barrier around it. It was the same kind that his creator, and the offspring of his creator, held.

Reaching out, Vyad smiled as his hand easily touched the blackened roots, cold under his touch. Running his fingers up the trunk towards the colored part, he felt the barrier imped him. It pushed his hand away from the tree, not allowing him to move any further.

Making a fist, Vyad's face reddened with anger. It had taken millennia for just the roots to turn black, but no matter. Vyad was a patient man when he wanted to be. Once he had Aoire, the process would go much faster. Once the tree was completely black, Vyad could use it to finally take over the world.

Vyad took a deep breath and closed his eyes. He reached out with his mind, searching for her. Around him, a great hall rose up. It was only one level, the floors made of black marble. The ends of the hall stretched out as far as he could see, the ends vanishing in the distance. There were no lanterns here, but it was well lit.

Lining the hall were millions upon millions of doors. Above each door was carved a name, and Vyad knew that behind the door was the dream world of that person. His boots echoed all around him, the only other sounds coming from behind each door as its patron dreamed away.

This was the Hall of Dreams, Vyad's own creation. He had created it as mankind grew across the earth and he felt his hold over them slipping. Here, he could freely enter the dreams of anyone with a door – a trick he learned from his creator. Once he was in their dreams, he could whisper to them and plant thoughts to alter their actions, or even bend them to his will. All those that had given themselves over to Vyad wore a glass bead someplace on their body, with their beads twin in Vyad's possession so that he could see them at all times using his viewing disk. All he had to do was open their door.

Not every door was open to him, something Vyad learned early on. While he had access to every soul on the earth above and now below, some doors he could not open, while others slammed shut in his face as soon as he opened them. Some vanished from sight, the walls absorbing the door. Others caused him great pain when he tried to open it, or he was cast out of the room and flung back into the hall like a rag doll. Vyad hated those rooms.

Moving down the hallway, something caught his eye. Stopping in front of one of the doors, Vyad looked at it.

"Interesting," Vyad said.

The door was exactly like all the others, but Vyad stood in front of it reading and re-reading the name written above the frame.

Ahearn Lionheart.

Just a few days earlier the name above the door had read -

Caz.

Reaching out a hand to turn the handle, Vyad paused. This was not the dream he was looking to invade. Not yet.

Moving further down the hall, Vyad's eyes scanned the rooms as he passed them. Her door was always moving, never in the same place that it had been the night before. A security measure from her father - his creator - no doubt. It was this simple act that had kept Vyad searching for her for twenty-two years.

Then suddenly, one day, her door appeared right in front of him when he entered the Hall of Dreams. It had taken Vyad by surprise, a feeling he found odd and vastly uncomfortable. This evening it didn't take him long to find her door. Her door was just like all the other ones, a fact that infuriated him. She was a celestial being, created by the highest nobility, and the humble nature of the door did not match her standing. What was the point of all that power if you weren't going to use it to your advantage?

Trying to grip the door handle, Vyad felt a strong barrier

around it. Grunting softly, he pushed against the barrier even more. Finally he broke through. Turning the knob, he pushed the door open. Warm sunlight filled the Hall of Dreams as the door swung open, revealing a lush valley. In the distance, he could see her.

Chapter Seventeen

Stepping into the sunlit valley, the door closed softly behind Vyad. Now, a single doorframe with no wall attached stood behind him, greenery all around him. Tall mountains with snow-capped peaks framed the valley. Not a cloud was in the sky, but a warm breeze ruffled the soft grass under his boots. A large lake lay off in the distance, bright yellow and purple-blue wildflowers coloring the ground around it.

He could see Aoire sitting on a hill in the distance, her back against an enormous tree with brightly colored leaves. Vyad made no sound as he approached, but her body stiffened the nearer he got.

"You shouldn't be here, Vyad," Aoire said, turning her naturally blue-green eyes to him. Bright gold flecked throughout her eyes and for a moment Vyad felt his heart ache. They were the same as his creators' eyes in every aspect - eyes that once had been able to bring him to his knees with a single look. A wind rustled the leaves above their heads.

"I was able to enter the presence of your father at will, who is to say that I can not visit you in your dreams?" Vyad asked, sitting down next to her. His hand brushed the scar on her left wrist and she snatched her hand away.

"I see you still have my parting gift," Vyad stated.

Aoire didn't reply, but looked off into the distance, her eyes brooding. Clouds began to appear above the lake.

"What has life been like for you now that you are on the run?" Vyad asked.

Aoire pulled her knees tight to her chest. "I would think you would know, since your spies are everywhere. How have you managed to create such a vast network of spies?"

"You don't know? I thought your father told you everything," Vyad snipped.

Aoire shrugged. "If you don't want to tell me, that's fine."

"My ways are for me to know and no one else," Vyad replied, running a hand across the top of the grass. It blackened and shriveled under his touch. "Besides, if I give away all my secrets, you will stay one step ahead of me."

"I will always be one step ahead of you, Vyad. You forget that you are already defeated, even if you try to deny it. My brother took care of that for everyone," Aoire said.

Vyad scowled, rising to his feet. "How are your dear father and brother? Still trying to gain back the love of a people that want nothing to do with them?"

Aoire looked up at him, her face emotionless. "Father and Brother do not have to *try* to gain love. You never understood that. I know who you are now Vyad, and how you work. I also know what I was created for and how this all ends for you. Even if you have not come to terms with it yet."

Vyad's top lip curled back. "Yes, we all know how this is 'supposed' to end. However, the human body can only take so much and while you are in this form, dear Aoire, there is no end to the amount of suffering that I can inflict upon you. There is nothing you can do about that."

"And why is that?" Aoire asked.

Vyad leaned over, pushing a curl away from her forehead, his fingers grazing her temple. Red blisters immediately appeared on her smooth skin. Aoire winced, but made no noise as Vyad pressed his face close to her. "Because it is not in your nature to stop events from unfolding that you know must. You are called to a higher purpose and everything else along the way doesn't matter, does it? All the people who die, and all the suffering that happens to you and yours, is insignificant next to the end result, aren't they?"

Aoire stared at him in shock. "Of course it matters! Life matters. People matter. What happens to me does not."

Vyad chuckled. "My dear, you are so naïve now that you are in a human body. Of course it matters what happens to you. It matters to the ones that love you, and so it is they that will suffer the most. Do they know what you are? What you really are?"

Aoire didn't reply, so Vyad pressed on. "If you continue down this path, continue to try and fulfill this destiny of yours, it is they that will ultimately suffer the most. You will be unable to do anything about it either, because you still blindly believe the end result of all this will create a better world for them."

Aoire stuck her chin out defiantly. "It will. I know it will."

"Was everything made better when your brother fulfilled his calling? If so, this world would never have come to pass, right? If what he did was for the good of all, then why is everyone living underground like moles and being killed by Bashers?" Vyad asked.

"Those are your demons, Vyad. Not Father's, or Brother's, creation."

"But they made a way for Bashers, did they not? Bashers are around because of the chain reaction leading from your brother's sacrifice to now."

"That had nothing to do with him. Humans have free will. Those who turned into Bashers were unwilling to be guided to a better future."

Vyad threw back his head and laughed. "What better future? A life fulfilled if they simply follow your father's will for them? Look around you, Aoire. Life is so destitute for everyone that they have no way of even seeing the future you want to usher in for them. What is to say that if you even do succeed, they will want that life? They have been living underground for so long that no one remembers the old earth. How can you possibly expect them to believe in a promise so profoundly fanciful? Humans will always cling to what is right in front of them, something tangible to pursue."

"And that is what you promise? A way out of their suffering if they simply give their lives to you? Protection from the evil of your demons?" Aoire argued.

Vyad smiled wickedly. "Yes. That is exactly what I offer, and they always accept with fervent desire. I show them a way out of their suffering, one right in front of them, while you can only offer something they have to wait to inherit. Who wants to wait for the promise of something good, when something better is right in front of them?"

"All wrapped up neatly in an eternity of servitude and despair," Aoire spat. "I bet you don't tell them that part."

Vyad shrugged. "Why would I? I simply have to whisper the prospect of a better tomorrow and they eat it up. They do not need to know the consequences of their actions. By the time they figure it out, it's too late for them anyway."

Aoire looked at him, shaking her head sadly. "That short-sightedness was always your greatest weakness. You believe it is too late for anyone, whereas Father, Brother, and I, know that even in the eleventh hour it is never too late for anyone. Your pride is why you lost everything in the beginning and why you will lose again in eternity."

Vyad's face twisted as her words sank in. Fury swirled in his black eyes. His voice came out like a hiss. "You will never win, child. If I have too, I will take you apart piece by piece."

The clouds that had begun to gather over the lake turned dark grey and then black, spreading swiftly across the entire sky and darkening the valley. A strong wind picked up as Vyad grabbed Aoire by her throat and slammed her back against the tree. Vyad tightened his fingers around her smooth neck, beginning to crush her windpipe. Aoire gasped for air, writhing under his grip. She clawed at his hand, but that made him squeeze harder.

Vyad felt her strike him in the ears with both her hands, her blow disorienting him. Slightly surprised by the pain, Vyad loosened his grip unwillingly. Landing sharply on the ground, Aoire gasped for breath. Red marks had appeared where he had held her. Shaking his head to stop seeing double, Vyad snarled and lunged at Aoire.

The valley erupted brightly as a jagged stream of lightning struck the ground between them. An invisible hand grabbed the back of Vyad's shirt and yanked him backwards, throwing him through the open door to Aoire's dram. Vyad collided with the wall in the Hall of Dreams.

Getting to his feet, Vyad launched himself at the door

again as it slammed shut. The door shimmered and then vanished, replaced by a smooth wall. Vyad rammed his fists into the wall, cracking it.

"Creator!" Vyad shouted, his skin turning red in anger. "Creator! You may be able to keep her safe for now, but I am coming for her! I am coming for your daughter, and I will do everything in my power to destroy her!"

Around him the Hall of Dreams melted away and he was back in his room. Smoke rose from his body, the red of his skin turning back to its normal golden hue as he worked to regain control over his anger. Going to his desk, Vyad began to pour over the maps again, a new hunger in his black eyes.

* * * * *

Aoire sat straight up, frantically ripping her blanket off. Gasping for air, she grabbed at her throat, her eyes wild as she felt the rough outline of Vyad's hand burned into her skin. Tears ran down her face as she tried to get her breath, her windpipe compressed from her encounter with him. She could still feel his hand around her throat, his skin burning hers.

Retter's face appeared through the black dots that danced in front of her eyes. She could see his lips moving, but the blood pounding in her ears made it impossible to hear anything.

"I can't...I can't...breathe," Aoire gasped, her lips beginning to turn blue. Laur and Ahearn also appeared in her field of vision.

Ripping open the top of her satchel as her vision narrowed, Aoire pulled out one of the leaves she had taken from the Dhunni tree back in End. She pressed it to her neck, feeling the millions of tiny hairs on the leaf come alive. They hooked underneath her burn, affixing the leaf to her. Her breathing slowly began to regulate itself as the pressure in her throat eased. Taking a deep breath, Aoire leaned back against the tunnel wall, her lips white.

"What in the gods happened?" Retter asked. Aoire could finally hear his voice as the pounding in her ears subsided.

"Vyad," Aoire replied. Dark bruises had already begun to appear all over her throat. Three red lines were across her forehead as well, bright against her pale complexion. She winced as she tried to swallow.

"Here?" Ahearn asked, looking around.

They had stopped for the evening in a wider part of the tunnel, the swirls on the wall not as bright so they could sleep. Long shadows were cast along the tunnel floor, but there was no sign of anyone else but them in their camp.

Aoire shook her head, closing her swollen eyes. "No. He was in my dream."

"What?" Laur burst out. "Vyad can reach you in your dreams and attack you there?"

Aoire nodded, swallowing gingerly. Her mouth was dry, and her head was pounding. The leaf, however, was cool against her skin, soothing the burn on her neck.

"Who is this Vyad?" Laur asked, her eyes wide.

"A very dangerous individual with major anger issues," Ahearn said.

"He was the one that hurt your wrist?" Retter asked. Aoire nodded.

"How?" He added.

Aoire closed her eyes as she swallowed. Her voice came out barely above a whisper. "He can move between dreams, enter any that he wants to, and he can affect the dreamer too. Whatever he does to you in your dream, happens in reality."

"And he can burn people?" Ahearn asked.

"Me. He can burn me," Aoire replied, pulling the leaf away as she felt its coolness wear off.

"Why you?" Retter asked, taking the leaf from her and handing her a fresh one. It had blackened where it had touched the burn on her neck.

"Because of who I am," Aoire said.

"Was it the burn on your wrist that caused you to pass out in End when the Khalefo appeared?" Retter asked.

Aoire nodded. "Yes. His touch is poisonous to me, and since the Bashers are an extension of him, I reacted when they drew near. A small battalion I could have handled, but thousands overloaded me."

"You seemed fine when we met," Laur said.

"We put her in the lake outside of End. The water healed her, as it did me." Ahearn pulled open the slash in the shoulder of her jacket to show Laur a thin white scar just like the one on her ankle.

"You didn't bring some of that water with you, did you?" Laur asked.

"The water in the lake has potent healing properties, but it only works there. The Dhunni trees have similar healing properties, but unlike the water, they can work anywhere," Aoire replied. The burning on her neck had subsided to a dull ache, so she pulled the leaf away and crushed it in her hand. As it broke, golden sap seeped out of everywhere the leaf had blackened.

"What is that?" Laur asked.

"Premena," Aoire replied.

"What is premena?" Retter asked.

Aoire reached into her bag, pulling out a small glass vial with a golden stopper. Pulling off the top, she wiped the sap onto the spout, watching it slowly drip down into the vial. It swirled counter-clockwise as it dripped, moving around at the bottom of the vial as if it had a life of its own.

"Premena is very powerful and rare. Just one drop will be able to transform anything into any form desired, or it can be used to cure any ailment. It can even bring the dead back to life," Aoire replied. "It runs in the veins of the Dhunni trees and their leaves, but it only presents itself when pure evil comes in contact with it. Premena is rare to see and even rarer to posses."

"So even though Vyad caused you harm, his evil act was changed?" Ahearn asked.

Aoire crushed the other leaf, adding more premena to the vial. "Yes."

"What else do you have in there?" Laur asked, eyeing the satchel.

"Whatever we may need," Aoire replied, fatigue washing over her. Her face was paler than normal and the finger marks around her throat stood out brightly, the skin red and broken with a rim of bruises.

"Get some rest, Aoire," Retter said, squeezing her hand. "We will keep watch."

Exhausted, Aoire curled up on the ground. Retter pulled the blanket up around her shoulders, sleep already taking ahold of her. Sitting down near her head, Retter watched her as she slept. She seemed smaller than normal, and even in sleep, her face was a mixture of exhaustion and pain.

"What is going on here?" Laur demanded, her staff across her knees.

"What do you mean?" Ahearn asked.

Laur looked at her and Retter, her face drawn tight and her eyes hard. "Do not take me for a fool, either of you. I have seen and learned more than either of you combined. I know that you two are Guardians. I know that Guardians learn everything about the people or place they are protecting. I also know that End was completely demolished by the Khalefo, and you three seem to be the only ones who got away. So I gather that you two must be protecting Aoire, but what I don't know is why. I also don't know why this Vyad is hunting her, or why that Narcissa woman is so bent on capturing Aoire. As I don't know how long I will be traveling with you, I can understand wanting to have secrets, but I do know that I am owed an explanation."

"I guess you do deserve to know what it is that you have gotten pulled into," Ahearn said, settling onto the floor of the tunnel at Aoire's feet. She looked at Retter who nodded slightly.

Ahearn took a breath, interlocking her fingers over her knees. "Aoire came to us about two weeks ago. Before that, no one knew she existed."

"What do you mean 'came' to you?" Laur asked.

"That I found her, may be a better way to say it," Retter said, his eyes still fixed on Aoire. "Every year the young women in End who have turned twenty-one come to the Birthing House to be processed and start their year-long training on how to become Birthers."

"Birthers. I read about those. I thought it was an archaic design that had long since died out," Laur said.

Retter shook his head. "It's a practice that until now, was very much alive. I do not know if any of these other cities practice a Birthing program, but in End it is - was - our way of life. Over that year, the young women study and are taught how to serve their city as Birthers, At the end of the year, on their twenty-second birthday, the Amesi brands those that are Birthers and those that are Unborns. No woman who is twenty-one is ever left unchecked in End. They all come to the Birthing House to be processed and trained, a way of life that is taught to our children from the moment they are born. Our women believe that it is their duty to help to bring new life into the world to replace those who have been lost."

"And Aoire? Was she present on this Processing Day?" Laur asked.

"Yes, but not at the Birthing House. Aoire is already twenty-two," Retter replied.

"Then how did she end up there?"

"Retter brought her to the Birthing House. From then on things escalated. Eimhir was not pleased to know that she existed, so she ordered me to put her in a confinement cell and Retter was taken to the NeverEver," Ahearn said.

"The NeverEver?" Laur asked.

"That's what Aoire called it. I don't know how I got there. One moment I was speaking with a fellow Guardian and then the next I woke up there. It was a place where nothing exists, but everything exists at the same time. In the NeverEver there is no concept of time, everything around me was pure white and completely silent. I don't know if I was floating, standing, or sitting. I could move around freely, but could not see or feel any ground underneath me. All around, I could sense the presence of others, but I couldn't hear or see them and when I tried to call out, the sound of my voice ended as soon as I had spoken. When I was there, I felt nothing - no pain, no fear, no sadness, and no joy. Nothing until Aoire got me out," Retter said.

"How?" Laur asked. "I thought she was locked in a cell."

"I released her once I found out what Eimhir had done to the Commander," Ahearn replied.

"Why the sudden change of heart?" Laur asked.

Ahearn shifted. "I never wanted to put Aoire in that cell, but at the time it seemed the only option. The unrest in End had grown increasingly worse each year, affecting even the Guardians and the Birthing House."

"Perhaps Aoire really did show up at the right time," Retter said.

"What do you mean?" Laur asked.

"Caz is correct – the unrest in End had grown worse, and it all started when Eimhir became Amesi. There were things happening in End that the effects of could be seen and felt even in the streets. I think Eimhir knew just how powerful and important Aoire is. You have seen how she knows things that others do not, even things we have not shard with anyone. She says it is because of whom her father is, and while I was skeptical at first, I have seen her do miraculous things in the short amount of time that I have known her. This may all be happening for a reason," Retter replied.

"The unrest is not just in End," Laur said softly, taking a long look at Aoire.

"What?" Ahearn asked, but when Laur did not reply, she continued where Retter had left off.

"About a week after Aoire revealed herself to all of End and freed the Commander, the Khalefo attacked. We found out that Eimhir had been working with Vyad and Narcissa. Eimhir allowed Vyad to attack End and all of the citizens in order to capture Aoire. Aoire had warned us that Vyad had a wide network of spies, but we never thought it would have been Eimhir," Ahearn said.

"Why?" Laur asked.

"She was the Amesi, the Mother of the Birthing House, and the one who was sworn to protect the Birthers and Seeders. The Amesi's sole task is to protect the unborn lives being created in the Birthing House, and to watch over the well being of everyone there. Each new Amesi is named by the previous on her deathbed, swearing her life to the service of the Birthing House. She is chosen over all the other Birthers of her generation because of her strength of character. I guess over time, Eimhir began to believe that she was master and protector of all of End and that even the Guardians were under her control," Ahearn answered.

"Aren't they?"

Retter scoffed. "Of course not! The Guardians do not answer to her, or to anyone. We are sworn to protect the Birthing House, but we are not hers to order around and control. We are one unit, our loyalty to one another our strongest asset."

"So what happened in the attack?" Laur asked, seeing Ahearn's eyes shift to the ground, her fingers picking at the hem of her jacket.

Ahearn looked back down the tunnel, back the way they had come, her eyebrows knitting together in remorse. "You said you walked through End. You saw what happened. The Khalefo attacked from underneath and above. We were completely unprepared even though Aoire had given us fair warning. It backed up what I had heard Narcissa say to Eimhir the night Aoire first appeared. Vyad would stop at nothing to capture Aoire and he made that very clear."

Laur's eyes softened. "From what I saw, there was no

way to prepare for an attack like that, even if you had been given ample notice. There was nothing that you could have done. It's a miracle you three even got out alive."

Ahearn blinked away tears. "The only reason we got out alive was because we *had* been warned. Knowing that Vyad was going to attack, and that he wanted to take Aoire prisoner, allowed us to devise a plan. I grew up in the Birthing House, exploring every inch of it, and I knew of secret passageways behind the walls. During the attack our brothers sacrificed themselves to allow us time to get out."

"Even the Sihir came to help. The last thing we saw before we were able to get away was the Sihir, our Protectors, and our Guardians, all working together to fight a particularly large Khalefo," Retter said.

"Was he dressed in black and covered in metal piercings?" Laur asked.

Retter nodded.

"His name is Fearg. I overheard him and Narcissa talking when I was in End. He seems to be the leader of the Khalefo," Laur explained.

"Did you see any survivors?" Ahearn asked.

Laur looked at the ground, the memory of the carnage overwhelming. "No. I saw nothing more than death and destruction. You three were the first souls left alive that I found."

A silence fell over them.

"But why does this Vyad want Aoire so badly, and why would he go to such great lengths to get her? Attacking End, sending Narcissa after you, even attacking her in her sleep – why her?" Laur asked, breaking the silence.

"All we know is what she has told us, but everything she has told us up until now has proven true. She possesses a great power and an even greater calling. I have seen much evil in my life, but I have learned that the greater the evil, the greater the good that defeats it. If this Vyad is as evil as we think, and it is her that he fears, then she must be an even greater force for good," Retter replied, brushing a lock of curly red hair away from Aoire's face.

"She is nothing more than a child. She doesn't seem like a threat to anyone," Laur said.

"She's stronger than you think," Retter said softly, a gentle smile on his face. Ahearn couldn't recall ever seeing the Commander smile.

"And what are your callings? The one that revealed her to her enemy, and the one who locked her up, are now what? Protecting her?" Laur asked.

"We are here because we choose to be. She will need all the help she can get. Especially now that we know that Vyad can get to her in her dreams, Bashers may be the least of our problems," Retter replied.

"And you are willing to do that? Willing to sacrifice everything for her?" Laur replied.

"We know this is where we are supposed to be," Ahearn said, her face set. Laur had read once that Guardians never turn away from their most sacred of duties. Laur wondered what they weren't telling her if protecting one person pulled them away from protecting their city.

"You two may know that, but I don't," Laur said. "As promised, I will come with all of you as far as City of Truth, but I still have questions. Questions that I intend to get answered before going any further with any of you."

Without waiting for them to reply, Laur rolled over so that she was facing the tunnel wall and clutched her staff close to her chest. Closing her eyes, she drifted off to sleep, but her senses didn't dull. It was a trick she had taught herself to allow her body time to rest, but also to be able to wake at a moment's notice.

Ahearn looked at Aoire, watching her chest rise and fall in shallow breaths. "What do you think is going to happen to us?"

"Honestly, I don't know, but I do know that we are alive. It's lucky that we got out of End at all," Retter replied.

"Lucky," Ahearn said flatly. "Would you really call us lucky?"

Retter looked at Laur. He had seen many Unborns and discarded Birthers with the same caged look in their eyes as Laur had - people who had experienced lifetimes of pain with no way to escape. "I would say that we are luckier than most. As bad as things were in End, we have not known suffering like Laur has. To be able to survive as long as she has against Hunters...she would have made a good Guardian, even as a woman."

Ahearn felt her heart begin to quicken. "Do you think being a woman would have made her any less effective as a Guardian?"

Retter leaned his head back against the tunnel wall, fatigue creeping into his voice. For a rare moment he let his guard down and spoke to Ahearn like a colleague and not as her Commander. "The whole system in End is archaic and has been from the beginning. It has always been our way for Guardians to be male, but I am not concerned about her gender and how that could affect her usefulness. Who is to say that anyone is better at any one job, simply because they are male or female? Perhaps more suffering could have been averted if women were allowed to be Guardians, and had not been forced to bear children until they were used up. It turned my stomach to see those innocent girls trapped as they were, but now that End is gone, we may never know how things could have been different."

Retter's voice trailed off as sleep began to take him. His chin dipped against his chest, but he did not move from his seated position by Aoire's head. Still asleep, Aoire found his hand. Retter's fingers instinctively curled around hers.

Turning away, Ahearn curled up on her mat and closed her eyes. Thoughts raced through her mind as she settled in, but the last image she saw before she fell asleep was the way that Retter looked at Aoire. She wondered if he would ever look at her again once he learned the truth about her.

Chapter Eighteen

Groaning, Aoire opened her eyes and blinked. Her head was pounding, and the pale blue-green light from the symbols hurt her eyes. Her throat was still sore, but she could breathe a little easier. After she had fallen asleep she hadn't dreamed at all - something that had never happened to her before - but instead, quiet darkness filled her dreams. She could feel Father's presence within the quiet stillness as she slept, strengthening her.

Retter was sitting next to her, his back straight as a board and his chin against his chest as he slept. Their hands were intertwined, his eyes opening when she gave his hand a small squeeze.

"How are you feeling?" Retter asked.

Aoire opened her mouth to reply, but nothing came out. She smiled weakly instead.

"Here. Drink," Retter said, handing her water-skin to her. Taking a few sips gingerly, Aoire winced as the cool water ran down her raw throat. As it soothed her throat, she was able to drink a little more. No matter how much she drank, the water-skin would always be full.

"We all fell asleep not long after you," Retter said, seeing Aoire looking at Laur and Ahearn.

"How long?" Aoire rasped.

"Have you been asleep? Only a few hours, it's not quite morning. I never thought that learning to count the hours by the light of the algae in End would come in handy anywhere else, but I guess these patterns work the same way."

"They tell a story," Aoire said.

Retter gazed at the symbols next to his shoulder. "They do?"

"It's a language, and a very ancient one. Older than this world, existing from a time before time began," Aoire replied, coughing slightly as her voice caught in her throat.

"What do they say?" Retter asked.

"They speak of creation, the story of everything and everyone. They tell of perfection, of life and love, of deep betrayal and unimaginable loss. They tell of struggle and pain, death and resurrection, renewal and perfection. They tell of life after death. They chronicle the history of this earth, and Father's role in it," Aoire managed. She took a long, slow, drink as her throat began to burn.

"Are you in there?" Retter asked.

Aoire smiled, nodding. "I'm mentioned."

"How long is the story?"

"It's still being written. It started before creation, and will continue for all eternity."

"There doesn't seem to be enough room," Retter observed.

Aoire laughed, and then coughed. "There is more than enough room, Retter. These tunnels run underneath the entire surface of the earth, connecting everything together."

"Where did the tunnels come from?"

"A great tree once existed on this earth, larger and older than any other tree. Its purpose was to give life, and it held the ability to take life away. Father used its roots to connect the whole earth together and to record the story as it unfolded."

"What happened to it?"

"It vanished. Lost to us during a great battle," Aoire said, her voice so soft and sad that Retter could feel the weight of her grief.

"Are we underneath the earth?" Retter asked, wanting to change the subject.

"Yes," Aoire replied.

"What is it like up there?"

"Uninhabitable."

"What happened?"

Aoire sat up and pulled her knees to her chest, circling her arms around them. "Human nature. Over the span of a few thousand years, things escalated and eventually imploded. Overnight millions were lost and your ancestors were forced underground."

"Where we all live now with no knowledge of our own past, apparently," Retter said, scowling. He looked at Aoire. "Vyad never seems to be far from a tragedy, how does he factor into all of this?"

"Vyad has been collecting souls to his side for many thousands of years. The same event that forced everyone underground also opened the door for Vyad's minions to repopulate the earth, this time as Bashers. His reach goes deep."

"Repopulate?"

"There was a time when Vyad and his followers roamed the surface of the earth freely, affecting the lives of humans on a daily basis. Through the sacrificial act of my brother, Father was able to release all from a future of bondage and sorrow. In that one moment, Vyad lost his dominion and he has been trying to claw it back ever since. That was nearly five thousand years ago. Sadly, the very event that forced humankind to live underground, also turned the tide for Vyad."

"Five thousand years ago?" Retter whistled. "How old are you?"

Aoire smiled. "Far older than you would suspect."

Retter eyed her skeptically, but continued. "So if we are all underground, then Vyad must be housed up someplace underground too."

Aoire nodded.

"Any idea where?"

"One," Aoire replied quietly.

"And that is where we are going?"

Aoire twisted a lock of her hair around her finger. "Eventually."

"Then I am with you every step of the way," Retter said.

Aoire felt her heart swell, but shook her head. "There will be a time that I will go where you cannot follow, Retter. When that happens, you will have a hard choice to make."

"What kind of choice?" Retter asked, but Aoire was unable to answer as her throat constricted, and she began to cough violently. The sound of her coughing woke Laur and Ahearn.

"You're awake," Ahearn said. "How do you feel?"

"Fantastic," Aoire replied hoarsely. The color had returned to her cheeks, but dark circles still lay under her eyes.

"More leaves?" Laur suggested.

Aoire shook her head. "They did all they could. The rest will heal in time."

"How far is City of Truth?" Laur asked, gathering up her blanket and water-skin. She paused. "And where are we going to put these?"

"Hand it to me," Aoire said, taking the blanket from Laur and pushing it effortlessly into her bag. The blanket vanished, the shape of her bag not changing.

Laur stared at her, leaning heavily on her staff. She was still keeping the weight off her left foot, even though it was healed. "How on earth do you keep so much in such a small bag?"

"The NeverEver," Aoire replied, taking Ahearn's blanket from her.

"What?" Retter asked, his head snapping up from folding his blanket. "You mean that place I was in, is inside your bag?"

Aoire clipped her water-skin to the side of her satchel. "Father created a portal within the bag to the NeverEver. He has placed everything we will need in the NeverEver, and in it we can hold an unlimited stockpile of supplies. Anything we need, I can reach easily."

"I thought the NeverEver was only in that room," Ahearn said.

"No, it's everywhere. There are many places throughout the earth where portals to the NeverEver are, and each of those portals leads to a different part of the NeverEver. One of them just happens to be in my satchel now," Aoire explained.

"Your father seems to be full of surprises," Laur said.

Aoire smiled wistfully at the mention of Father. She adjusted the strap on her satchel so it did not pull on her burned neck. "We should get going."

"Are you okay to move?" Retter asked.

Aoire nodded. "I'll be fine. We can't stay here."

Checking to make sure that they didn't leave behind any sign they had been there, Aoire scanned the tunnel behind them for any sign of Narcissa. No matter how far down the tunnels they went, she could still sense Narcissa's evil presence. How she was able to stay in the tunnels was beyond Aoire, the light from the symbols made of unrefined purity. No evil could withstand this level of purity for long. Continuing towards Truth, the bright symbols on the walls faded back to normal long after they passed by. The only thing that didn't fade was Narcissa's presence.

* * * * *

Narcissa crept slowly after Aoire and her party. For the past few weeks she had been following them by their soul trails, unable to pass where the symbols were glowing. Anytime she drew close to the symbols, her body felt like it was on fire. Narcissa could feel her frustration growing as the glow of the symbols halted her pursuit time and time again. All Narcissa wanted was to have Aoire within her clutches, but she could not seem to draw any closer to them.

Waiting for the symbols to fade, she could hear Besit urging her forward, whispering into her ear that the light could not kill her. Running her fingers lightly across to top of the rainbow trail closest to the ground, the most glorious scent filled Narcissa's nose. It was sweet and light, and the moment she smelled it, Besit went into a feeding frenzy. Narcissa felt her body lurch forward, hungry for the source of the smell.

Pain hit her like a battering ram, a cold fire that threatened to tear her apart at the joints and burn her up simultaneously. All thought was forced from her mind and she was unable to move forward or go back. She could feel white-hot needles pierce her mind and for a split second, she was sure she was dying all over again.

Curling up into a tight ball, Narcissa tried to protect herself from the pain. The blue-green light grew brighter around her, the symbols vivid behind her closed lids. Along with the brighter light, the pain grew. Narcissa's body began to convulse.

In a fit of pain, her hand fell on one of the symbols on the wall. The smell of burning flesh filtered through the pain in her mind, but she couldn't discern the pain of her burning hand from the pain in her whole body. She could feel the barriers she had put up in her mind to protect herself begin to weaken amidst the pain. As they did, shadowy forms of her victims appeared in her mind's eye.

The sound of their voices, muffled and distant, accompanied them. The figure in front was the most solid, blue eyes as brilliant as the clearest lake tearing straight through Narcissa. Pulling her arms around herself, she curled even tighter, shaking her head to make them go away.

Slowly, after what felt like eons, the forms in her mind vanished back into submission as the pain in her body subsided. Blinking, Narcissa uncurled and looked around. The light from the symbols had faded.

Lifting her hand up, she saw that a perfect remnant of the symbol she had touched was now burnt black into her skin. Running her fingers along the burn, Narcissa blinked when his eyes flashed through her mind again.

It had been longer than she could remember since seeing those eyes. She had forced them away long ago, unable to face the question that still lingered, unanswered, within them. It was the same question she saw in the eyes of all her victims – *why?*

Narcissa had no answer, nor did she feel that she needed to supply one. She never thought of them again after taking their lives, but the longer she was in the tunnels, the harder Narcissa found it to control her thoughts, or them. Memories of a past life, a life she had forgotten, began to force their way into her mind.

When first in the tunnels, she could easily brush away the memories, but it was getting harder to subdue them. She even found herself lingering in the memories for long moments, old emotions and longings surfacing within her heart. Anytime they did, she felt Besit tighten her grip painfully around her heart. Narcissa fought the anxiety rising within her as she felt control over her mind slipping away, but she couldn't turn back and risk facing Vyad. He would make sure that she suffered far worse.

Getting to her feet, Narcissa pushed forward until she reached the next group of illuminated symbols. She eyed the trails in front of her, wanting more of the scent of the rainbow trail, but wary of the pain she had just been through. She figured the trail and scent belonged to Aoire, wondering just how much more delicious her soul would be to devour if just a small taste of what she left behind did that to Besit.

Every trail shimmered in the air at chest height and glowed a certain color depending on the person. A soul path didn't glow very vibrantly, just a gentle shimmer in the air left behind as they moved. The paths that Vyad or the Sihir left were colored based on their power, and another of the paths she followed was different from the others. It was purple, a trail Narcissa had never seen intact before.

The purple trail intrigued her. She had seen remnants of a few other purple trails, but their owners had long since died. To see a living purple trail out in the open...she had heard rumors of what Purples could do, powerful and frightening magic. Curiosity of if they were true now that she knew there was a Purple alive in this world, overtook her curiosity of what she may taste like.

Following the path as it forked to the right, she stopped. The tunnel had bowed out here, making a large rounded area. The soul trails intersected each other in a jumble, and then continued down the tunnel.

"This is where you stayed the night, isn't it girl-child?" Narcissa murmured.

Reaching her hands out, she plunged her fingers into the soul trails. As soon as she touched them, a jolt ran through her body and her pupils dilated. Four shadowy figures appeared around her, perfect representations of Aoire and her companions, except that the one with the purple trail appeared as a shadowy mass. Narcissa had yet to meet this one, so she could not see them in her mind the way she saw the others. The same light, sweet, smell rose up around her and Narcissa had to force Besit to calm down.

Moving her fingers through the trails, the scene sped up until Aoire's figure leapt up from her bed, screaming silently and clawing at her throat. Narcissa smiled cruelly as the others frantically tried to help her, a mark of some sort around Aoire's neck. Narcissa could see a faint outline of a similar mark on her wrist.

"You left your mark on her again, didn't you, Master?" Narcissa said.

She watched the rest of the night play out in front of her, frowning when Aoire pressed something she couldn't make out against her neck. The playback from the soul trails were always shadowy remnants of what really happened and so much detail was lost. Still, Narcissa did not like the look of relief that crossed over Aoire's face once she pressed, whatever it was, against her neck.

What other tricks do you have up your sleeve, girl-child? Narcissa thought, pulling her hands out of the trails once everyone had gone back to sleep. The scene vanished, along with the smell. She felt Besit quiet within her, but could feel the hunger for souls growing.

Her eyes following the soul trails up the tunnel, Narcissa smiled. She knew she wasn't much more than a day or two behind them. The way into City of Truth was hidden within a labyrinth that tested even the strongest of mind and spirit. Aoire would be her prisoner before they would even be able to find the entrance to Truth. Her main concern wasn't getting to them within the tunnels, but getting to them before they were able to enter Truth.

Narcissa had traveled between the main Five enough to know that the closest city to End was Truth. It was a long journey to get there and not one that many made anymore. Some had tried when the cities had first been found, but they had been lost amidst the labyrinth of tunnels. Narcissa often found remnants of those who had traveled and failed, barely anything left of their soul trails.

Truth had a specialized defense mechanism against Bashers. For most, it worked perfectly the first time, but for Narcissa it took a bit longer. She had trained herself to compartmentalize pain and fear over the hundreds of years she had been alive. That was the only thing that helped her to cope with what Truth did to her. Other Bashers were not as lucky, but Narcissa prided herself on being more resourceful and intelligent than they were. Desire to appease Vyad wasn't the only driving force for Narcissa.

Drawing closer to the next group of illuminated symbols, Narcissa blinked as the tunnel melted away and she was suddenly standing in front of a room full of people dressed in vibrant colors. The tunnel walls were replaced with rough stone and warm colored wood.

Round wooden tables spread out in front of her with mismatched lamps on each, casting a ring of dim light around them. Couples nestled close to each other and in darkened corners, whispering promises to each other. The husky smell of old earth had been replaced by the smell of bourbon and stale perfume.

Narcissa's whole body felt warm and alive as she looked out at the faces, an excited energy coursing through her body and making the blood pound in her ears. Young women and men in black and white outfits, deftly wove their way through the room, refilling drinks and handing out plates of food as the conversations continued in a low hum. Every now and again the room blinked from view and then came back again, replaced for a split second by clean white walls and a single blue light that illuminated Narcissa.

"Ready?" a deep voice asked. Narcissa felt her heart skip as a handsome face with blue eyes as brilliant as the clearest lake came into view. A domed ceiling of rough stone hung low over them, bright lights on either side of her casting a warm glow over the wooden stage they stood on.

"I am always ready when I have you by my side, Lucien," Narcissa replied, slipping into his arms. She smiled as he kissed her forehead.

"They may only be a hologram, but knock 'em dead *mi*

amore," Lucien said, kissing her lightly again before sitting down in front of a beautiful piano.

Taking a deep breath, Narcissa stepped forward to the microphone that hung from the ceiling. Opening her mouth, she began to sing. Her voice was soft at first and then grew louder, its sultry notes filling every inch of the room. All conversation ceased.

After a few bars of only Narcissa's voice, Lucien began to play. His melody merged perfectly with her singing, haunting and pure. As they harmonized, vibrant images flashed across the ceiling above the audience. Not a single person moved.

Once Narcissa's last note faded away, the silence continued.

"Narcissa St'Autry!" Lucien said, rising from his piano bench and holding out a hand to Narcissa. Applause erupted from the room as everyone leaped to their feet. Narcissa felt joy wash over her, pushing any nerves she had out of her mind. Lucien appeared at her side, his hand intertwined with hers.

Rising from a low bow, Lucien whispered into her ear. "After this, you will be the most sought-after singer in all of Paris, *mi amore*. No more singing only in your home, now the whole world will know you. This is only the beginning."

The room faded away and Narcissa now stood with Lucien in the white room, the blue light bathing them both. Lucien turned her towards him and their lips touched. The memory faded away to be replaced by a stream of others that flooded her at once - Narcissa and Lucien singing in front of larger and larger venues, Narcissa beginning to see her face all over the television, Lucien asking her to marry her in front of a hologram of the Eiffel Tower,

Lucien's beautiful smile flashing once more in front of her eyes, Narcissa saying yes to a hooded man standing in her living room, and finally Lucien's empty eyes staring up at the night sky as it exploded in fire.

Deep within she felt Lucien stir, but as always he kept quiet.

Dropping to her knees, Narcissa dug her fingernails into her hands, trying to break free of the stream of memories and the grief that was building within her. The memories were even more jumbled now, but the sharp pain of her nails in her palms broke the onslaught from her past. Trying to gain control over her mind again, her body trembled. A final memory flashed in her mind – Lucien's empty eyes staring upwards as a mushroom cloud of ash filled the sky and all of Paris burned.

Narcissa slammed her fists onto the ground as she felt the grief within her explode. With a scream, she flung her arms out by her sides. The walls and ground around her to cracked as she expelled all of her grief and heartache.

Getting to her feet, Narcissa conjured up an image of a vault in her mind. Once open, she shoved her past and her memories into the vault and slammed the door shut. As it bolted shut, an icy calm washed over her, numbing her to everything.

Setting her jaw, Narcissa now moved faster down the tunnel, her back straight. She no longer felt any pain when she drew closer to the blue-green symbols or when she stepped into the light. She would catch up with them soon enough and Aoire would be hers for the taking. Moving further down the tunnel, her skin began to blister and smoke.

Chapter Nineteen

"That's City of Truth?" Laur asked as the tunnel opened up to reveal a massive cavern. A thin ledge with a steep drop-off jutted out past the tunnel opening, allowing them a bird's eye view of the vast city below.

"It's so different from End," Ahearn said, her hands on her hips. Laur leaned against her staff, taking it all in.

"It's black," Retter frowned, his arms crossed over his chest.

Laur looked him up and down, her finger following her eyes. "*You* are not okay with that? I would have thought that black was your favorite color."

"I prefer reddish-brown for a city, like in End. Black is too stark," Retter replied. Aoire hid a smile as she pulled her cloak up a little higher. Any movement of air sent shivers down her spine when it brushed against her burn.

"I think all of you will find that Truth is in every way different than End," Aoire said. She lightly touched her neck when her burn began to tingle.

A winding canyon at the bottom of the ledge spread out between them and City of Truth. The only way down was a crude ladder that was cut directly into the rock face. Past the canyon, City of Truth sprawled out behind a great wall that rose up from the floor with a sharp lining. The wall was square and from this distance they could see a white mass piled up against the front. It's shape changed slowly.

There was no visible doorway in or out of Truth. The city was laid out in a square pattern, each section nestled within the last. It gave Truth the effect of a city made of square rings. Thousands of tall rooftops came to sharp points within Truth, a tall wall separating each section. Directly in the middle of Truth was a blue lake identical to the one in End. It was the only splash of color within the city or cavern. Even the dirt that filled the canyon below was black.

"One question," Laur said, peeking over the side of the ledge and snapping back quickly as her stomach turned, "how do we get from here to there?"

A deep rumbling of stone scraping against stone filled the cavern, small plumes of dust rising up from the canyon.

"We will have to go down into the canyon," Aoire replied. "Once there, we have to find the doorway into Truth. It set somewhere in the cavern below."

"Find it? You don't know where it is?" Retter asked.

Aoire shook her head. "The canyon protects the entrance to Truth. The door is down there, but it moves around on its own. We will only find the door if Truth decides we are worthy to enter – it's why no Basher has ever been able to."

"And how is it that we are expected to get down there?" Laur demanded.

"I think I can help with that," Narcissa said from behind them. Spinning around, they all stared at her.

Narcissa stood in the mouth of the tunnel, the exposed skin of her body blackened and smoking. No pain registered on her face even though her burnt skin was cracked and bloodied. Her eyes were black pools, an effect that Aoire had only ever seen on Vyad. Her lips, which were normally blood red, were now as black as her hair and the bead that hung around her neck was nearly invisible. She took a few steps forward, so that she was clear of the tunnel. As soon as she saw her, the tingling in Aoire's neck intensified. She felt her throat constrict, as if Vyad was choking her again, but the pain was not as debilitating. The leaves had done their trick.

"You followed us through the tunnels?" Aoire asked in disbelief, staring at her. She had never known any Basher who could withstand the power of the tunnels. Within the fury in Narcissa's eyes, Aoire could see something else burning just as brightly underneath - a calm resolve to succeed.

Now free of the tunnels, Narcissa's body stopped smoking and slowly her skin began to heal itself. The dead skin flaked and peeled away as new skin grew underneath. Narcissa locked eyes on Aoire, watching her without blinking, dark smoke forming around her body and filing the entrance to the tunnel. It blotted out any light around her and began to curl towards them, low whispers in a strange language coming from within the smoke.

Taping into her *opari*, Aoire's power coursed through her veins. She didn't have to look over her shoulder to know exactly how far they were from the canyon floor, or what little time she would have to react to any attack from Narcissa. All she had to do was get the others as far away from Narcissa as possible.

Narcissa lifted a cracked finger, wagging it slowly. She could feel Aoire tap into her power, and with it smelled the same faint sweetness she had in the tunnel. "I wouldn't do that girl-child. This close to each other, and any transportation spells you do will pull me along with you. Shields will also be useless."

"You don't have to do this, Narcissa. I am the one that you want, leave them out of it," Aoire said.

"Well isn't that sweet? After all this running and hiding, you have decided to sacrifice yourself to protect them," Narcissa scoffed.

Aoire spread her hands. "It's me that you were sent to find, they have only been protecting me. Now it's my turn. I am willing to go with you, if you promise me that you will spare them."

Narcissa cocked her head to the side, pressing a finger to her cheek. She studied them for a moment before shaking her head. "No."

Before Aoire could blink, she felt a sharp pain in her sternum and then nothing but air beneath her. Her hip popped loudly as she hit the ledge and rolled over the side, pain blossoming behind her eyes.

Tumbling through the air, Aoire landed flat on top of one of the stone pillars in the canyon below. Her head snapped back against the rocks, and for a moment everything went black. There were sounds of fighting from above and then the impact of boots on either side of her. Gasping for air, Aoire blinked as Narcissa's face filled her hazy vision.

Kneeling down and pressing a knee into Aoire's dislocated hip, Narcissa grabbed her by the front of her tunic. She lifted her up so their faces were inches away from one another. Still trying to get her breath back, Aoire felt it driven from her again as sharp daggers of pain radiated out from her hip.

"I will never understand why he is so afraid of you,

girl-child," Narcissa said snidely. "You don't seem like much to me at all."

Aoire's eyes widened as Narcissa twisted her knee, pressing it down even further into her hip. She could hear other voices yelling something, but the pain was so intense that everything came to her from far away - even her own screams. Finally, Narcissa pulled her knee from Aoire's hip. Aoire gasped in relief, gripping her hip as tightly as she could. Everything swirled in front of her.

Narcissa closed her eyes and breathed in deeply through her nose. "It is a shame that he wants you all to himself. You do smell divine."

"You don't have to do this," Aoire gasped. "You don't owe him anything."

Narcissa threw back her head and laughed. "I don't owe him anything? Girl-child, I owe him *everything*. He is the reason that I am as powerful as I am today. I gave him my soul and he gave me eternity in return. I have grown strong enough to rival anyone, including him. If he wants you, and I can't understand why by the looks of you, then I will bring you to him," she ran a hand over Aoire's head. "But in what state you are in is entirely up to me."

Grabbing her by her hair, Narcissa yanked Aoire to her feet. Pulling her close she kissed Aoire, and for a moment everything stopped. Aoire could feel the deathly poison of her kiss enter her body, and then a shockwave rose from inside her, pushing the poison from her body.

Narcissa's eyes widened, shock and pain mixing on her face. Shoving Aoire back, she screamed as her kiss reversed itself. Black lines began to spread out from her lips, covering her entire face. As Aoire fell, she twisted her body to get her hands underneath her and swept her good leg across Narcissa's ankles, before rolling off the edge of the pillar.

Dangling exhausted from the top of the pillar, Aoire tried not to loose her grip. Her arms shook, the canyon still swimming in front of her. Mustering what energy she had left, Aoire slowly and painstakingly climbed down. Collapsing when she felt soft sand beneath her feet, Aoire held her dislocated leg as tightly as she could, gritting her teeth against the pain. Everything was still spinning far too fast.

"Aoire!" Ahearn's voice echoed through the canyon.

"Here," Aoire replied weakly. Laur and Ahearn's faces appeared as Aoire opened her eyes, snapping them shut again as their faces spun in opposite directions.

"My hip. I think it's dislocated," Aoire explained as Laur tried to help her sit up. The canyon floor pitched violently and she shook her head, breathing heavily as Laur helped her lay down again. Her heart pounded in her ears, unable to hear what Laur was saying to Ahearn.

"What are you-" Aoire began, but shut her mouth to keep from screaming or throwing up as Ahearn pulled her leg out sharply, popping her hip back into place. Sweat covered her body. "Thank you," Aoire said meekly.

Her eyes jolted open when a thought filled her mind. Aoire sat straight up. "Retter, where is he? Narcissa didn't kill him, did she?"

"No," Ahearn replied, laying a gentle hand on Aoire's shoulder. "After Narcissa threw you over the ledge, Retter went after her. Narcissa must never have fought a Commander before, because he was faster than I am sure she expected. He managed to keep her occupied for a bit.

But once Narcissa saw you lying on top of that pillar, she abandoned her fight with him and came after you again."

"So where is he?" Aoire asked, struggling to get to her feet.

"Maybe you should rest a bit more?" Laur suggested.

Aoire shook her head. "I don't have time to rest. We have to find Retter before Narcissa does."

Looking at each other, Laur and Ahearn each grabbed one of Aoire's arms and hoisted her to her feet. Laur handed her staff to Aoire, who leaned against it thankfully. It sank a little in the soft sand, but held her weight.

"I think he may have gone after Narcissa. The Commander had that look in his eye when he is solely focused on one task," Ahearn said. She pointed down the canyon. "He went that way...I think. Aoire, he won't stop until his task is finished."

Aoire could hear the concern creep into Ahearn's voice. She looked towards where Ahearn had pointed and used her *opari* to scan the canyon for any sign of anyone else, frowning.

Something was wrong.

She could sense the three of them easily enough, but if she tried to expand her *opari* out further, it bounced around. It was nearly impossible for Aoire to sense any other presence in the canyon clearly. The only thing her *opari* did do, was alleviate some of the pain in her body.

"We need to find him, and quickly. This canyon will not stay this shape for long, and we do not want to be caught in here when it changes," Aoire said.

As if on cue, they heard the sound of stone scraping against stone again, followed by the sound of smaller rocks tumbling down the canyon walls. Gripping Laur's staff tightly, Aoire gingerly put one foot in front of the other.

"What is that noise?" Laur asked as the three of them slowly made their way through the canyon. Up close, they could see that the soil and rocks were not completely black, but instead a rich dark brown color with grey and black veins of color. Much thinner threads of bronze ran throughout the entire canyon. Even the sand under their feet had a bronze sheen to it.

"No algae," Ahearn observed, craning her neck back as far as she could to look up at the sides of the canyon. The pillars around them rose hundreds of feet into the air, and even though they were at the very bottom, everything was still brightly lit. Leaning closer to one of the pillars, Ahearn saw that light emanated from the bronze threads, bouncing off of the walls to create a natural glow.

"It won't grow here. Has no reason to," Aoire said.

"What is that noise?" Laur asked again, as the sound of stone scraping on stone echoed loudly. The ground shook slightly, various sized rocks falling from above and landing with a dull thud in the sand.

"Look behind us," Aoire replied. Turning around, Ahearn and Laur's jaws dropped.

"It's gone! The way we came, it's gone!" Laur exclaimed.

Behind them, the canyon walls had closed together, blocking their way back. Rocks of various sizes had fallen around where a large pillar was now wedged into the opening in the canyon. All around them, they could hear constant rumbling and scraping, collecting into a never-ending song.

"The pillars and the walls of this canyon move. It's an ever-changing labyrinth down here and many have lost their minds, or their lives, to this maze. Be careful where you step. Even the smallest disturbance could set off a chain reaction," Aoire said, continuing to hobble forward. "Our best bet is to keep moving, find Retter, and then get to Truth before Narcissa finds us first."

* * * * *

There was no time to react, it had all happened so fast. Retter had been so fascinated with the cavern and the city below, that he hadn't sensed her presence until it was too late.

Retter had spent his whole life in End, walking the streets of the four districts and getting to know the people, that he thought he had seen it all. He thought End was the only city in the world, therefore it had always seemed a metropolis to him. Now, looking down at City of Truth, Retter realized that all of End could fit within the smallest section. He had been marveling at the sheer magnitude of the city in front of them that he hadn't even sensed her coming until she was upon them.

Narcissa.

Even with her burnt and cracked skin, Retter knew it was her. The sight of her covered in burns of that magnitude, with no pain anywhere in her face or eyes, was enough to chill even his blood. Her eyes were the most terrifying part of it all, pools of darkness and rage. She fixed her gaze on Aoire, and his entire Guardian training kicked in. Even the smallest detail became focused as his mind cleared.

A single thought entered his mind – *protect Aoire*. It was the same thought he had the first time he saw her by the lake outside of End. Retter felt his muscles tense, felt the familiar itch between his shoulder blades where his swords had been. It only took a moment for him to be battle ready.

It took half as long for Narcissa to send Aoire flying from the ledge and into the canyon below.

Thump-thump. One.

Time slowed in front of Retter's eyes. He heard her hip dislocate as she bounced off the ledge and tumbled over the edge.

Thump-thump. Two.

Closing the gap between he and Narcissa, Retter saw surprise flash across her face for a second. Moving his head slightly to the right, Retter felt the air whistle as he dodged Narcissa's strike. Putting up his palm, he batted her fist away and struck her in the ribs, feeling them crack. He shot Ahearn a glance and she nodded, reading everything she needed to in his eyes. She and Laur inched towards the ledge. The sound of Aoire hitting one of the pillars below met his ears.

Thump-thump. Three.

Narcissa's nails dug into his face and blood began to drip down his face. He didn't let the blood dripping in front of his eyes, or the pain, stop him. Guardians are trained to see with more than just their sight and Retter could tell that Narcissa was slightly off balance. Out of the corner of his eye, he could see that Laur had begun to descend down the ledge, Ahearn watching in case he needed help.

Thump-thump. Four.

Grabbing her wrist in his hand, Retter spun and twisted, flipping both of them onto their backs with her arm pinned between his legs. Just before he kicked her in the temple, he caught a smile on her face. In one quick move, Narcissa landed on top of him, slipping free of his grip fluidly.

Blowing him a quick kiss, she vanished over the ledge. As Retter scrambled to the edge, he saw her straddling Aoire.

Wiping away the blood, Retter could feel the deep gashes Narcissa's nails had left. Snarling as Narcissa dug her knee into Aoire's hip, making her scream in pain, Retter shouted to Ahearn and Laur to get to Aoire. He would take care of Narcissa.

Standing up to follow them down the ladder, Retter felt panic rise within him as he watched Narcissa kiss Aoire. It quickly faded as the kiss backfired. He saw Aoire sweep Narcissa's feet out from under her, just before vanishing from view over the other side.

"You're mine," Retter growled, watching Narcissa slink off into the canyon.

* * * * *

Running through the canyon with her hand over her mouth, Narcissa felt the pain of her kiss fully. For a split second she had tasted the sweetness of Aoire and her power, a sweetness that Aoire's soul trail scent paled in comparison too. If Aoire was everything that Vyad said she was, Narcissa supposed it would make sense that her kiss backfired. She had never tried to take the soul of a being that powerful before, but the part that really perplexed Narcissa was that man - that handsome man in all black.

She had never met anyone that would be able to match her speed and precision for *any* amount of time. She had come across plenty of people in her travels who were as swift as her, even for only a moment - rare times when the human instinct to survive kicks in and they can do unexplainable things - but almost always it was the unexpectedness of that act that surprises them the most and leads to their downfall.

It wasn't the same with this man. There was something vaguely familiar about him. He seemed in complete control of his actions, and his speed. She wondered, could all Guardians do this? Or was this a trait only a Commander possessed? Was this why he was the Commander? She had managed to take a piece of his face, but even that had proved difficult.

Following behind them back in the tunnels, there had been nothing in his soul trail that had led her to believe that he was anything special. He had no color to suggest that he possessed some sort of hidden gift, and she had seen no foreshadowing of the speed and strength she had just encountered. For her, the battle did not last longer than four heartbeats, and she knew it was the same for him. As close as they had been, she had seen into his eyes, and she knew that he was trained to kill. He would protect Aoire at any cost. He could prove a much more formidable foe than she had thought.

Leaning against a pillar, Narcissa lightly touched her face. The burns on her skin were completely gone, most of the skin on her hands healed as well. She could no longer feel the poisonous veins around her mouth that had spread when her kiss backfired. Anger overshadowed her momentary relief. Narcissa hated surprises, but she hated losing even more.

The sound of stone scraping on stone was everywhere. As she leaned against the pillar, she felt it begin to shake. Stepping away, she stumbled backward a few steps, as the great pillar was pulled quickly back across the canyon to become one with the canyon walls, cutting off the corridor she had just come from. Rocks rained down from the force of the pillar merging with the canyon.

Looking around, Narcissa realized that the landscape of the canyon was changing right in front of her. Her way back was now blocked and any markers to indicate where she had come from were gone.

Turning around in a small circle, she felt fear settle in the pit of her stomach – a fear not brought on by Vyad, or Besit, for once – but by knowing that she may not make it out of the canyon. In all her travels to Truth, she had never come this way. Her passage into Truth was always through one of the water portals, but even using those had gotten increasingly harder the more souls she took. She wouldn't even be able to track them by their soul trails here, the lingering remnants of old trails broken apart until they nearly vanished.

Narcissa closed her eyes and listened intently for any sign of the humans at all. Slowly, voices drifted through the canyon towards her, bouncing off the walls and echoed all around her. For now, they were all female, but that was no matter. All she needed was for Retter to appear, and then she could use him to get to the others. This close to Truth, they would not enter the city without him.

Sitting on the ground near the only entrance to her section of the canyon, Narcissa would wait, as long as she needed, for him to show up.

Chapter Twenty

"I think we came this way already," Ahearn said, her black-gloved hand blending in with the pillar she was touching.

"Everything looks the same, how can you tell?" Laur snapped. They had been walking for hours and seemed no closer to finding a way out than before. Laur cringed as she heard the pillars shift again, sighing deeply.

"Aoire, is there any way that you can transport us to Retter and get us out of here?" Laur asked, leaning against the side of the canyon.

Aoire shook her head. "I don't know where he is. Transportation only works if I can see where I need to go. In this canyon, we could re-appear inside of a rock."

Groaning, Laur sank to the ground and stuck her legs out in front of her. "I can see why people lose their minds here."

Aoire smiled gently, pulling a package of wafers from her satchel. She tossed it to Laur. "Eat, Laur. You need to keep your strength up."

Ahearn came to stand next to Aoire. "How are you feeling? You took a pretty bad fall."

"I'll be fine. My body will heal. Retter is more important right now," Aoire replied.

Ahearn laid a gentle hand on her shoulder. "You are still human, Aoire. Your body will only be able to take so much before it shuts down. Take care of yourself first. You are of no help to anyone dead."

Aoire looked at her, her eyes searching Ahearn's face. It was like Father was speaking through her. Eventually, she conceded. "I guess it wouldn't hurt to rest for a bit."

"Good. You two sleep, I will keep first watch. I need to see if I can locate the Commander anyway, and I can not do it properly with any noise coming from either of you," Ahearn said, looking over her shoulder at Laur. "That means you too, Laur. Get some rest."

"No argument from me. Maybe after sleeping we can find our way out of this cursed canyon, or the doorway to Truth will suddenly appear to us," Laur grumbled, curling up on the soft sand. "Crazy witch woman trying to kill us every chance she gets, and a canyon that changes its look whenever it fancies. I traded Hunters for this?"

"Stop your grumbling and get some sleep," Ahearn ordered, her voice taking on a Guardian edge. She walked away, not seeing the glare that Laur shot at her, and hoped on top of a large boulder far enough away from them that she would not be distracted. Settling down on top, Ahearn focused all her energy on the canyon in front of her. It was harder to track how sound moved here, bouncing off the walls and echoing around them similar to how light moved here. Listening intently, Ahearn began to slowly separate the sounds that echoed around them.

Further back, Aoire watched Laur rest. She knew that even though Laur wouldn't admit it, the day's events had shaken her up. Exhausted, Aoire sunk onto the sand. She closed her eyes, drifting off to sleep quickly.

Blinking, Aoire lifted a hand to shield her eyes. The canyon, Laur, and Ahearn were all gone, and she could no longer feel any pain in her body. Even the rumble of the canyon was replaced by silence.

Aoire was not on her hill, but stood on hot sand. The sky was bright with harsh white sunlight that beat down on her mercilessly. Everything was so bright that she couldn't see much around her, except the sand under her feet. It was eerily still.

A figure appeared on the horizon, its form broken up by heat waves rising off the sand. Aoire blinked, straining to see who it was from under her hands. A large smile broke across her face as he came into view.

"Brother!" Aoire cried, running to him and throwing her arms around his neck. She buried her face in his soft curls, breathing him in. He had the same curls she had, but brown instead of red, and he smelled just like Father. Brother wrapped his strong arms around her, holding her tightly.

"How are you?" he asked once their embrace ended.

Aoire shrugged. While she couldn't feel any pain in this place, the marks Vyad had left were still there. "As well as can be expected. I know in time these will heal, as yours did."

Brother smiled sadly. "But they were no less painful."

Aoire dug the toe of her boot into the sand, looking around. "Why are we here, Brother? What is this place?"

"Father and I wanted to remind you of your task."

Aoire's face flushed. "I don't need reminding."

Brother chuckled. "Perhaps. In this form, while your

body is incredibly strong, it is also vulnerable. Humans have an innate capacity to withstand immeasurable amounts of pain, if the purpose they are serving is worth more to them than their own lives. You are in the unique position of having seen the earth from two perspectives, but it can be easy to forget something when you don't see it all the time. We simply wanted to remind you of what it is you are fighting for."

Brother snapped his fingers and immediately the scene around them changed. A windstorm kicked up, blowing the sand around them away and revealing the hard, broken earth.

Everywhere around them great slabs of concrete were torn in two, rising out of the ground like infant mountains. Buildings were toppled and crushed, their metal innards jutting out violently from the ground like the bones of fallen sentinels. Wind whipped all around them, great screaming tempests threatening to topple them both. They stood underneath a large outcropping of stone, Brother holding her close as the wind threatened to tear her away.

Above them the sky had turned blood-orange, great pillars of smoke rising to connect with mushroom clouds of ash that were tinged yellow. Off in the distance, a massive lightning storm raged without any thunder, striking the ground a hundred times a minute. It was hundreds of miles away from where they were, but it stretched across the entire horizon. Nothing caught on fire where the lightning struck, the ground so barren that nothing grew. The shadow remnants of bodies lay wherever they looked.

Snapping his fingers again, Brother called back the sandy landscape. The harsh white sky returned, but now brilliant blue waves crept in and out of the white light.

"Its gotten worse hasn't it?" Aoire asked, dropping to her knees.

Brother knelt next to her. "Yes. Your journey will resemble the surface in many ways. It will not get any easier, and there will come a time when the whole earth will see and remember what happened to it. You must be ready when they learn the truth."

Aoire wiped a tear from her cheek. "This is harder than anything I have ever done before."

Her brother nodded. "I remember telling Father the same thing once. Different time and place, but this is the cup that was passed to you because only you can drink of it."

Getting to his feet, Brother curled his gentle fingers warmly around her hand. Aoire could feel the rough callouses that being a carpenter had left, but underneath they were warm.

Pulling her to her feet, Brother kissed her forehead. "Narcissa is one of the keys. You cannot do this without her. Make sure she meets Father. The manifestation of her true identity will be a crucial part to all this."

"Narcissa?" Aoire asked in disbelief, but everything vanished from view.

Pain and exhaustion crashed back around her, overwhelming at first. Opening her heavy eyes, Aoire saw she was back in the canyon. Groaning slightly as she lifted her head, Aoire looked at Ahearn who was still sitting on her boulder. Gritting her teeth, Aoire pulled herself to her feet and approached her slowly.

"You need to get some rest," Aoire said.

"You need to get more. You can barely walk, Aoire," Ahearn said, her eyes still scanning the corridor in front of them. She didn't look at Aoire as she spoke, all her attention focused on their surroundings. Ever since Narcissa showed back up, the hairs on Ahearn's arms and back of her neck had stood on end.

Aoire leaned against the boulder. "I'm fine. It feels better if I move."

"And your shoulder and head?"

"What about it?"

Ahearn shot her a look before turning back to the corridor in front of her. "I am a Guardian, Aoire, I am not blind. I know that a dislocated hip wasn't the extent of your injuries."

Aoire felt the large lump that had risen on her shoulder blade from when she hit the pillar. She could also feel dried blood on the back of her neck. Coupled with the constant ringing in her ears and stiffness in her arm, Aoire knew that her wounds would need more tending to soon.

"I'll heal," Aoire said, brushing off Ahearn's concerns. "What about you, Ahearn?"

"What about me?" Ahearn asked, an edge to her voice.

"We never got a chance to talk about what happened in End," Aoire replied.

Ahearn's body stiffened, but she said nothing.

Aoire continued, her eyes watching Ahearn's face carefully. "I know that it can't have been easy for you to have seen all your fellow Guardians, and kinsfolk, killed by Bashers."

"I'll be fine." Ahearn said, her voice flat.

"Are you sure?" Aoire asked, laying a hand on hers.

Ahearn snatched her hand away. She turned her eyes to Aoire, her face covered by her Guardian mask.

"I said that I was fine," Ahearn said coolly. "What

happened in End was tragic, but it happened. There is no use dwelling on things that cannot be changed."

"Have you located Retter?" Aoire knew she was not going to get any more out of Ahearn.

The empty look faded away and Ahearn's usual spark returned to her eyes. She shook her head, her eyes searching the canyon again. "Everything here is so confusing. Sound bounces around the same way light does. Every time one of the pillars of the walls shift, I can't tell if it is happening right next to us or across the canyon. It's impossible to know exactly where the Commander would be in relation to our position. Or Narcissa."

"It was the same when I used my power to try and find him. It would seem as if we are meant to find Retter, and the entrance to Truth, the old-fashioned way. Keep trying, Ahearn. I know you can do this," Aoire said. Leaving Ahearn again to continue trying to locate Retter, Aoire hobbled back to where Laur was and settled onto the soft sand again.

"Did you get some rest?" Laur asked Aoire, looking at her from where she lay.

Aoire tapped the corner of her eye. Laur immediately sat up and started frantically digging through the hidden pockets in her clothing.

"Relax, Laur. Caz didn't see," Aoire said gently.

Laur did not slow down until she produced a small vial filled with a thick, dark brown liquid. Pulling the stopper out, she downed all of it at once. Aoire said nothing as she watched Laur's eyes turn from purple to deep grey.

"What was that?" Aoire asked.

"It's called ndryshim. I got it from a peddler in Rarities," Laur replied.

"That is a powerful and ancient magic Laur, magic that no one uses anymore because it had terrible consequences. How did you get ahold of it?" Aoire asked.

Laur shrugged. "The peddler said that it had been in his family for generations, but that it was of no use to him anymore. He gave me enough for one use and I have been making more as needed."

"You have the original recipe with you?" Aoire asked, her eyebrows arching.

Laur nodded, pulling a small, worn leather book, from her breast pocket. "I transcribed it in here, so that if the spell was lost or ruined, I would still have a copy."

Aoire took the book from her and flipped through it. She could see Laur's strong handwriting throughout all of it, alongside drawings. Many of the spells were ancient and powerful, no longer used because of their destructive side effects. Finding the page with the recipe for ndryshim, Aoire looked over it and then handed the book back to Laur.

"This magic is far too advanced for just anyone. The last to use this form of magic died nearly three hundred years ago. Who taught you?"

Laur's face darkened slightly. "No one."

"You taught yourself?" Aoire asked.

"Well, I had to, didn't I?" Laur snapped, hearing the surprise in Aoire's voice. "I lost everything when this curse came upon me, and learning how to protect myself was the only option I had. My life was suddenly fair game for anyone to take. Ndryshim allows me to keep not only myself safe, but those around me safe. What if Caz finds out? Or Retter? Whoever wants me dead would pay them a lot of money to turn me in, but they would not hesitate to kill any of you if they thought for one moment you were helping me."

Aoire moved to sit next to Laur. Placing her hand over Laur's, she let a small thread of her *opari* course into Laur's body.

"There," Aoire said. "Now no one will find out, and you will not need ndryshim anymore. Your eyes will stay grey until you decide to trust someone with your burden. If you do decide to trust Caz or Retter, you should know that neither of them would sell you out for just a few glass chips."

"What makes you so sure of that?" Laur asked.

Aoire laughed gently. "Because I have watched them for a long time now. They value life over anything else. Just be careful Laur. Keeping secrets may feel like it keeps you safe, but the longer you withhold who you are from those closest to you, the more distance it can create."

"What would they possibly know about keeping secrets?" Laur asked bitterly.

"Caz knows more than you may think," Aoire said softly, looking back at Ahearn.

"Why Caz?"

"That is for Caz to tell, as is your secret," Aoire replied, turning her eyes back to Laur.

"What if I am not ready?" Laur asked.

Aoire squeezed her hand reassuringly. "You will know when you are."

"Found him," Ahearn interrupted, standing up on her boulder and pointing down a thin corridor branching off to the right. "We should hurry though. He seems to be moving quickly. I also found Narcissa, and Retter appears to be going after her."

"How far away is Retter?" Aoire asked, allowing Laur to help her to her feet.

"Not far. It took me longer to locate him because of how

sound moves here. If we leave now, we should be able to catch up to him." Ahearn said as they approached her.

"How can you tell?" Laur asked, hearing their voices echo around them.

"I have been studying sound since I was very young. Every person creates their own unique sound when they move, and I was taught how to use those to track a persons movements," Ahearn replied.

"Sound is how you will find him? And how can you possibly tell he was going after Narcissa?" Laur asked.

"Their sounds have overlapped each other a number of times. The Commander has one of the most distinct sounds I have ever heard. I just had to locate it and then track it back to where he is," Ahearn replied.

"It's an advanced form of tracking, similar to using sound to hunt. It comes in handy here, where the ground is too soft to leave defined footprints. At one point in time, there were animals that used this same form of tracking to hunt in darkness. They would let out a high-pitched screech and when the sound bounced off of solid objects, they could see what was around them in very dark or very large places. Caz learned how to use it backwards. Still very effective, none-the-less," Aoire explained.

"Are these animals still alive somewhere? I would like to study them to see how they track. I wonder if the Guardians learned it from them, and if so, I would like to know how," Ahearn asked, turning down a slightly wider corridor. The canyon snapped shut behind them, blocking their way back. Aoire felt the hair on her arms stand up the further down the corridor they traveled. Something was waiting for them.

"One day you may meet them," Aoire said.

Ahearn turned sideways when the canyon walls narrowed, and then stopped when it opened into a large clearing, pointing across the way at the middle of three corridors. "This is where his trail stops, and then it picks up again over there."

In front of them, five enormous pillars rose out of the sand in the middle of the clearing, creating a ring. A sixth pillar rose out of the center of the ring, the pillar face completely smooth. The five outer pillars were so massive, and rose up so close to the clearings edge, that the only way to the other side was through the middle. A reverent hum ran throughout the clearing.

"What is this place?" Laur asked, looking at the pillars in awe. She couldn't believe the simple beauty of what they were looking at.

Aoire didn't hear, all her attention on the clearing. She could see a network of power running through the sand, like the roots of a tree, glowing with a bright light. The network originated at the base of the sixth pillar and extended out, connecting all the pillars together and then disappearing into the canyon walls. The ground under Aoire's feet hummed with energy exactly like her *opari.*

The pillar closest to them was red-brown in color, with an outline of a Dhunni tree carved near the top. The second pillar was the same color as the canyon they were standing in, a small door carved near the top with lines rushing into it from all directions. The third pillar was gold in color, with a hammer carved near the top. The fourth pillar was greyish, with a starburst pattern near the top. The fifth pillar, set across from the red-brown pillar, was a mixture of every color and had an eye carved near the top. Each pillar was smooth, with a wide base and tapered to a flattened point above where the symbols were carved.

Instead of rising to incredible heights, most of the sixth pillar was broken or melted off. It was made of roughly hewn stone, not smooth like the others and it leaned to the side. It was pure white with a opalescent sheen, black scorch-marks marring the place where the top of the pillar had shattered. A great crack ran down the front, splitting the pillar in half. Something powerful had struck the pillar and shattered it, cracking the foundation and melting the stone.

Feeling a tug at her *opari,* Aoire approached the pillars reverently. As she stepped into the clearing, the glowing roots under her brightened when her foot landed on them. She felt a jolt run through her as the lines of power ran up her leg and over her body, the magic of the clearing merging with her. Drawing closer to the broken pillar, she could feel unchecked power coursing from it. Small lightning sparks ran up and down the inside of the crack as the power built and needed to be released.

Reaching a hand out, a large spark of lighting spilled out of the crack, and tethered her to the pillar with a jagged line of pure, unrefined power. Aoire went rigid as the lightning branched and hit her body in multiple places. Five other bolts of lightning came from the crack and hit each of the pillars, connecting all of them.

"Aoire!" Laur cried, trying to enter the clearing.

"Wait!" Ahearn said, pulling Laur back as a jagged piece of lighting lashed out and nearly hit her. They shielded their eyes against the brightness in the clearing, no longer able to see Aoire.

After what felt like an eternity, the light began to dissipate. Aoire came back into view as the lighting died down around her. Once the final bolt left her, she still stood in front of the pillar. It was no longer leaning and the pillar was now one complete piece. It was still the same height, but all melted areas had been smoothed.

"What happened?" Ahearn asked. When Aoire did not answer right away she strode into the clearing with Laur at her side.

"Aoire, what happened?" Ahearn asked again as they neared her.

Aoire turned around to look at them, stopping them in their tracks. Her skin was luminescent and her eyes were crystal clear. All traces of fatigue, pain, and worry were gone. Power sparked at the edges of her eyes, but it was the color that took them by surprise. They were no longer just one color, but swirled with every color imaginable. They were even older and wiser than before, as if they held the whole of history within them.

"That which was once wronged, was righted," Aoire replied.

"What?" Laur asked, still staring at Aoire's eyes.

"You asked what happened. Restoration happened," Aoire said. She bent down to pick up Laur's staff, tossing it back to her. All childlike features were gone from her face and body. She was now more womanly and defined, her body moving with a grace and fluidity it didn't have before.

"We need to get to Retter before Narcissa does. A display like that would not go unnoticed, and I do not want to leave Retter alone any longer," Aoire said, crossing the clearing quickly.

"Aoire, what was that place?" Laur asked, jogging to catch up with her.

"It's called the Fivefold. It used to be a holy place where

the elders of the Five would meet. Long before the event above, the elders made this clearing to pay homage to the unified work that was done to create a safe haven for earth's inhabitants. They each built a pillar to represent their city, and the middle pillar was gifted to them. It was blessed by my father, serving as protection against the Bashers, or anyone else, who came to the Fivefold with evil intent," Aoire replied.

"What happened to it? How did it get broken?" Laur asked.

"In the beginning, the Fivefold functioned as it was meant to. Twice a year, each leader of the Five would meet here to speak about what was happening back in their cities, both good and bad. They were all in perfect harmony, respecting each other and working to come to an agreement on how to handle any situation within the cities, no matter how long it would take. Unity thrived within this underground earth, until there was a battle over the power of the pillars.

"As the pain and suffering in the cities escalated, some elders came to believe that the protective power of the pillars could be transferred to their respective cities. They thought that by doing so, it would be an even better protection against the Bashers and once the idea that the power of the five pillars could be transferred took root in some of the elders' minds, it didn't take long to take root in their hearts. When a thought takes root in the heart, there is nearly nothing that can be done to reason with it.

"Fear is a powerful force, and it was this fear for the livelihood of their loved ones that drove them to consider defiling the first law of the Fivefold: No power freely given, can be forcibly taken. One elder did tried to sway their decision, but he was forcibly cast out and sent back to his city. After, the others attempted to move the pillars and when they did, lightning struck the middle pillar. What they didn't know was that the middle pillar served not only as a protective barrier, but also a doorway where Father could hear them. As long as the hearts of the elders were true, Father would grant them their wishes. But now that it was broken, the power left. The elders quickly realized that the power they had so callously tried to take was never theirs in the first place. It had been a gift. Now that it was gone, the unity of the cities broke."

"Where did the lightning come from? A Yellow?" Laur asked, climbing over a boulder.

Aoire shook her head. "No. Father sent the bolt to destroy it."

"And you restored it?" Laur asked.

Aoire nodded.

"How?"

Aoire smiled. "Unity unites that which disunity disconnected."

"Do you think the Fivefold will come back?" Ahearn asked, pausing at a fork in the canyon. After a moment, she led them down the left corridor.

"Father may decide to restore the Fivefold one day. If he does, the pillars may not have the same purpose," Aoire replied. She halted as she almost ran into Ahearn, who had suddenly stopped in front of another clearing.

"He's here, but something is wrong," Ahearn said, her brow furrowing. The clearing opening looked no different from all the others, but there was a distinct chill in the air and the rumbling of the canyon was louder here.

"What's in there?" Laur asked, trying to see past Ahearn.

"Truth," Aoire said.

Chapter Twenty-One

"There it is," Aoire said, pointing at the canyon wall across the clearing from them. This clearing was no different from any of the other clearings they had walked through, except that it was the smallest by far.

They stood in the middle of the clearing near a large pillar with only two corridors leading in or out – the one they had entered from, and another on their right. Just barely visible in front of them was an ornate arched doorway carved into the stone of the canyon. The doorway was outlined with black gold, making it hard to see. Even still, the effect was beautiful.

Similar to the doorway in End that had housed the NeverEver, words in the ancient tongue were carved into the top arch. They were bordered on each side with a thin line. Inside the arch was a carving of an ornate tree with branches that fanned out, only stopping when they connected with the border. The roots of the tree disappeared into the soft sand. A cold wind ruffled their hair and clothing, pulling them gently towards the doorway.

"It's beautiful," Laur breathed.

Ahearn trailed her fingers along the door, tracing the outline of the tree gently. "I can see why it is hard to find."

"Where is Retter?" Laur asked, looking around. "Caz, I thought his sound stopped here, so shouldn't he be here?"

Ahearn frowned, turning around. "It did stop here."

"So where is he?" Laur repeated. Aoire felt her stomach drop as she heard the sand shift behind them.

Retter stood in front of Narcissa, one arm twisted behind his back so violently that he was forced to lean backward at an unnatural angle. Three scratch marks marred his face, running from above his right eye to his cheek. His eye was already swollen shut and sweat ran down his face, making small rivulets through the blood on his face. Narcissa stared at them over his shoulder, her exquisite face twisted with fury.

"Commander," Ahearn whispered under her breath. The knife that she kept concealed in the sleeve of her jacket appeared in her hand with an almost imperceptible flick of her wrist.

Ahearn blinked as Aoire's voice entered her mind. *Don't. Let me handle this. If you attack her now, she will kill him before you can take a breath.*

Aoire's voice also echoed in Laur's mind as her hands tightened around her staff. *You too, Laur. Stand down. I will take care of Narcissa.*

"Are you alright, Retter?" Aoire asked, stepping in front of Laur and Ahearn so she was face to face with Narcissa. She felt her *opari* begin to agitate within her, the ball of fire spinning faster.

"He's fine," Narcissa replied. "Aren't you, Retter?"

Retter opened his mouth to reply, but Narcissa twisted his arm, making him rise to his toes. He bit the inside of his cheek to keep from crying out, tasting blood. Nodding curtly, he closed his eyes, his shoulder straining to stay in its socket.

"She is going to kill him," Ahearn hissed. "If you are going to do something, do it now!"

Narcissa's eyes flicked to Ahearn and a nasty smile spread across her face. "Such loyalty. Is that something that is common among Guardians? Or simply due to your own predisposition?"

Aoire put a hand out as Ahearn's whole body tensed. *Don't, Ahearn. She is trying to bait you.*

Ahearn didn't move any closer, but her eyes were hard as her knife danced deftly between her fingers.

"Your battle is with me, Narcissa. Leave them out of it," Aoire said.

"I don't think so, girl-child. If I have learned anything over the past few hundred years, it's to never allow yourself any weaknesses. You, my dear, have three. I just need to apply the right amount of pressure," she twisted Retter's arm a little more and there was a loud pop and crack as his wrist broke and his shoulder dislocated, "and you will be my willing slave."

"Ahearn, don't!" Aoire yelled as Ahearn darted past her, her knife grasped tightly in her hand.

Narcissa watched calmly as Ahearn closed the gap between them. Drawing near, Ahearn lunged at her. Narcissa barely moved, but suddenly Ahearn was disarmed and Narcissa was holding her wrist tightly. Narcissa's other hand still grasped Retter.

Narcissa pressed her thumb into Ahearn's wrist, making her drop her knife and driving her to her knees. Striking Ahearn across the face, Narcissa sent her flying into the pillar. Ahearn's body collided with such force that the stone cracked. She crumpled to the ground and lay completely still.

All around them a loud rumbling grew. The pillar Ahearn hit began to shake, her impact forcing it off balance. Rocks rained down around them as the ground pitched, sending them all off balance. In that moment, Retter and Aoire's eyes locked.

Using the rolling ground as leverage, Retter slammed the back of his head into Narcissa's nose. She stumbled back as the bridge of her nose snapped, blood flowing down her face. Retter darted away from Narcissa and scooped up Ahearn's limp body, rolling out of the way of the shaking pillar with her cradled safely in his good arm. Laur fell backward, using her staff to steady herself as the canyon continued to rumble and shake.

In a flash, Aoire was at the doorway. Pressing her hand firmly against the carving of the tree, right in the heart of it, Aoire allowed her *opari* to surge forth. The ball of fire within her nearly doubled in size. Like a tidal wave, it flowed into the door, transforming the black lines into solid gold. The light from the gold bounced off the bronze threads running throughout the canyon, causing it to begin to glow.

Snarling in anger, Narcissa zeroed in on Aoire. In a heartbeat, she was right in front of her. One hand still on the doorway, Aoire focused a portion of her *opari* to create a shield around herself.

As Narcissa's attacks deflected off of thin air, her anger rose. Aoire could feel the strain on her body to divide her *opari* between two strenuous tasks. She had never had to divide her *opari* like this before and it caused her strength to leave a lot faster than usual.

Just as the last of the doorway was nearly gold, Aoire felt her shield weaken. She saw Narcissa's hand fly at her in slow motion, striking her across the cheek and sending her sprawling across the sand. Spreading her fingers out towards the door, Aoire sent a thread of her *opari* through the sand as she rolled, lighting up the rest of the tree. Slamming into the canyon wall, Aoire tried to get to her feet in a daze.

A sharp click came from within the fully lit door, and then they heard the sound of giant gears from deep within the canyon wall. With a hiss, the outer edge of the arch began to glow brighter, and then the familiar sound of stone scraping on stone.

Pushing everything in front of it back without slowing, the door began to extend from the wall. A golden line began to extend down the middle of the door when it stopped, slicing it in half. Once it reached the sand, the door began to open with a loud groan. Eventually, the two halves of the door slammed loudly against the canyon wall, echoing throughout the whole cavern.

"The way into City of Truth," Narcissa said, a gleam in her eye. She got to her feet and stared at the dark entrance.

"Truth is not for you, Narcissa. Not as you are now," Aoire said, finally pushing herself to her feet. A bruise had already begun to appear on her jawline from where Narcissa had backhanded her.

Narcissa turned around to look at Aoire, her body framed by the open doorway. "Now that I know what the entrance looks like, I can get into Truth anytime I want to. You three have no place to hide that is safe anymore."

Aoire moved so that she was between Narcissa and the others. "We do if I defeat you."

Narcissa laughed. "Defeat me? Girl-child, I have beaten you down more times than you can count. What makes you think you are any match for me? I can tell your strength is nearly spent. How will you defeat me if you have no energy to lift a finger, much less use your magic?"

"She won't have to if we kill you first," Retter said, pushing himself to his feet with his good hand. His other arm hung limply at his side. Ahearn was still lying on the ground, deathly pale and barely breathing, with Laur crouched by her side.

Narcissa laughed again. "Taken down by a Guardian who is crippled, and a girl who can barely stand? Please. I could kill all of you in my sleep."

Laur rose to stand next to Retter, gripping her staff so tightly that her knuckles were white. "Try it, demon. See if you get close enough."

Narcissa sighed and stuck out her hip. She looked at Aoire whose legs were shaking from exhaustion. "Is this really the best you can do, Aoire? This rag-tag group is not strong enough to do any damage to anyone half as powerful as me. Do you really want to sacrifice them on the altar of your crusade? Is their blood something that you want to carry the rest of your life?"

Aoire hated to admit it, but Narcissa was partly right. She was exhausted and her body ached. Aoire searched deep within, deeper than she had ever before, to find any ounce of strength that could help her.

A single word entered her mind. With it, everything quieted.

Remember.

Immediately her *opari* raged to life, brighter than ever. Now it was a swirling mass of color, outlined in gold, silver, and bronze. Aoire felt the energy surge through her with an intensity she had never felt before, consuming her, and immediately everything hindering her vanished.

All fear was gone. All confusion was gone. Aoire suddenly saw everything differently, saw it all so clearly now. In her mind's eye, she could see Narcissa, but also the faces of every victim she had ever killed. They appeared one by one in front of Narcissa, and then the demon Besit - the one that had taken her body hundreds of years ago - rose above her. She could see evil swirling around Narcissa like a web of slick tar that imprisoned her, originating from the black bead around her neck.

Turning her eyes to Laur, the life Laur had been subject to appeared before her eyes, but also the powerful woman Laur would become. A crown was upon her head, purple light radiating from her body. She saw the loyalty of her heart and the fire of her spirit pouring forth in waves, terrifying her enemies into submission. She saw Laur's true self, rising from within her in all its glory and might. She saw her leading the Sihir, the acceptance of her identity breaking her chains.

Aoire turned to Retter, a strong and good-hearted man, standing tall beside Laur. She saw the extent of the damage done to his arm, but knew that he would never admit to how much pain he was in. An image appeared above him - a powerful warrior-king with an equally powerful warrior-queen by his side. Together they were defeating their enemies in waves.

Beside Ahearn's prone body, Aoire saw Ahearn's true identity kneeling. She saw the burns from the fire that had killed her parents on both her and her true identity, light bursting from them as the fury of her strength and might spilled out through the scars of her past. She saw Ahearn as a powerful General leading thousands, their loyalty to her second to none.

Turning her eyes back to Narcissa, Aoire knew what she had to do. In this state, with the full force of her *opari* flowing through her veins, Aoire was connected to everything. She could feel the heartbeat of every soul on earth and hear their thoughts. She could see now just how important Narcissa was, how important she had always been, and why Vyad had chained her. Aoire couldn't allow him to have control over Narcissa any longer.

"As I said before, Narcissa, you will not enter City of Truth as you are now. It is time that you come face to face with who you have become. It is time that you come to learn the truth of your identity," Aoire said.

"You can't touch-" Narcissa cut off as Aoire vanished, appearing in front of her less than a heart beat later. Before Narcissa could react, Aoire reached out and lightly touched a finger to Narcissa's chest.

The concussion of air that impacted Narcissa from Aoire's touch blasted her backward. Hitting the rock wall next to the doorway to Truth, Narcissa fell into the sand. Trying to get up, Narcissa's eyes widened as Aoire immediately appeared in front of her.

Aoire knelt down and gently lifted Narcissa's chin so she was looking into her dark eyes. Aoire's face was completely serene, her eyes swirling with every color imaginable. When she spoke, her voice was gentle and compassionate. "I told you this would happen. The creature inside of you has no right to you anymore. It must be defeated, so that you can finally be free from this prison."

Looking back over her shoulder, Aoire smiled softly to

her friends. Turning back to Narcissa, her eyes faded to white. Narcissa tried to pull away, but she could not break from the touch of Aoire's fingers.

White light extended from Aoire's body, radiating out like starlight and enveloping her and Narcissa. It grew so bright that it seemed to drown out all other light and sound. As the light grew, Retter and Laur shielded their eyes. With no sound at all, the light vanished.

Blinking, Retter shot to his feet.

Aoire and Narcissa were gone.

Chapter Twenty-Two

Narcissa gasped for breath, shooting straight up on the hard bed she was lying on. It felt like every bone in her body had been broken. Her hair spilled wildly around her shoulders, and her chest was tight where Aoire had touched her. She couldn't see anything in the darkness around her.

Swinging her legs over the side of the bed, Narcissa gripped it tightly while she waited for her eyes to adjust. The light from Aoire had been so bright that it had seared into her eyes and blinded her. It was so brilliant that she could still see it when her eyes were closed.

Still waiting for the darkness to lift, Narcissa began to realize that she wasn't blind, but the room she was in was pitch black. The darkness was thick, but there was a soft ball of light hovering above her. It gave just enough illumination for her to see that she was lying on a crude bed. Narcissa reached a hand out past where the light was and it vanished in the darkness, as if her arm had been cut off at the elbow.

Pulling her arm back, she strained to hear anything in the darkness and only silence replied. She could sense an oppressive presence in the darkness that seemed to encroach upon her. Closing her eyes to try and make it go away, the bright light from Aoire was all she could see.

Narcissa opened her eyes again.

Nothing. Not a sound.

Narcissa decided she couldn't just sit on the bed and wait. Holding herself tightly, she pressed her feet on whatever invisible ground was beneath her. It had no reflection and wasn't hard or soft, nor was it hot or cold. Standing up, even the sound of her dress against the sheets of the bed was swallowed up in the void around her. The ball of pale light rose as she did, never hovering more than a few inches from her head. Narcissa looked up at it, frowning. It just floated in the air, giving off a pale light that wasn't even warm or comforting. The light simply...existed.

"Hello?" Narcissa called out, surprised by the hesitation in her voice. It suddenly hit her that not only was it silent all around her, but she could no longer feel or hear the souls within her. A cold dread blossomed in her chest.

"Hello?" Narcissa called out again, this time a little louder. When there was no reply again she felt the dread turn to panic.

She couldn't sense anything around her, or within her, or near her. Taking a few steps forward, Narcissa could still feel ground underneath her feet and the light followed her. As the panic within her rose, her feet flew faster. She began to run in any direction she could, trying to find someone or something, other than herself.

Running around blindly for a while, Narcissa stopped. Her chest heaved and hot tears ran down her face. It had been so long since she had felt this alone, that she had forgotten what it did to her. Searching within for Lucien, she tried desperately to let his voice fill her mind once more. She didn't care if he yelled at her, or didn't speak to her, or said hurtful things, she just wanted him with her. She didn't want to be alone again. She had never wanted to be alone ever again.

"Narcissa," a deep voice said from behind her.

Narcissa spun. Lucien stood behind her, tall and handsome in his dark blue suit - the very suit he was wearing when he died. His beautiful blue eyes looked dully at her, his face expressionless. There was no color to his skin, no spark to his eyes, no sign that he had life in him, but Narcissa still felt her heart skip a beat. She hadn't seen him since the night she had been granted her kiss. A second orb of light hovered above him, but it cast no shadow anywhere on his body.

"Lucien? How? How are you here? I-" Narcissa cut off, a sob threatening to escape.

"Killed me?" Lucien finished for her, tilting his head to the side slightly. "I remember. I remember not only that, but so much more. In fact, memories are all I have anymore. Memories are all that we, your prisoners, have anymore. I remember how much I loved you, more than life and performing together. I also remember how you exploited my love for you. The pain of dying pales in comparison to the eternal pain of being your prisoner."

"So you are here to punish me," Narcissa stated, pulling into herself.

To protect herself, she had forced herself to forget how much she had loved him. Now that he was here, all those feelings came rushing back. Narcissa never wanted to lose Lucien, she had wanted him to be with her forever. The night he had refused to become like her – oh, how he had looked at her when she revealed what she had become - his rejection of her hurt more than anything else.

The kiss happened so fast, almost like a reflex. She hadn't meant to kill him, but she could also remember the joy of knowing that he would be with her forever once she felt his soul inside of her. Narcissa felt her stomach turn at the memory now that Lucien stood before her, a shell of whom he had been. The body without the soul is nothing, and she knew now that it was the beauty of his soul that she had loved.

Lucien stared at her with emotionless eyes. "As much as I would enjoy punishing you for what you have done, he persuaded me to come. He knew that you needed me far more than the level of my disappointment in you. I am more of a guide than anything else."

"Who asked you? Vyad?" Narcissa asked, trying to ignore the hot pain in her heart as she looked at her first love.

"No. The Creator," Lucien replied.

"Who?" Narcissa asked, taking a step closer to Lucien. She had head Vyad speak that name before.

"The Creator," Lucien repeated. "He is the one who created everything, who watches over all, and he has been waiting a long time to finally meet you."

Narcissa swallowed as her mouth went dry. Meetings with Vyad had never been in her favor. "Why would he want to meet me?"

"For some reason, he wants to extend grace to you. If it were up to me, I would allow you to suffer for the choices that you have made and the hurt that you have caused, but I am not he," Lucien's eyes seemed to bore straight through Narcissa, but then they softened. "You have chosen an evil life for yourself *mi amore*, one that I still cannot understand. We were happy, and you threw that happiness away for this. How has this served you so far, *mi amore*? Do you feel any less lonely now than when we were alive and in love?"

Wrapping her arms tighter around herself for protection from Lucien's words, Narcissa felt a tear run down her cheek. This place seemed to undo her and now that her first love - and her first kill - was standing in front of her, it was more than she could bear.

Pushing her feelings back down, Narcissa looked all around her. "Well if this Creator wants to see me so badly, where is he? As far as I can tell, it is just the two of us here. If he's as powerful as you say, why wouldn't he show up himself? Why put me in this place with you?"

"This isn't familiar to you?" Lucien asked, spreading his hands. "This is the darkness that not only you live in, but the prison you have trapped me in along with every soul you have taken. You built this long before you became a Lefeela, through your thirst for glory. Creator believes that in order for you to be free, that you need to face the reality of whom you think you are."

"So this is all my own creation?" Narcissa asked, her arms still around herself.

Lucien nodded, extending his hand to her. "Look around you. This is your soul, Narcissa. This is how black your soul has become, but you have the chance to change that. You have the chance to take what evil you have done in your life and turn it towards good. All you have to do is take my hand as invitation."

Narcissa felt the ground tremble slightly beneath her feet as he spoke. She heard Besit's voice begin to whisper to her. Small cracks began to appear in the darkness around them. Black ooze as thick as tar dripped from them, flowing towards her in thick lines. Narcissa felt it collect around her ankles, slowly rising up her legs, cold and thick.

The darkness around them filled with the last words of those she had killed, deafeningly loud. She threw her hands over her ears to try and shut them out, but they just grew louder. Lucien watched her as fear filled her heart, his hand still outstretched.

"Lucien!" Narcissa cried out, hot tears running down her face. She looked at him with pleading eyes, his outstretched hand so close. The tar was now up to her chest, pulling against her, trying to pull her away from him.

"Take my hand, *mi amore*. Do not be afraid," Lucien said more gently as the black ooze reached her shoulders.

Narcissa strained to take his hand, her eyes wild with fear. Just as the tar began to force its way into her mouth, she lurched forward and managed to grasp Lucien's hand tightly. White light shattered the darkness and swept the tar away. A scream the likes of which Narcissa had only heard once when in Vyad's presence filled the room. Narcissa closed her eyes, gripping onto Lucien with everything she had. Lucien pulled her close, and she felt safe in his arms as she had long ago.

"Well done, *mi amore*," Lucien whispered into her ear. She felt his lips, soft on her forehead, and then he let go of her. The ground vanished from underneath her feet and Narcissa began to fall. There was nothing around her as she fell, just soft colors streaming past her, and then she landed gently in a soft bed. All fear left Narcissa, peace pushing it away. The sound of a woman softly singing filled her ears.

I know that song, Narcissa thought, her forehead furrowing. *That's not possible.*

"Open your eyes, *cher*," the woman said. Narcissa felt her heart leap. She had been twelve the last time she had heard that voice.

Blinking against the soft light, the room came into view. Dust danced in the sunlight filtering through an old window with a white curtain, lavender set beneath the windowsill in a long planter box. Four bedposts held up the white canopy that cascaded down around the bed, a thick rug underneath the bed. The walls of the room were washed white, exposed beams of the same rich golden color as the floor, rising up the ceiling to a point.

A girls white dress hung on the back of the door, little purple flowers adorning the ruffled hem. At the end of the bed lay a black and white kitten curled up on a small white pillow. Narcissa recognized her great-great grandmother's childhood room immediately. It was identical to the only family photo that Narcissa's mother had owned, even down to the kitten.

Warm sunlight illuminated the woman by the window, her black hair falling to her hips with a slight wave to it. Her arms were crossed under her breasts and her hip was out as she looked out the window. The sunlight lit up her white dress, giving her an ethereal glow. It was a simple dress, but made of the finest material. Hearing Narcissa move, she turned around, the corners of her dark eyes wrinkling as she smiled. She had the same features as Narcissa, but she was a bit older, with a single streak of grey running through her hair at her temple.

"*Mère*?" Narcissa asked, shock hitting her like an anvil.

Narcissa's mother's smile broadened. She knelt in front of Narcissa, placing her hands around Narcissa's face.

"*Mon coeur!* How you have grown up!" Her mother said,

her eyes misty. Narcissa felt a lump rise in her throat as her mother's soft hands caressed her face.

"How are you here?" Narcissa asked, blinking away tears.

Her mother sat next to Narcissa on the bed, the mattress creaking softly. "He wanted me to be the next face that you saw. Lucien did his part in getting you this far, and we were hoping that this place and my presence would be soothing to you. Oh my dearest, I have watched over you for so long. I have waited with such longing for you and I to be together again."

Narcissa felt shame pierce her heart. "You have watched over me? You have seen the things I have done?"

Her mother nodded, squeezing her hand. "*Mon coeur*, you have been confused for so long. I fear I left you too soon and because of that, you have been trying to find your way back ever since. I never wanted to leave, but my body was broken beyond repair. I was so tired, and he was calling me home. I know how tired you are as well, *mon coeur*. I know you have been searching to fill the void my death left behind, searching for a way to never feel alone again."

Narcissa laid her head on her mother's shoulder, not realizing she was crying until hot tears fell on the back of her hands. "What do I do? I have done terrible things."

"Stop running *mon coeur*. It is tearing you apart inside. You have always been strong, is it any wonder that the demon that took you was almost as strong? Creator offers a way out of the darkness, but only he can give you that peace. It has to be your choice. I cannot make it for you, no one can. I made my choice a long time ago, and I would make the same were I given the chance," her mother replied, wrapping her arms around Narcissa.

"I don't know if I can. Vyad will make sure that I suffer for all eternity if I turned away now," Narcissa said.

Her mother looked deeply at her. "You *are* suffering, Narcissa. Your soul is suffering every time you take a life. If you do not turn away from this life now, you may never be able to. You have the strength to do this and I do not wish to see my only daughter given to an eternity of torment because she chose fear over providence."

"Were you scared?" Narcissa asked.

"Scared to die?" her mother asked in turn. "Or scared to choose?"

"Yes," she continued when Narcissa stayed silent. "Yes. I was so like you *mon coeur,* so sure that I could fix myself and not need anyone's help, but I was in so much pain and heartbreak. Only Creator had the answer I was searching for. Once I found him, I found an unexplainable peace. It made dying not so terrifying, because I knew that I was going to a better place. I was going to a place where everything was at it had first intended to be. A place of no fear, pain, death, or sickness, and one where I could still be with you *mon coeur.*"

"After what I have done, why would he care for, or want, a creature like me?" Narcissa asked.

Her mother gently took her face in her hands and stared intently into her daughter's eyes. "Because to Creator, you are a treasure among treasures. You are worth fighting for, and there is nothing in your past that can ever make him stop pursuing you. You are *mon coeur,* my heart, and also his. Creator can redeem even the vilest things that you have done."

The room shook gently and small cracks appeared on the walls. Black ooze began to seep from the cracks, but this time it moved slower than it had in the black room. Narcissa could hear Besit's voice in the tar, calling to her.

"Where is Creator?" Narcissa asked, eyeing the tar. She pulled her feet onto the bed as one trail slowly snaked its way towards her.

Her mother smiled and pointed at the door with the dress. The tar touched her foot, but she didn't seem to notice.

"Through there. He's waiting."

"Will you come with me?"

Her mother shook her head, sorrow filling her eyes as more tar crept down the walls around them. "Sadly, I must leave you again. This journey is your own. It is your path to walk. Lucien and I have simply been here to help you, but the choice, in the end, is yours. No matter what you choose, I will always be looking over you, *mon coeur.* Always and forever."

Her mother kissed Narcissa's hands. Rising from the bed, Narcissa embraced her mother for as long as she could before she felt her resolve weaken. She knew that she could easily stay in this place forever, stay in her childhood room with her mother whose presence and touch she had been without for most of her life, but she also knew that she couldn't. Narcissa had already lost everything; she figured she might as well see what this Creator could give her.

Narcissa finally tore herself away from her mother as the ooze closed in around her feet. She could feel the cold grip of Besit within it, trying to hold Narcissa there. Looking at her mother one last time, Narcissa flung open the door. If Narcissa had thought the first time she had to say goodbye to her mother was painful, this second time tore her apart.

Golden light from the doorway spilled onto her mother and the bed behind her, the black and white kitten blinking sleepily. Narcissa heard Besit hiss in pain and anger as the golden light fell upon the ooze, making it pull back and shrivel up in protest. Just as her resolve to leave was almost gone, Narcissa leaned back and allowed herself to free-fall into the golden glow.

Narcissa felt the sensation of falling from a great height, the golden glow all around her. She felt the rush of the air around her body, the outline of the doorframe with her mother standing in it growing smaller as she fell. The door closed and she was gone again. Continuing to drop, the sensation of falling from a great height was replaced with one of floating.

Narcissa saw nothing around her but soft, golden light. The air was warm on her face as she fell and for the first time in her life, she felt nothing. No fear, pain, or heartache. She had no concept of time as she fell. Narcissa closed her eyes and spread her arms, allowing herself to be lost in this feeling of nothingness.

Opening her eyes as the air began to warm, Narcissa blinked. Below her, she could see some sort of shape. Drawing closer, she could see it was a massive ball of opalescent fire rimmed in gold, silver, and bronze, swirling in the abyss she was falling through. Growing closer, Narcissa noticed that her descent had begun to slow. She could also feel herself being pulled towards the fireball.

Bracing herself, Narcissa felt nothing as she entered the ball of fire. No searing heat, or pain of impact, but instead the golden light around her was replaced by curls of opalescent fire. Immediately her descent stopped and she found herself floating in the middle of the fireball, enveloped by gentle warmth.

Floating in the middle of the ball, bursts of different colored flames spurted up around her at different intervals. One flared up right in front of her, bright green in color, and Narcissa reached out. A small ball of green fire stayed in her palm when she pulled her hand out of the flames, dancing an inch above her palm. It was cool to the touch and carried the sensation of life.

Opalescent threads swirled amidst the spurts of colored flame. Letting the green flame go, she reached out to touch the threads. An image of a stone striking a giant of a man in the forehead and killing him appeared in her mind as the thread lit up from her touch. Snatching her hand from the thread, the memory blinked out of her mind as soon as the light vanished. Narcissa felt someone else's triumph wash over her.

Moving her hands around her in lazy circles, Narcissa could feel a gentle pressure around her, holding her up. As her hands and feet moved, ripples of color extended out from her body and vanished into the ball of power. Narcissa's chest burned and she realized she had been holding her breath this whole time.

A heartbeat came from under her, sending a ripple of white light towards her. It crashed into her, exploding into millions of tiny colored lights that expanded out in every direction. They were cool to the touch and wet, like tiny droplets of water. Narcissa touched one with her finger and it exploded into even smaller droplets.

Breathe.

A deep voice echoed through the fireball. Narcissa both heard it and felt it within her soul. Panic settled into the fringes of her mind as the burning in her chest intensified and black dots danced before her eyes.

Another heartbeat crashed into her.

Breathe, my child.

Unable to hold it any longer, Narcissa gasped for air. She felt the warmth from around her fill her lungs and then her body. It strengthened her, making everything around her more vivid.

She took another deep breath and another, each one making her stronger than before. The more she breathed in, the more she felt Besit weaken within her. Another heartbeat radiated around her and Narcissa could feel the presence more palpably. She didn't know how she knew, but she knew it was to whom the voice belonged.

"Who's there?" Narcissa asked. She hadn't spoken the question, but instead had thought it and then heard it reverberate around her through the fire. Black ooze began to drip around the outside of the fireball, coating it.

I am.

"Who are you?"

Creator. The rightful owner of this land and all its inhabitants. I am Father to all who choose me, granting my children great and powerful gifts, including everlasting life. I have the power to turn thought into reality, and give emotion and color a form. I never lie, I am incapable of it, and I do not use fear to force others to do as I wish. I am the one that you have heard of, the one Vyad fights against and whose offspring he fears. I am the answer out of the loneliness you have felt your whole life, working so hard to escape.

"Why would you think I am trying to escape anything?"

I exist from a time before time began and I will exist long after it ends. I have walked this world that I created, above and below, with the people I created. I have seen the deepest desires and fears of your heart, my child. I know it was your fear of being alone after your mother passed that drove you into alliance with Vyad, allowing Besit to take residence in you. As much as Lucien loved you, and you still love him, Vyad showed you a way to quell that fear, didn't he?

Narcissa swallowed. She had a feeling he knew the answer, but was waiting for her to speak. "Yes."

Even after Besit took you, and even after you have added all these souls within your body, do you still feel alone, my child?

"Yes," Narcissa could barely utter the word, the cold weight of her disparity hanging over her like a wet blanket. The words that Creator was speaking filled her with a small spark of hope. Vyad was the only other one that she had experienced powerful magic from, but his came with a painful price. Creator felt warm and strong around her.

Vyad can offer power and might, he can offer great strength, but he cannot grant you what I can. I can show you a way out of the pain and suffering that will be eternal, a new life full of purpose. You will no longer be beholden to Vyad, and you will finally find what you have been searching for. Instead of being his slave for death, you will be my instrument for freedom, transformed into a powerful weapon against Vyad.

Narcissa could feel Besit squirm as Creator's words pierced through Narcissa. "I have done many evil things. How can you ever make that right?"

It was not you that did those things, but the demon Besit within you. Vyad knew how powerful you would be once you accepted who you truly are, and he has done all he can to keep you from that.

"There is no way to come back from what I have done."

There is. My way. You do not understand the full extent of the prison that you have built for yourself. You have allowed Vyad to fool you into thinking that you are invincible because of the evil power that he has bestowed upon you. Vyad works in the shadows, exploiting the darkest desires of the heart to entrap and ultimately kill.

"And you? How do you work?"

I work in the light. I take that which is broken, and I use it for good. I work with the willing, the ones who no longer want to live in pain and brokenness, and who want to have a higher purpose for their lives. You are my dear creation, and I know what you are fully capable of. You are not so broken that you cannot change, my child. You are incredibly powerful, more powerful than you even know.

Narcissa felt her heart stir from his words, his claim of her as his own blossoming in her chest. She felt the cold hand of Besit tighten around her heart painfully as a feeling of belonging grew there. Narcissa gasped, the familiar pain of swaying from Vyad's hold over her amplified here. This time, instead of giving in, Narcissa fought. Creator's words had stirred deep within her, showing her love and mercy.

Now that she had tasted it, she no longer wanted to live in darkness. Gasping in pain as Besit tightened her grip even more, Narcissa nodded her head.

"Yes," Narcissa managed to get out between gasps.

Immediately the fireball roared, doubling in size. The black ooze crystalized and exploded away in sharp shards, a vicious female scream ringing out as it did. Every color within the ball intensified and began to swirl around her like a whirlpool. The colors rushed into her body through her eyes, nose, and mouth. The fireball began to shrink as it all flowed into Narcissa.

Pain exploded in her chest. Narcissa's back arched, white-hot fire raging throughout her body, twisting her muscles and causing her whole body to contort. She could feel a great battle rage within her between Besit and the purity of Creators power that had entered her body. It was the most excruciating pain she had ever felt in her life. She wanted to scream, cry, or pass out, but couldn't. She could only wait in agony for it all to end.

Narcissa felt sharp claws rip at the inside of her chest, her back arching even further back. She watched, floating in the air and unable to move, as the same black ooze that had been following her erupted from her chest. It formed into a ball above her, collecting right above the black stone around her neck.

The ball undulated, its surface fluid. It grew as more of the ooze was pulled from her body and collected in it. Narcissa could see Besit within the ball of ooze, pressing against the edge of the ball as she tried to escape. A clawed hand shot out from the ball, trying to grab onto Narcissa. Narcissa vaguely felt its claws graze her neck near where her necklace lay.

Once all the ooze was out of her, the last of the fireball she had been floating in clamped around it. It created an opalescent shell around the tar and then they both vanished. At the same time, the black bead hanging around her neck shattered.

Narcissa felt the power that had poured into her body settle behind her navel, her exhausted body hanging limply in the sky. Beneath her a valley had appeared, with a lake in the distance. The soft grass cradled her exhausted form as darkness clouded her vision. Aoire's boots were the last thing she saw before darkness took her.

* * * * *

"Well that was a surprise," Vyad said as he picked himself off the floor of his chamber. He looked at his viewing module and frowned. A great, jagged crack had appeared down the middle of the bronze disk, and the place where Narcissa's bead had been was blackened from the explosion. Smoke rose from the charred bronze disk where the lightning had struck, blowing Vyad back.

The last thing that he had seen before the black lightning surged and overpowered the disk, was Narcissa giving her life over to Creator. His power had entered her body, casting Besit out of her, and at the same time shattering the stone Narcissa wore around her neck. Vyad had not expected Narcissa to turn so easily, or for the explosion of the stone on her necklace to be mirrored by its twin that he had here.

Vyad did not like being surprised.

Running his fingers along the jagged scorch marks on the viewing disk, Vyad frowned. He knew he could fix it, but if one of his Generals could be turned that easily, he needed to tighten his grip on them. Black lighting radiated through his eyes as his initial shock turned to anger. Narcissa had chosen her path. He would have no problem punishing her appropriately.

Spinning around to gather Fearg's stone from his desk, Vyad's eyes snapped to the tree. Stepping closer, he stroked his beard and felt his anger replaced by another feeling. For the second time in a short while, Vyad found himself surprised.

A single opalescent leaf with golden veins and bronze tipped edges had appeared on one of the branches.

The Tree of Life was beginning to awaken.